LACEY KING AND LAU

The SNITCH:

An Agent Without a Badge Based on a True Story

outskirts press

The Snitch
An Agent Without a Badge

v7.0

The authors may be contacted at:
- Lacey King - lacey328@yahoo.com
- Laurence E. Sturtz, Esq. - lestu@aol.com

Outskirts Press, Inc.
http://www.outskirtspress.com

ISBN: 978-1-4787-9555-1

Library of Congress Control Number: 2018901129

PRINTED IN THE UNITED STATES OF AMERICA

To David,
A wonderful friend
whom I admire - Wishing
you enjoyable reading.
Lacey King

DEDICATION

To Alan, my beloved, whose love and patience
helped me finish this book.
Lacey King

To my wife, Maureen, who has supported me with
enduring patience, devotion, and love throughout
our marriage and my demanding law career.
Laurence E. Sturtz, Esq.

[illegible]

ABOUT THIS BOOK

This work is based upon a true story; only the names have been changed. The events and characters described in this book were real. It is a conspiracy story about a psychopathic career criminal, his two criminal associates, the FBI, and an innocent young man who gets caught in between them and loses his life. The book is based upon the original trial transcripts (edited for brevity), published newspaper articles depicting every detail of the trial, and the written recollection of the lead trial attorney recorded immediately after the trial in 1976. This book portrays the culture of the FBI during the 1970s and the crimes committed by an infamous bank robbery gang in the United States at that time. The opinions expressed in this book are solely those of the authors and do not represent the opinions of the publisher.

FOREWORD

The Snitch: An Agent Without a Badge is an account of a kidnap-murder trial that occurred in Ohio during 1976. All names have been changed, but most of the facts of the trial have been kept to give authenticity to the story.

The trial begins as David and Goliath, when the defense attorney is faced with a prosecution team fortified by the mighty forces of the FBI, federal attorneys, and a healthy bank account. The defense attorney is hand-picked by the presiding judge because of his national reputation for representing high-profile individuals and companies, and presenting and winning two cases before the Supreme Court of the United States before his thirty-fifth birthday. However, he is awarded a measly budget of $1,500, which could barely pay the cost of paper copies required in this capital murder case that lasts eight weeks.

In this case, the FBI uses bad guys—snitches—to carry out crimes in hopes of catching their comrades in the act and thus breaking up gangs who rob banks, sell drugs, kidnap, deal in stolen goods, steal cars, participate in organized crime and corrupt union activities, etc. An underlying ruthless nature of the FBI is revealed, in that they do whatever it takes to cover up their involvement in this crime, thus reducing themselves to the level of their criminal subjects under the pretext that the end justifies the means.

The defense attorney is basically a good guy who takes

the case because he feels it's a challenge, because he likes the notoriety, and because he believes in equal justice and thinks the law should be applied equally no matter who you are. The prosecutor is a tenacious lawyer, yet gentlemanly and fair. The judge, sixty-two years of age, is experienced, strong, fair-minded, stern, but pleasant. He leans slightly in favor of the defense. The defendant is a not-too-bright psychopath, whose IQ is reportedly 95. He displays no conscience whatsoever. However, he possesses the gift of friendly charisma, making him attractive and compelling to anyone who would listen. He uses that gift to manipulate and leverage himself in difficult situations. The jury—a group of twelve from a rural area—has the capacity to step back and figure out the conspiracy and try to do the right thing in their decision regarding the bad guys.

CHAPTER 1

October 1976

So, it's true. Time really does slow way down when death is imminent, like an echo traveling along an endless tunnel. Larry heard the unmistakable low rumble of a helicopter before he saw it. At first, he simply wondered what a helicopter would be doing in this rural area of Ohio. How odd—in all the years he had lived here and driven the back roads between Columbus and Newark, he had never seen a helicopter. A crop-dusting plane, yes, but never a helicopter. Confusion turned to apprehension, the second Larry remembered what Rocky had told him. First a helicopter, then the cars.

The uneasiness Larry had felt in the pit of his stomach ever since the beginning of the Rocky Hamilton court trial was now replaced by fear that shot through his body like a lightning bolt. Accompanying thoughts of imminent death is always a flashback of the last few seconds of life. Why does the brain bother to record such things? Does the person think he will live to tell it? In such cases of gut-wrenching fear, the brain always goes into high alert. Some people freeze, some immediately begin planning their escape, and some who think the situation is hopeless lapse into a flashback.

Just seconds before, driving along a country road, Larry

Strong had seen the cornstalks, shorn of their edible ears, still standing tall and green, lining the fields on either side of the road, swaying in the breeze. He had seen a mud-splattered light-tan late-'60s Chevrolet station wagon, the first car to pass him in the past ten minutes going the opposite direction on Ohio State route 161. The heavy-set, puffy-cheeked mom driving dangled a cigarette out of her ruby-red lips. Matching red blouse. The little girl, tenish, bouncy, dark-blonde ponytail, talking animatedly to her mother. The deep ravines banking in front of the fields on both sides of the two-lane highway proving no escape was possible.

That flashback reverie lasted, what, maybe half a second? The sound of the helicopter grew louder. Fear gripped him hard, ferociously. Larry's thirty-five-year-old heart pounded in a futile effort to leap right out of his long, lean body. His fingers, white-knuckled, bent around the steering wheel of his 1975 Trans Am—you know the one, white hoop scoops, fuel-injected 440 horse power engine, low-slung and sexy. A rich man's hot-rod. The beauty of the late-afternoon Indian summer day evaporated as he stared up into the sky searching frantically for markings on that damn orange helicopter which was now twisting in broad circles above him. His eyes were glued to it, but he could find nothing. *They don't let planes fly without markings! They just DO NOT!*

The unmarked orange bird stayed right with him, swirling loud and low. Way too low.

Just like Rocky said it would.

Which side was after him? Couldn't be the Mafia; even they would have trouble pulling off the 'copter thing. Wouldn't they?

WOULDN'T THEY?

Of course, they would.

Larry, roaring forward, rounded a curve. His heart fell to his stomach; his stomach jumped to his throat. Less than a hundred yards in front of him, a large, four-door plain brown sedan had pulled perpendicular across the road. He could make out four white male heads with knotted ties at their necks and short-cropped hair—two in front, two in back—straining to look directly at him. Larry's eyes darted rapidly to his rearview mirror.

Shit!

A twin brown sedan, harboring four more seemingly cloned and similarly attired all-American types, was closing in on him fast from the rear. The deafening din of the helicopter boxed him in along with the front and back door cars on the road. Entombing him.

The end. The brilliant, brash, hot-shot defense attorney, married father of two, cut off in his prime.

Tomorrow's headlines…

Suddenly, an explosive jolt of energy pierced the rapidly forming casket shadows around Larry, shooting his body with a final surge of adrenalin—the kind that could set off a nuclear reactor. It riveted him into hyper clarity. Clarity that lasered his attention to the sedan behind him and the man leaning way out the left, rear window, aiming a sawed-off shotgun straight at him. Ahead, in the other car, two guys were doing the same damn thing!

Just like Rocky said they would.

But Rocky had also told him that those sawed-off shotguns could not penetrate the metal of his car. They would get him through the window.

The meager seconds left of Larry's life ticked off the clock.

Fight? Flight?

"Screw you!" said Larry aloud, his heart still trying to

drum through the skin underneath the white dress shirt he was wearing. "I go down, you go down, you bastards!" He reached over to the passenger seat for his .38, loaded with armor-piercing bullets—the kind that *could* penetrate metal—which he always carried with him these days. He down-shifted abruptly, almost—but not quite—stalling his Trans Am. The car behind him skidded, matching him in the slow-down.

They had him. The helicopter pulled back, taking the cacophony of its blades and engine with it.

Nano-seconds passed. Part of Larry was still moving in almost comically exaggerated *s – l – o – w – t – i – m – e.*

Tick... tock... tick... tock... Like a freaking metronome!

But the greater part of Larry was in a state of primal terror, operating on rapid survival instinct.

Sons of bitches! A hail of bullets you want? A hail of bullets you'll get!

Another micro-second passed.

The lead car straightened out and began creeping slowly forward. Head-on at him. Larry frantically pretzeled his body, bending at the waist, miraculously managing to keep the butt of his 6'4" frame in his seat and squishing his head and neck under the steering wheel while plunging his long left arm through it, locking the steering column in place under his arm as he reached down violently, grabbing the clutch pedal. His right foot remained on the gas pedal. Gun in hand, he curled his right arm over his bent body and pointed his automatic weapon straight out the side window. Six powerful bullets at his disposal. He'd empty every last one into them before he went down.

Damn it!

His senses stood at attention, critically acute. Red alert does that. He could hear the lead car approaching him. Hell, he could ***feel*** the damn thing, as its nose pulled close to his front end. Good God, they were going to come alongside him and blast him through his driver's side window. The one that now held his .38 with those attention-getting, metal-piercing, flesh-imploding bullets. He'd been trained to always double shoot in rapid succession. Bam, bam. Bam, bam. The first bullet slows 'em down; the second one throws the body into shock and stops the heart.

Bam, bam.

Would he be able to get off three doubles? He couldn't go down without a fight, without some justice.

He couldn't.

He wouldn't.

In slo-mo, the oncoming car breached the side of Larry's vehicle, which had come almost to a complete stop, just rolling forward. As the two cars drew parallel, instinct demanded! ACT! When the driver of the approaching car saw Larry's revolver sticking out the window, he hit the accelerator at the very same moment that Larry pulled hard, popping the clutch of his sports car with his left hand. The Trans Am shot forward, squealing tires peeling rubber, flying from 5 mph to 75 mph in seconds. Larry's body shot up from under the steering wheel, deeply relieved and unbelieving that not a single shot was fired. His right foot kept the gas pedal floored. 105 mph. Through the rearview mirror, he saw the two cars behind him growing smaller as the distance between them grew larger. Those damn shit-colored sedans. Wrapped in nondescript brown, like porn shipped through the mail. Like that fooled anybody.

Plain brown sedans.

FBI. Corrupt to the bone.

Just like Rocky said they were.

CHAPTER 2

Ten Months Earlier
January 1976

Larry got off the elevator on the third floor, turned right, and walked partway down the dimly lit white plastered hallway, pausing in front of the office door with the opaque puckered glass inset with Judge Franklin C. Abbot in large blue letters sprawled across it. Instinctively he straightened the red silk tie he had carefully selected earlier that morning. It complemented his French-cuffed white shirt and tailor-made, dark-gray pin-striped suit, which he had also carefully selected. His black Allen Edmonds shoes were buffed to a flawless shine. It wasn't that Larry was fussy, and certainly not effete, but clearly he was precise. "Natty" and "successful professional" were synonymous to him, and Larry was always natty. Had to be. He had already successfully argued before the United States Supreme Court, not once but twice, and all before his thirty-fifth birthday. Which, by the way, was exactly three days ago. Success, as well as his handsome face, fit basketball-player-height body, and easy gait gave him an air of self-assuredness. More of a swagger than an air, but he wore it well.

He had left his black cashmere overcoat in the back seat of his car in case the predicted snow actually arrived with all its projected fierceness. He was macho, not stupid. Blizzards and coats went together, even for him. But for the most part, his style, if not his politics, was more John F. Kennedy. Coatless and hatless whenever possible.

"You must be Mr. Strong. Good morning," greeted the trim, middle-aged woman, interrupting her typing, and smiling up at Larry as he entered the surprisingly decent-sized outer office. Her smile lingered on him just a tad long, and then she nodded toward the open door to the inner sanctum. "Judge Abbot is expecting you."

"Thanks," Larry replied, lighting her face with his own demure smile. He strode past her work station and peered inside the adjoining room to a large oak desk that dominated the area. Behind that desk was a figure even more imposing than the furniture on which he was leaning.

Santa Claus.

No beard, no red suit, no sleigh full of toys. But the spitting image of Santa all the same. He was on the phone and motioned Larry to a seat in front of the desk. Rotund belly, unlined face in spite of his sixty-plus years, bright eyes tinged with intelligence and bemusement. And, of course, ruby-red cheeks. His voice was even, with a broad lilt. Not southern, but with that genteelness.

Santa.

His Honor finished the call quickly, sat down, held up his wait-just-a-minute index finger, swiveled his worn tan leather chair away from Larry, then sneezed and blew into his handkerchief. *Could be the culprit behind those rosy cheeks,* thought Larry.

Judge Abbot pocketed his hankie, swiveled back around, and rose himself up to his full 5′10″ stature. The two men shook hands. "Mister Strong, have yourself a seat. Glad you could make it."

"Thank you, sir," replied Larry amiably as he settled into one of the two chairs positioned in front of the desk.

The judge paused, eyeing Larry for a moment, absently stroking his chin like a bearded man would. "There's a fellow over there in our Licking County jail by the name Rocky Hamilton, who claims to be an FBI snitch, and that's probably true. But he also claims to have been working undercover when he got involved in the aggravated murder felony for which he's been indicted. Normally, I would be more hands off. But something about the set-up doesn't set well in my craw. The accused knows too much about the inner workings of these guys from—what is that farm out there in Virginia? Quantico?"

"Right. Quantico."

"Hell, Hamilton is practically running weekly seminars on the FBI as well as the inner workings of bank robbery gangs for our law enforcement personnel. He's become something of a minor celebrity. The guy is good, chattering away like a magpie, drawing police and even members of your profession from neighboring counties. Friday afternoons in our jailhouse may never be the same...." His Honor shook his head and let out a rueful laugh, which led to a sputtering cough. Another round with his handkerchief, a swallow of stale black coffee, and he returned his attention to Larry. "All things considered, I think I'm going to feel a whole lot better about this if we can level the playing field a little before we get any further into the game. Now, don't get me wrong, Mr. Strong, we have excellent attorneys in our little area here in Newark, Ohio, and I've already assigned a very good criminal one to this case. We've got a good prosecutor, a good defense attorney. Even-Steven. But then we factor in the long arm and resources of the FBI."

"No more even-Steven," smiled Larry.

"Right you are. And that's why you're here today. I need someone with a national reputation who can handle the heat and the clout. Justice doesn't have a prayer of working if it's not a fair game."

"It's interesting, Judge, but I don't know that I'm your man. I've never tried a capital murder case. You know I'm usually more immersed in constitutional law. Give me a First Amendment case and I'll bring it home for you like a Christmas turkey."

Larry gulped silently. Jeez, had he really voiced a Christmas euphemism to Santa? Hopefully, His Honor hadn't noticed.

"Well, sir," replied the judge with aplomb, "you might bag the bird here, too. Who knows? I don't. Why not expand your venues? Clearly you are experienced in taking on the big boys, and that's what this case needs. 'Course, you won't make any money to speak of. The State doesn't give me many options. On the other hand, I can promise you this: it *will* be entertaining."

"David and Goliath, huh?"

"Go for this one, Strong. Lead chair. You'll have a hell of a ride."

"I'll think about it."

Judge Abbot handed him a thick folder. "Take a look at what we know so far. You can use one of my conference rooms."

Larry reviewed the file. Rocky Hamilton, the defendant, had been indicted for aggravated murder and kidnapping of Assistant Bank Manager Jamie MacDonald of the Detroit National Bank. Two other assailants had been indicted as well, but one had been given immunity to testify against Rocky. The defendant was claiming to be a snitch for the FBI and was involved in this case simply to keep them informed. Without going any further, Larry knew this case had teeth to it, and he wanted to hear what the defendant had to say.

Before he could return the file, Judge Abbot appeared in the doorway. Larry's nod was the only indication the judge needed to know that Larry was agreeing to take the case. As Larry walked out of the courthouse and across the street to the county jail, he glanced at his surroundings. On the few occasions he had been to Newark, he had never paid much attention to the downtown area with its plain, modest, and tidy storefronts. The residential area began just one block away—rows of small houses, mostly of stucco and worn paint.

Larry glanced at his watch. Almost noon. He walked past a tea shop, which was the only place he knew of to get a hot sandwich, but all the seats were taken. Children out to lunch from a nearby school took up many of the tables. So, he decided to skip lunch and go on over to the jail and talk with his new client.

The room was nothing more than a small, cold, dingy, sterile box, 8′ x 8′ x 8′ at best. An ancient, scarred, oblong table and four web-backed, metal-based chairs were its only adornment, not counting the small, barred window near the upper right corner. Larry didn't. His focus was on the man clad in the orange jumpsuit sitting across from him. Average height, clean-shaven, well-groomed, leaning to flab. Definitely not a gym rat. So this was his newest client, or as Judge Abbot put it, the "smooth, smooth talker."

Larry had his game face on. He was a pro. His open, impassive face reflected that to perfection. Defense attorneys are always skeptical in early meetings with all those poor, innocent people accused of dastardly deeds, but Larry was not about to let his newest client become aware of that tidbit.

Besides, after his talk with Judge Abbot, he was a little more inclined to give "the benefit of the doubt" its due.

"Rocky, I'm Larry Strong, and I'm—"

"I sure do know who you are, man," interrupted Rocky affably. "I already heard the rumor that they was looking to get you as my lawyer so I been checking around about ya." He shook his head and smiled broadly. "I'll tell ya what. I thought they was gonna stick me with some two-bit, starving Public Defender. Man. I hit the jackpot with you. You're like a celebrity. I need to tell you right up front that I am *not* guilty. No, sir, I am absolutely *not* guilty. I did not kill that kid from the bank. I been workin' for them FBI boys all along. They knew about this snatch from the time we first started plannin' it. I was their inside man. But, boy howdy, I sure do need someone smart enough to prove it. Them Feds, they bailed on me when things got dicey, and now they're settin' me up. I'm screwed. But now," Rocky said looking Larry straight in the eye, "I got some pull on my side. I needed a heavy hitter 'cause the FBI, man, they don't mess around. I just know that you, my man, are gonna save my ass."

"Listen, Rocky," said Larry, "heavy hitter, celebrity—it's all bullshit. None of that matters. What's important here is that you understand that you're now in an attorney-client privilege relationship and that every time we talk it will be under that protective umbrella. Your life depends on understanding that, and on being absolutely straight with me, telling me everything so that I can defend you. The State wants to fry you, pal, and if you withhold information and I get surprised in court because of a lie or omission on your part, you are going to help them accomplish their goal. You tell me everything, and I will decide what to do with it. Capisce? It's your life, so don't be stupid about it."

"Yeah, sure, okay. But we already got a problem."

"What's that?"

Rocky looked up at the overhead light and said, "Them Big Boys play by their own rules." Then without making a sound while pointing upward, he broadly mouthed "bug in light."

"What!" exclaimed Larry.

"See for yourself," replied Rocky, still pointing up.

Larry climbed onto the rickety table and unscrewed the cheap light fixture with a dime from his pocket. "I'll be damned!" he muttered as he peered into the bowels of the fixture. There it was, plain as day. He ripped out the listening device, replaced the dirt-and-insect-encrusted glass globe, and climbed down from the table, electronic bug in hand.

"Good God," said Larry, holding up the device and shaking his head. "Wiring an attorney's client conference room in a jail or courthouse is illegal in every state and federal jurisdiction in this country. It's a felony."

"I'm tellin' you, man, the FBI don't do felonies. The FBI does the FBI," Rocky said, picking up the electronic bug. "There could be more of them things in here. Next time, bring a portable radio or somethin'. Ain't no problem for them to replace that thing the minute we leave this room, and then there is them spike mikes...."

"They can pick sound up from outside the building," finished Larry.

"Right."

"I'll bring the radio."

In high spirits, Rocky was returned to his cell and immediately picked up a ball, maybe an inch or so in diameter—like the size of the one you'd get in a game of jacks or one of those paddle ball gizmos sold at the five and dime store. He bounced it rhythmically from the cinder block wall of his 6′ x 8′ cell into his hand then back to the wall, then to his hand, then the wall. He sat there in his orange jumpsuit, the uniform he'd worn for most of his life courtesy of one state or another, his butt propped on the edge of his cot with its skinny mattress. The ball shot back at him. Contraband. It pleased him to have some. It always had. He snagged the rubber missile out of the air with his left hand, instantly propelling it toward the wall again at an angle that would force it to boomerang to his right side.

Back and forth.

Forth and back....

He still had it. Hell, yeah, he still had it. As long as he could still spin it, he was in control. It had always been that way with him. He could remember back to when he was five, living in Detroit's hood, his alcoholic old man slapping him silly, slamming his pint-sized head around like some kind of bloomin' punching bag. So hard he saw stars. And his mom—hell, she was all over the place. She was a high-pitched, whiny, angry broad—hard on the sauce herself. God, he hated whiners! She had a helluva backhand made worse by her ratty wooden spoon. She was a terror, all right. Except when she wasn't. Except when she didn't yell or hit. Didn't drink. Didn't....

You just never knew.

By the time young Rocky was six, he had pretty much figured it out. If he could entertain them, spin a story, stay in their good graces, he could deflect his father's rage and his mother's unpredictability, and somebody else would get the brunt of it. Rocky didn't give a shit who it was as long as it wasn't him. His newfound, first-grade-level wisdom wasn't exactly salvation, though. It didn't keep him—it couldn't keep him—out of trouble. After all, he was still in the hood. But it did let him feel in control. And in many ways, he was, as he wormed his way out of situation after situation. At six, he had the cunning strategy of a delinquent; at twelve, he had the JV record to match it. At fourteen, he walked out of school for the last time. Hail, hail the gang's all here. He hit the streets with his cronies, and quickly found himself immersed in the revolving doors of jails and prisons.

And just like that, a lifetime criminal was born.

Whap! The ball careened back into Rocky's left hand. No, the guards ain't gonna give *him* no grief. He made sure of that. They're suckers for insider dope. So he set himself up to be the friendly bearer of the news they wanted to hear. How do the gangs really work? He'd drop tidbits here, making sure, of course, that they knew he was just reporting, but not a part of that. What about the inner sanctum of the FBI? He'd drop tidbits there, making sure they knew that he *was* a part of this. They became his buddies; he became their buddy, and now Friday afternoons were his. He'd hold court once a week for two or three hours, speaking to whatever group of deputies and law enforcement had gathered and regale them with his insider scoops. Yep, he took care of them, and in return, they took care of him. Worked like a charm. It always had.

Oh, yeah, he still had it, alright. Damn right. Look at him, stuck here in this county jail, not a penny to his name, with them Feds trying to ram this murder rap up his ass, and Mr. Bigshot Attorney was now pimping for him. High-falutin' Mister Larry Strong was now representing Mister Rocky Hamilton.

Yep, by golly, he's still got it.

CHAPTER 3

Friday, December 5, 1975
8:28 a.m.

This can't be happening. It's like something out of The Twilight Zone. *It's a dream, a Rod Serling-level, Class A nightmare. It must have been that pickled fish from last night that Mother loves so much. It reminds her of the old country. Not me. I was only seven when we left Scotland, and I have never liked fish. When I wake up from this nightmare, I'll have to ask my sister if she and the kids got sick, too.*

Because ***this just can't be happening!***

How could it be? Thirty seconds ago, I pulled into my bank's parking lot, turned off the engine, and checked my watch. Damn, I had wanted to get here earlier. The audit is coming up and there's all this extra work. I slammed the door of my old Pinto, shivering against a blast of cold air. Detroit in December – jeez! So, here I was reaching into the back seat, grabbing my briefcase and the manila file folder I threw on top of it when I ran out of the house this morning. The dog-gone file slips out of my hand and a few papers scatter onto the floor. I lean further into the back seat to collect them, and that is when I hear a voice, calm and clear – almost genial – coming from a guy on my right. "Don't make any noise, buddy. I got a gun in my pocket and a bullet that's got your name on it. You get my drift, bank boy?"

Good Lord in heaven, what is happening here?

"You make any noise or fast moves, and you're a dead man." On my left, a more excited, rapid-paced male voice. "Yeah, that's right, asshole. Back out of the car right now!"

Stay calm, I say to myself. Stay calm. Remember the instruction manual they gave you when you became assistant branch manager last year. There's a card in it telling you what to do on the off chance that something like this occurs. But who pays attention to that crap? It's like getting the safety directions from the stewardess when the plane's about to take off and actually expecting to have to use the flippin' life jacket. Who thinks like that? No one would ever set foot on a plane. No one would ever work in a bank.

Good God! What did the card say?

What did the damn card say?

Just stay calm, Jamie. You'll remember.

I back out of the car slowly and pull myself up to my full height – all 5'5½" of me – and begin to raise my hands in the air. It takes every ounce of my will and pride to keep from peeing myself. Oh, God....

"Put your friggin' hands down and act natural," the voice on my right says, now not so calm. My hands drop to my side. I look up at the guy – 5'10", flabby. Probably 190, 195 pounds. I may be short, but I'm fit. I think I could take him. Except that his right hand is in his jacket pocket and a sharp bulge is pointing directly at me.

*That card. Damn! I **cannot** remember.*

*What the hell **am** I supposed to do?*

Then I look at flabby man's face and... and he's wearing a mask. One of those flexible, rubber Halloween types that look real from a distance. Up close, it's clearly a mask. He has blond hair and sideburns that flare out a little near his earlobes, same as mine. I know I am supposed to remember details; that's the only authentic detail I can be sure of.

Memorize it, Jamie, I tell myself, so that if you get out of this mess you can describe these men to the authorities.

Not if, Jamie, when. ***When*** *you get out of this.*

I look away before I can even think to catch the color of his eyes. I feel a little wet dribble slither down my left thigh. Oh, God, how embarrassing even in front of these two slobs!

The guy on my left, skinnier, shorter – maybe 5′8″ or so, dark unkempt hair, Arab-looking mask – sidles in close to me; the guy on my right does the same. I am sandwiched tightly between them, and they quickly hustle me into the front seat of their blue Chevrolet precariously parked perpendicular to my car, engine running. A Monte Carlo, I think. I was so preoccupied with getting into the bank, I never even saw or heard them pull up!

Arab-mask is in the driver's seat, blonde sideburns is in the passenger's seat, and I am stuffed between these two creeps. The driver points to a car slowed at the alley entrance next to the parking lot. Joyce, a bank clerk, stops her car and looks at me, almost frozen. I probably look the same as I stare, wide-eyed and desperate, back at her. Then she sees they have noticed her and she speeds off. Arab-mask peels rubber as he races out of the familiar safety of my parking lot. By the time he turns right onto the street, Joyce's car is nowhere to be found.

I am alone now, and more terrified than I have ever been in all my twenty-five years. Ninety seconds – two minutes tops – have passed since I first stepped out of my Pinto this morning. Ninety seconds….

A lifetime ago….

Dear God, let me wake up. Please, I am begging You; let me wake up.

Because, ***this can't be happening!***

CHAPTER 4

July 1976 – Deep Throat

It bruised Larry's ego to do so, but on this incredibly hot and humid night he had to acknowledge that his Trans Am had a lot more pep and fire than he did. Which only frustrated him more. He prided himself on being a man of boundless energy. It helped him maintain that competitive edge. But tonight, after another irritatingly protracted day at the courthouse and dungeon-like jail in Newark, followed by the long, sweaty, and stifling commute back home to Columbus, it was a no-brainer. Machine had bested man, hands down.

He wearily pulled his car to a stop in front of his house and turned off the engine, leaving gravelly-voiced Rod Stewart mid-lyric. Larry's foul mood notwithstanding, the music continued unabated to Larry's brain after the radio fell silent. He couldn't remember the exact words of the song, just something about a man's desire and his heart on fire. Well, maybe Rod's got a point, thought Larry as he finished collecting his briefcase and endless extraneous papers from the trunk and trudged up to the front door. Getting laid might be exactly what the doctor would have ordered—had one been around.

With that in mind, Larry opened the door and forced out a cheerful hello which, in spite of the lights that were on, was met with dead silence. A bold note tacked to the message board next to the mustard-colored wall phone in the kitchen informed him that his wife, Letty, and their two sons had given up on him for the night and gone to the movies for popcorn and air-conditioning. "Air-conditioning" was underlined, all caps, double exclamation points. Chicken salad in the fridge.

Swell.

So much for trying to redeem the day.

He pulled a beer out of the fridge, opened it, and plopped heavily on an olive-green cushioned dinette chair, perfectly coordinated with the gold/olive/yellow wallpaper print prominent in the room. Leave it to Letty; she always pulled everything together—their social life, their kids' lives, the comforts of their home. They were, from his point of view, a textbook couple. Normally that thought would bring a smile to his face. Tonight, his only response was another large swig of his beer. He glanced down at the newspaper Letty had left out for him on the table, as she did every evening. Dayton, having run out of excuses, was finally being strong-armed into the last quarter of the twentieth century. Whether they liked it or not, their schools were going to be forcibly integrated in September. Larry, politically conservative but socially liberal, would have let out an alleluia, had he not been so damned tired. And so damned pressed.

He had hit a wall with his FBI snitch case starring the infamously psychopathic Rocky Hamilton. Or was he? Maybe he was just some poor bastard, not overly bright, who came up the hard way and got caught in the middle. After a day like today, who the hell knows?

Crap....

Larry's thoughts drifted to today's court session. But Your Honor, the prosecution has the full resources of the State—what with its lawyers, police, and investigators—*and* the seemingly limitless reserves of the FBI to help in the research and preparation of its case. Hell, they've practically got the entire *federal government* behind them, and, dollars to donuts, those bozos are going to lie through their damn teeth. *And* here the defense stands, empty pockets turned inside out, and we can't get bupkis to help our cause. Shit, we have trouble getting a lousy buck and a quarter to cover the cost of copies at the local office supply store, for God's sake.

The Court: Sorry, Mr. Defense Attorney. It ain't fair.

Larry: But Your Honor, after I pay my office staff, long-distance telephone bills, travel between here and my home in Columbus and going up to Detroit to check out physical evidence that the FBI can't seem to get down here, I'll be lucky to break minimum wage.

The Court: Pro bono sucks, son.

Larry: Your Honor, I have not been able to get the proper documentation, records, and exculpatory evidence that the prosecution is required by law to surrender to the defense. Nada. No lists, no telephone records, no nothing.

The Court: Mr. Prosecutor, what do you have to say to this?

The Prosecutor: I'd say the defense counselor is way in over his head and needs to hire more staff to help him in his investigation.

Larry: Screw you!

The Court: Now, boys. Let's make nice. I don't intend to get involved in any rhubarb between you two counselors.

Larry interrupted his internal replay of the day just long enough to get up and grab another beer out of the refrigerator. Of course, Judge Abbot and the prosecutor hadn't actually said those words in court, although they might as well have. Larry hadn't said them either. God knows, if he had, he'd be spending the night in that rotting Licking County jail along with good ol' Rocky Hamilton.

Here it is July, only four months until trial date, thought Larry, *and I haven't been able to get peanuts from either the prosecutor's office or from the FBI.* Back in late May, Larry had gleaned some information from the trial of Skip Nowalsky, who had been found *guilty* for actually stabbing Jamie MacDonald to death. In connection with that trial, articles in *The Detroit Press* and Newark's newspaper, *The Advocate,* had informed the public of the FBI's role in the crime. Larry took a bulging manila folder from his briefcase. It held all the newspaper articles his paralegal had clipped relative to the kidnapping and murder of Jamie MacDonald and the Nowalsky trial. One headline blared, *"Did mistakes by kidnappers and FBI cause banker's death?" Hell yes,* thought Larry, *and I am going to prove it.*

The author of the article probably had it right when he wrote "it appears that the biggest mistake made by MacDonald's suspected abductors was that they had no plan beyond kidnapping him and demanding a $250,000 ransom. While MacDonald was taken to a house in Ohio by one of the kidnappers, the other remained in Detroit and made telephoned ransom demands. The original attempt to collect the ransom failed when a bank official arrived an hour later than the kidnappers had instructed. Subsequently, several appeals were made on radio and television broadcasts for the kidnappers to get in touch with bank officials and arrange the $250,000 ransom drop. Although the kidnappers never came up with an alternative spot, they kept looking for one. While doing so, they mistakenly believed they were spotted by police surveillance. That mistake, which caused the kidnappers to panic, is believed by the FBI to have led to MacDonald's death."

The article continued to then point out the mistakes

made by the FBI. "Obviously, the most critical mistake made by investigators of the kidnapping came when FBI agents who had set up surveillance of the house where MacDonald was being held did not rush in and capture him, for fear that the abductors would kill him at the first kick of the door. Instead, while waiting, they failed to notice when MacDonald was taken from the house shortly before midnight on December 9th, and driven to the woods on County Road 216 in Eden Township about three miles away, where he was stabbed to death. His body was found two days later on a pile of dead limbs on the side of this desolate rural dirt road."

Larry couldn't wait to get these bumbling FBI agents on the witness stand and embarrass the hell out of them. The blaring ring of the phone saved Larry from slipping further into the rabbit hole. He snatched it up and said abruptly, "Strong here."

"I am going to make this your lucky day, Mr. Strong," the male caller said with a slight Midwest twang. Chicago. Those flat a's were a dead giveaway.

"Who are you?"

"Let's just say I am your Deep Throat."

A shot of adrenalin rushed through Larry's body. He pressed the phone closer to his ear. He couldn't detect any white-haired geezer in the voice on the other end of the line, but still it was mature enough to have been around the block a couple times. Probably late thirties. The anonymous caller spoke in cool, almost clipped tones. Not an ounce of good ol' boy camaraderie here. All three-piece suit with matching button-down vest.

"I am with the FBI. Don't get your hopes up too high. I am never coming out of the closet, you will never be able to identify me, and I will never testify. I value my job and pension too much to allow that."

"Okay, then. Why are we talking?"

"I've been reading about your case in *The Detroit News*. I know that everybody is negating your claims that the FBI is involved in a massive cover-up. I want to tell you that you are 100% on track. We screwed up. The kid died, and your client got dumped. I know that if I sit back and do nothing, your man will be executed. I will not permit that, because we were involved up to our necks. So here is what I will do. I am going to feed you information and document numbers that validate the information. You'll never get the information you need without the numbers. When you ask for these documents by number, they will know you have somebody on the inside. That might actually be your best ploy for leverage."

"All right. But you will see me make references to you. That will be leverage, too," said Larry. "I want it in their face that I have an inside source, and I'm going to suggest that this source may testify."

"That, of course, is not going to happen."

"Of course not. You'll never testify, because I'll never know your name. But I'm a bluffer, and I'm going to bluff my way through this, because that may be the only chance I have of getting anyone to tell the truth under oath. If they believe I've got a real Deep Throat for this case, and he's going to take the stand, then maybe—just maybe—they won't lie. Speaking of not lying, how do I know that you're for real?"

"Got a pencil? Let me give you a few specific documents by number."

Larry scribbled rapidly.

"You make your requests for production of these papers. You will see what's in them and know that I am very real."

"What's next?"

"I'll follow your progress through the news and contact you. Code name: Protectorate."

A click, followed by a dial tone, let Larry know the call was over.

CHAPTER 5

Friday, December 5, 1975
10:30 a.m. (maybe)

I have no idea how much time has passed. It seems like forever, although I still can't breathe, and all I can think to do is cooperate. That's got to be what the manual says. What else would the bank want me to do? Attack these guys with my nail clippers? Cooperating is what I'm doing, and it's what these two jerks are telling me to do. "Cooperate and you'll be home before the day ends," they keep saying to me. So, I let them move me into the back seat without protesting. Not that I had much choice. I'm crouched down with my face flattened against the bottom of the seat, my coat tossed over my head, and, oh yes, my hands tied behind my back with some kind of thick rope. So now I'm a friggin' contortionist.

What is wrong with me? I really did feel like crap when I woke up this morning. I even thought about calling in sick.

Calling in sick….

I could have called in sick….

WHY THE HELL DIDN'T I JUST CALL IN SICK!!

How hard would that have been? But no, of course, Jamie MacDonald wouldn't call in sick. Jamie is always the good guy, always the responsible one, always taking care of things, always being the dutiful employee.

WHY THE HELL DIDN'T I JUST CALL IN SICK!!

Uh-oh. The car has stopped again. Genial-voice is speaking to Arab-mask (at least that's how he looked when last I saw him). "Watch him. I'll go talk to Jason."

"What!" exclaims Arab-mask.

"For Pete's sake, Skippy. You don't just bring somebody by without asking!"

Oh please, spare me. It's turned into a damn freak show. Amy Vanderbilt surfaces in the midst of a kidnapping. ***My*** *kidnapping. What kind of insane alternate reality am I stuck in? Beam me up, Scotty. For the love of God, beam me up!*

Please, dear God, *let me wake up from this.* ***Please*** *let this be over.*

Minutes—probably only three or four—pass in silence. The front passenger door opens. Genial-voice says to the newly-named Skippy, "Bring 'im in after me and take 'im downstairs. Make 'im keep his head down so he don't recognize you. Make sure he knows to keep his mouth shut."

Footsteps move away from the car, then Skippy pulls at me. "Come on, asshole, get out of the car. You heard 'im. Head down and mouth shut. I'm carrying, man, and I'll use it if you as much as fart, so don't try nothing funny."

Coat thrown over my shoulders, head down, mouth closed, I am led through the door into a narrow hallway. Skippy nudges me in front of him to go down the steep steps. I am shaking so badly that I stumble on the first one. Skippy's quick reflexes, grabbing my arm and yanking it back toward him, are the only thing that keeps me from tumbling head long from top to bottom. The room is unfinished and dimly lit. He orders me on the cold cement floor, face down.

"Eyes closed," he commands. And I am not willing to provoke him by trying to sneak a peek. The next thing I know, his knee is in my back and a cloth with a paint-smell residue is being wrapped around my eyes. I lose control of the panic and start to wriggle.

"Hold still," he says menacingly, only asking the impossible.

With all my might, I focus on my breathing, trying to slow it down. I feel the rope being wrapped around my ankles and pulled tight. I am now more helpless than a trussed turkey.

Footsteps. Two sets descending. Genial-voice and someone I haven't heard before.

The new guy, nasal-voiced like he has a cold, says to me, "Hey, buddy. We have to figure out how much to get for you. How much are you worth? Think we can get a million?"

"It's possible, I think. But they would have trouble putting that much cash together. I don't know how long it would take. It would take a lot more than a few hours."

"What will them guys do quick?" This from genial-voice.

"Well, it's like this, every bank employee from janitor on up is insured for three hundred thousand dollars. Anything under that is probably more doable in a short time frame."

"Then, let's go for two-fifty," pipes in nasal-voice. "Two hundred fifty thousand dollars it is."

Unexpectedly, the smell of adhesive floods my nostrils as tape goes around my mouth. Breathe, remember to breathe. You can get through this, Jamie. Breathe.

Then hands – I don't know whose – reach underneath me and – Oh no, God no. Those hands fumble with my belt and undo my zipper. I hear my own muffled sounds emerge from underneath my duct-tape gag, as my pants are pulled down roughly, my penis catching on the cold concrete, my naked ass exposed.

NO! NO! NO!

Suddenly, I am attacked by a giant hornet on my left hip. A damn giant hornet!

Through my panicked, fuzzy brain, I hear the new guy say, "Damn, man! You gave him enough to knock out a friggin' horse!"

And then… nothing.

CHAPTER 6

July 1976 – Pre-Trial Discovery
Licking County Courthouse

"Your Honor, if it pleases the Court," said Larry rising, dangling a stack of papers in the air, "what in the world am I supposed to do with these? Initially, the defense can't catch a break as far as getting the FBI to turn over documents pertinent to this case, and then when I ask for specific documents, by number, no less, this is what I get." Larry slaps the offending sheaf down on the defense table with just enough force to make a point, but not enough to rile His Honor. Judge Abbot may have initially reminded Larry of Santa, but weeks ago his first five minutes in pre-trial motions had demonstrated for Larry the validity of the old saw. Looks are deceiving. Clearly, the man that Larry would spend the next several months referring to—more often than not—as the Court was no pushover. Neither was he a prick. Actually, Larry detected a guarded sympathy from time to time from Judge Abbot regarding Larry's inability to gain access to information he needed. Judge Abbot was indeed the one bright spot so far in the case. Well, actually now there were two—the Court and the Protectorate.

Let's see if the latter will pay off.

Larry grabbed the top sheet, strutting toward the bench

with it. Pointing with his black horn-rimmed glasses for emphasis, he showed the judge what he was complaining about. The redacted document had a name and number on it, a partial opening line and, near the bottom of the page, a half-assed closing line. The rest of the sheet was totally blacked out. Not so much as a preposition or a pronoun in sight. Larry, with his long stride, crossed over to the defense table and brought the rest of the similarly redacted stack up to the bench.

"We have this motion before the Court today, to compel the government to give the defense the unredacted documents that we have requested. The suggestion that all of this blacked-out material represents a national security risk is ludicrous. The government and the prosecution want us to believe that the release of this information will blow covers and give away trade secrets. Nonsense! The only cover that this data will blow is the FBI's complicity in and responsibility for the crime for which my client stands accused. This is the government at its worst, Your Honor. We saw it in spades three years ago with the scandalous Watergate. Unbent, our government is still using the same corrupt tactics—"

Prosecutor Gary Lansing's "Objection!" rang out with a healthy dose of theatrical pique. "The defense is standing on a soap box, Judge. It's irrelevant!"

The Court, with furrowed brow as he peered over the half-glasses precariously perched on the tip of his nose, replied, "Well, this is pre-trial, Mr. Lansing. There's no jury here. So we'll allow it for now. But, Mr. Strong, don't stray too far."

"Thank you, Your Honor. The prosecution, the FBI, and the US attorneys who have an interest in this case have placed a stranglehold on the defense. As can be plainly seen, the government's unusual and avid interest in this case is demonstrated by the fact that we once again have an assistant US attorney sitting at the prosecutor's table today. It is, in fact, the government's corrupt tactics that go to the heart of our case. Admittedly, until three years ago, Mr. Hamilton had been a career criminal. A thief. But never had he been charged with a direct act of violence. He was a bank robber who was arrested for a parole violation in Albuquerque, New Mexico, and cherry-picked by the FBI to become an informant. They wanted to nail the ringleaders of the most notorious gang of bank robbers of our time, most of whom Rocky had hung out with since he was a boy. They also wanted to catch the notorious bank robber and kidnapper, Chuck Wilson, who had slipped out of their clutches just a few months earlier, and whom Rocky Hamilton had also known most of his life. They needed to get the egg off their face by nabbing Chuck in the act to ensure he could never walk out of their grasp again. And how do they do that? In today's world, how does the FBI make sure that their evidence is irrefutable? Not by preventing the crime, not by stopping it mid-process, but after the fact. They catch the robber outside the bank, after the crime has been committed, holding the bag of money. That's how they do it, and that's what they were looking for when they recruited Rocky to work for the Federal Bureau of Investigation."

"Objection!" exploded Gary Lansing. "Spare us, please! Is Mr. Strong almost done with his rambling fantasy?"

"Your Honor, I am simply laying out the basis for our case. Rocky Hamilton became one of the most productive and highly paid snitches in the history of the FBI, and now they are trying to run from him faster than a rat runs from a sinking ship. Rocky was working for them at the time of this crime. They are claiming he wasn't. Rocky informed them of his whereabouts and the situation during the course of this crime. They claim he didn't. I must have access to the information on these documents so I can prove the government's involvement and complicity. For you to deny me that would be to deny me my defense and Rocky Hamilton a fair trial."

The Court said, "Are you alleging then that anything that your client might have done in this case he did on behalf of the FBI as an agent? Your theory is that he was an employee?"

"If it pleases the Court, we're still in discovery. But basically, that's it."

"Let's get your witnesses up here, Counselor."

FBI Special Agent Jacob Jones from Albuquerque, New Mexico, was sworn in and took the stand. His lanky frame was clothed in the standard agent uniform—conservative suit, conservative tie, typical white long-sleeved shirt, polished shoes, conservative short hair, clean shaven, minimum sideburns. His pose was relaxed and somewhat in charge.

Larry started right in, "Are you the FBI agent who got Rocky Hamilton to sign up?"

"I don't know that I would put it like that, but yes, I did recruit him."

"How did you find him?"

"He was picked up for a parole violation—carrying a concealed weapon—and was being held in a city lock-up in Bernalillo County. I approached him, and after a few days he agreed to talk. He gave me information on two bank robberies which we had under investigation and a fugitive we were looking for."

"Was the information good? Authentic?"

"Yes."

"What did he tell you?"

"He told us who robbed the banks."

"He was in a local jail on a parole violation. Did you have

any interest in getting him out of those charges for information received?"

"I think that may have been a possibility."

"A possibility or probability?"

"Objection," intoned the prosecutor.

"Withdrawn. Was this *possibility* in fact a reality in this case?"

"No. He just appeared one day and said he was out of jail."

"And you had no idea how he got out? You played no part in that?"

"No."

"Agent Jones, did you lead Rocky to believe that you had played a big part in getting him out to get further information from him?"

"I may have alluded to that."

"Were you in the courtroom in Albuquerque in 1973 when the concealed gun charge against Rocky was dismissed and the gun returned to Rocky, a convicted felon wanted in Detroit for parole violation, in that very courtroom?"

"No."

"And you had nothing to do with that?"

"Of course not."

"Of course not. Whatever could I have been thinking?" interjected Larry sarcastically.

"Mr. Strong..." admonished the Court.

"Sorry, Your Honor. Agent Jones, do you have any idea about how Mr. Hamilton's bond, which had been set as a $5,000 property bond when he was incarcerated in Albuquerque, was suddenly dropped to a $500 surety bond during the two months that you had your three or four in-person contacts with him?"

On cue the prosecutor piped in with his favorite word. "Objection!"

"If he knows, he may answer," responded the Court.

"Agent?" probed Larry.

"I have no idea."

"Did you have any knowledge that there was an Alcohol, Tobacco, and Firearms warrant on Mr. Hamilton when he was in your jail?"

"It's not my jail—and no, I did not."

"And that, too, just disappeared into thin air, like the bond reduction just sort of appeared out of thin air?"

"Objection!" cried the prosecutor.

"Sustained."

"Agent Jones, are you aware that there was an extradition proceeding being filed against Mr. Hamilton to get him back to Michigan while he was in your friendly city?"

"I would assume Michigan would take the proper procedures to get him back."

"That's non-responsive, Agent. Did you have any part in terminating the extradition?"

"No."

"That just happened out of thin air also, and you had no knowledge of how that happened either?"

"I never had the foggiest idea."

"In the two months in which Mr. Hamilton was under your jurisdiction, before you turned him over to the Detroit FBI office, did you ever furnish him with a phony driver's license?"

"Objection!"

"Now what?" asked the Court.

"The defense is on a fishing expedition."

"Mr. Strong, is there any relevancy here?"

"Shows a course of conduct."

The Court said to Agent Jones, "Well, did you do it or not?"

"Yes."

"Did you do that because Mr. Hamilton was wanted by the law?" bulldozed Larry rapidly.

"Absolutely not."

"You know the phrase 'Absolute power corrupts absolutely?'"

In a flash the prosecutor was on his feet. "Your Honor, that's outrageous!"

"Save it for the jury, Mr. Strong," tsk-tsked the Court.

"Well then, Your Honor, until there's a ruling on these redacted documents," petitioned Larry, once again using his glasses as a pointer, gesturing toward the stack of papers still sitting in front of the judge, "and I can get more proof of these allegations, my hands are pretty much tied."

"Well, you're free to ask any questions that you wish."

"That doesn't mean I am going to get proper answers, sir."

Larry thought he detected a slight look of understanding cross the face of the judge, who then looked at his watch. "Considering the hour, we'll adjourn until tomorrow morning, 9:00. I'll hear your next witness and give my ruling then."

"A couple of quick things, if I may, Your Honor," interjected Larry.

"Go ahead."

Larry had decided to seize the opportunity to plant a bluff. He wanted to put the FBI on alert that he might call his "deep throat" to testify in hopes of keeping them honest. He had also put word out on the street that he might be seeking immunity for a gang member to testify, and that rumor had caused all the gang members to leave town. Although there were no witnesses to call, Larry said, "I would like to petition the Court for immunity of an unnamed defense witness."

"Your Honor!" Prosecutor Lansing was on his feet. "The defense knows quite well that there are no provisions in the statute for defense to get immunity for witnesses."

Yes, Larry knew that the statute allowed only the State the privilege of seeking immunity for witnesses, but he argued for equal protection. He knew that Judge Abbot already suspected the FBI was guilty of withholding evidence and a cover-up. Much to Larry's satisfaction and the chagrin of the prosecutor, Judge Abbot said, "I will allow it. And what is your second request?"

"We ask the Court for an order instructing the prosecutor to immediately release certain benign personal items that belong to Mr. Hamilton that were taken from him at the time of his arrest."

"Your Honor, the prosecution is not prepared to move forward on that request at this time."

"Oh, for Pete's sake. It's a wallet, a notebook, a cheap watch, a couple of family pictures. It's as threatening and complicated as a peanut butter sandwich on white bread. Give the man back his stuff."

The Court said sternly, "Work it out, gentlemen. Tonight."

Larry wanted to take advantage of meeting with Rocky while he was in Newark for the day and headed for the jailhouse.

"Rocky, tomorrow I am going to put Agent Howard Bolton on the stand. Can you tell me something about your relationship with Bolton?"

"Okay. My specialty, if you want to call it that, was in the escape routes," began Rocky. "Anybody can rob a bank, but not everybody can get away. That takes a special plan. It's not something just anybody can do. I was a bag man, too."

Larry interrupted, "You would actually participate in the bank robberies?"

"Yeah, of course, man. How else do you think I could stay on the inside?"

"But how could you avoid getting shot when you came out of the bank carrying the loot?"

"We had them masks—the ones that was in the car when they took me in. You always keep your equipment with you. The FBI had pictures of them masks, so they could always know which one I was and let me escape."

"What?" Larry couldn't believe his ears.

"Yeah, man. I didn't want them shootin' me. So I told 'em in advance which mask I would be usin' when I was workin' a case for 'em. And I give 'em a picture. While they was roundin' up the others, I would fake a narrow escape. When you're on the inside, you're always playin' a role. You're always actin'. All right now, my deal with them FBI guys was that whatever was in my bag, I got to keep."

"That was your deal with the FBI?" Larry asked, still not believing what he was hearing.

"Yeah, man, during them early days it was. They claimed they couldn't pay much per job from the FBI, so they let me keep the bag money. After a while, that got changed. By the time I got handed off from Ed Marshall to Howard Bolton in Detroit, they was payin' me with the reward money instead. They fixed it for me to get some or all of the reward that them banks always put up or whatever the FDIC paid the bank. They told me not to worry about it, that there wasn't no loss to the bank or its depositors or shareholders. They was insured for this kind of loss by the FDIC."

Rocky continued, "When I got arrested last December, I was up for $2,500 from one bank and $10,000 from another. They'd told me it was in the works, but I ain't heard a word about it since I been in jail."

"So Jacob Jones in Albuquerque handed you off to Ed Marshall when you went back to Detroit?"

"True. Then when Ed left the FBI in February last year, my contact was Howard Bolton. But Ed never really left, you know. The FBI was in 'im. So I continued to talk to Ed and meet with 'im more than Howard, and Ed would relay information for me when I couldn't get ahold of Howard. Ed understood what it was like on the street. That something could go down at any moment and that I'd need to be able to reach 'im right away, man."

"And were you?"

"Able to reach Ed? Sure. Always was. I had his home number, his mother's number, his girlfriend's number. I could find 'im almost any time. But not Howard. He runs a different way. He don't get it, man. He don't get the street."

CHAPTER 7

July 1976 – Pre-Trial Discovery

The following morning, Larry arrived at the courthouse a good fifteen minutes before starting, as was his habit. He walked rapidly toward the assigned courtroom, but stopped abruptly when he heard voices coming from around the corner. One voice he recognized as Agent Jones, whom he had grilled on the witness stand the previous day. The other he assumed was this morning's target, FBI Special Agent Howard Bolton. Larry needed to squeeze a little more confirmation, or at least suspicion, of dirty tricks out of Bolton to secure a favorable ruling on his motion before the Court. That's what discovery was all about. Jerk 'em around a bit in pretrial, then nail their asses on the witness stand during the trial in front of the jury.

Larry stood motionless. Between the low tenor voice and obvious agitation, Jones's voice carried easily. "That pompous-ass lawyer must have somebody inside feeding him those document numbers. Some disloyal bastard in our ranks. I'd like to get my hands on that son of a bitch!"

"Stay cool," commented the unfamiliar male voice. "That arrogant sewer rat lawyer is nothing but a strutting pretty boy. We're not giving him anything but a bunch of shitty blacked-out documents. He doesn't have a snowball's chance in hell of winning this case. The FBI will see to that!"

Larry clicked into gear and with two quick strides rounded the corner. Knowing they had been overheard, their startled, drop-jawed faces met his cheerful, "Good morning, gentlemen!" Oh, for a camera. Larry forced himself not to laugh out loud until he got inside the courtroom. Priceless....

"All rise!" sounded the bailiff, and court was in session.

"If it pleases the Court," said Larry rising, "the defense calls FBI Special Agent Howard Bolton to the stand, and asks the Court to keep in mind that Agent Bolton is a hostile witness."

"Objection!" imposed Prosecutor Lansing.

What else is new, thought Larry.

"Well, now, Mr. Strong, we are not in front of a jury, so I am not going to declare him a hostile witness at this time."

"But Your Honor—"

"Noted, Mr. Strong; now move on."

"The defense calls Howard Bolton."

Bolton, blond hair turning subtly to gray, buttery around the edges of his 5′8″ frame, strutted to the witness chair and was sworn in.

Larry began with a strut of his own stuff. "In 1975, Mr. Bolton, what area of investigation were you assigned to for the FBI?"

"I worked bank robbery, kidnappings, interstate communications, and stolen property."

"When did you first come in contact with Mr. Hamilton?"

"It was on February 24, 1975."

"Where?"

"At the home of a mutual friend."

"A friend. And perchance was this *friend* also a special agent in the employ of the FBI?"

"Yes."

"Who?"

"Ed Marshall."

"And you met at Ed's house?"

"Yes."

"What was the purpose of the meeting?"

"To turn Rocky Hamilton over to me."

"To turn him over to you how?"

"As an informant."

"Had Mr. Hamilton been an informant for Mr. Marshall prior to that time?"

"He had."

"Had he furnished reliable information to Mr. Marshall before that time?"

"To my knowledge."

Larry darted a purposeful glance at Judge Abbot, and looked askance at Howard Bolton. "I'll take that as a yes. But for the record, I want you to confirm it. Was the information Mr. Hamilton gave to Mr. Marshall accurate or not?"

"Yes, it was."

"Fine. Now that wasn't so hard, was it?"

"Objec—"

"Withdrawn. Mr. Bolton, what kind of information did Rocky Hamilton provide to you between February 24, 1975, and late October of the same year when you claim you terminated him as an informant because his data wasn't useful?"

"He furnished me information regarding bank robberies, narcotics, fugitives, both from our department and from other federal agencies, intelligence information, arson, and that is all that I can specifically recall at this moment."

"You used the term bank robberies, so I assume there was more than one?"

"That is plural, correct."

"How many bank robberies did he give you information on?"

"Just as a rough guess, I would have to estimate that the confirmed information that he gave us would be approximately six banks."

"You used the term, 'fugitives from your department as well as other federal agencies.' Is that plural also accurate?"

"Yes, that is plural also."

"What were the circumstances—the number and circumstances of these?"

"Five would have been in the area of bank robberies, one would have been in the area concerning the Treasury Department, one in the area of Alcohol, Tobacco, and Firearms, and I can't remember any others at this time."

"You say he gave you intelligence information?"

"Correct. Well, let me refine that a little bit for you. It was information concerning the activities of persons believed to be associated with organized crime in the Detroit area."

"What kind of crimes?"

"Arson would have been one, and perhaps loan sharking, I believe."

"What about murders or attempted murders?"

"I don't recall."

"How about kidnapping?"

"I can't recall any of that."

"Mr. Hamilton was one of the highest-paid informants for the FBI. Ever! Yet according to you, during the eight months you were handling him, you paid him only one stipend of $55, and that was on July 10, 1975."

"That is correct."

"You've reviewed your notes prior to coming into court

today? Notes, I might add, that the defense does not yet have," Larry added to emphasize his point to the judge.

"Yes."

"So, tell me, exactly and specifically, what did Mr. Hamilton give you for that $55?"

"The identification of an individual who had committed arson, and information concerning activities of a prominent Detroit bank robbery gang, and information concerning the location of a fugitive wanted by the FBI, and information concerning activities of a Detroit area loan shark, and information concerning the location of the activities of two bank robbers in the Detroit area."

"Was this information accurate?"

"Yes."

"And did this information cause you to be able to secure the arrest of several criminals?"

"Yes."

"You got the bad guys behind bars?"

"I've already said yes!"

"For all of that—all of the information leading to all of the apprehensions of all of those criminals—you paid $55?"

"Yes."

"Was Mr. Hamilton permitted to retain any proceeds from any bank robberies while giving this informant information to your office?"

"No."

"Did your office arrange for Mr. Hamilton to receive the reward money, or a part of the reward money, from banks who, as a result of Rocky's information, recovered their losses?"

"Absolutely not!"

"Fifty-five dollars? I'm glad I don't have to work for you!" Larry turned and quickly waved off Gary Lansing before he could get the objection out of his mouth. "Never mind. I'm done with this witness. For now." Howard Bolton, shoulders squared, brimming with anger, left the witness stand and the courtroom.

The instant the door closed behind Howard Bolton, Larry immediately jumped to his feet to address the Court. "At this time, if it pleases the Court, the defense asks for a ruling on its motion to receive unredacted documents and on its motion for a continuance while we gather the data we need to present at trial."

Suddenly, another world heard from. The man sitting to the left of Prosecutor Lansing for the past two days rose to his feet. "Your Honor, may I introduce myself to the Court? Allen Robarts, Assistant US Attorney for the United States Government."

"Mr. Robarts, sit yourself down this minute before I hold you in contempt. This is not a federal court; it is a court of the State of Ohio, and it is *my* court. You are here as a courtesy I extended to the prosecution, but neither you nor the government of the United States has any standing here. Sit down and stay quiet."

No longer looking like anyone's grandfather, Judge Abbot's flushed cheeks and stern demeanor left no doubt that he had clearly exerted his authority and marked his territory by taking the stance that government attorneys were allowed in his courtroom but were in essence totally unwelcome.

"Now here's what we're going to do. We'll set up a procedure wherein the government will produce each requested document in both unredacted and redacted formats for the Court. The Court will review the documents in their entirety, and if I think there is something significant to the defense being redacted, I will order its production and give the defense appropriate access to it. So, Mr. US District Attorney, you are not going to get a chance to hide pertinent data under the guise of national security, and all that nonsense. As far as I can see, there's nothing pertinent to this case that is going to endanger the world if we know about it."

Larry's heart was doing a victory dance. Obviously, Judge Abbot had had an epiphany. He, too, was now convinced of the FBI's cover-up and was most likely as disgusted as Larry by the lies spewing from the FBI agents on the stand. Larry's inward celebration was short-lived when Judge Abbot said, "As to your second motion, Counselor, one more continuance, but that's it. We'll meet here on Friday morning at 10:00—no, we'd better make that 10:30—to set the trial date."

A quick tap of the gavel and court was adjourned.

CHAPTER 8

July 1976 – Licking County Jail

Larry's empty stomach drove him to practically sprint out of the courthouse and head to the corner diner for an early lunch, musing about what it would take to break the back of the FBI, to say nothing of the sweltering heat wave which continued to dominate as autocratically as the Feds. He slid into an empty booth in the swamp-cooled local haunt, ordered a burger with cheddar, rare—no pickle, no onion. Fries. Something about tearing into semi-raw meat felt psychologically appropriate to him today.

In spite of the help he was getting from Protectorate, the stonewalling of the FBI was a major pain, as was the current culture of the general public's romance with the FBI itself. Like maybe all those primarily WASP special agents—male, of course—were only two steps to the right of Jesus Christ. The stalwart knight-in-shining-armor portrayal of the flawless, super-patriotic Bureau had been liberally disseminated over the airwaves weekly by Efrem Zimbalist, Jr.'s hit television show, *The FBI.*

How long had that been on—nine, ten seasons? A Sunday-night staple. *That should be a fifteen-yard penalty for piling on, for God's sake,* he thought. What few people knew, including all the good white folks here in Licking County, was that each episode of the television show was produced with the endorsement and cooperation of the FBI. The real one. They controlled their image and the storyline. Hell, they even controlled the casting. The *pièce de résistance,* of course, was that each episode was not only subject to general Bureau approval, but also personal approval by HRH himself—Director J. Edgar Hoover, until his death. May his parched, paranoid little being rest in peace.

Make that a twenty-yard penalty….

And this state of public consciousness, accepting without hesitation the lily-white hands of all those oh-so-special, special agents was nestled deep within the gene pool from which Larry was going to have to pull his jury. A rural jury, at that.

Swell.

The burger came. Larry had to force himself not to swallow it whole. Still, he ate rapidly, wiped his hands and mouth with a paper napkin, and tossed it on the plate. He nodded at the haggard waitress, left her a healthy tip, and headed over to the county jail.

Rocky was waiting in the suspect conference room, drawing deeply on a Lucky Strike cigarette when Larry arrived, portable radio in hand. He took the seat across the table from his client.

"We just received one more continuance from the judge. We've got maybe six, maybe eight weeks before we're dealing with a jury, so we've got a lot of ground to cover, Rocky. So talk to me about the days leading up to the kidnapping of Jamie MacDonald."

"All right, now, this is how it was."

"Begin with December 4th, the day before the kidnapping."

"That would be a Thursday," confirmed Rocky. "Well, Chuck, Skippy, and me, we met up at Blue Diamond

Restaurant a few blocks from the bank around eight o'clock in the morning, or so. In that area. All right, we had somethin' to eat and then we drove from there to one block down, still in the process of casin' the bank. We was on the street that we thought Mr. MacDonald would use when he got off the freeway. We'd already worked his house."

"What did you know about him so far?"

"We know where he lives; we had already worked it. We know there's a big, loud dog in the next door yard which makes a snatch at the house outta the question. We also know when he came to work in the mornin', and that he normally closes the office at the end of the day, and gets a cup of coffee or two... he gets a carry-out bag; I take it for granted it's coffee. His arrival time at the bank is never the same each day. At this point we haven't got 'im on a set pattern yet, but we're gittin' close. He drives to work one way, or I should say he drove home one way and he comes back to the bank a different way. He drove a blue Pinto."

"Did you know what job he held at the bank?"

"We felt we knew he was either an assistant president or president of this branch bank."

"How did you know this?"

"From observations. He was the one that locked the bank up at 5:00 on Monday, and he was generally the first to arrive."

"Okay, so on December 4th the three of you are staked out near the bank. Then what?"

"We stayed 'til about 10:00 that morning. We hadn't seen MacDonald, so we took a ride by the bank to see if his car was there. It was, and we in turn left the area and went back to the restaurant."

"What transpired there?"

"Well, we got Dwight Fisher to join us and we had a

meetin'. Dwight was gonna help us with a place to stash MacDonald until the ransom was picked up."

"Where was that?"

"The basement of the medical clinic he worked at. And we could get drugs from 'im that we would need. Or Chuck—he had a stash of stolen ones, too."

"Was Dwight an equal partner in this?"

"No. Just an auxiliary. As far as the money goes, the three of us would split it equally and Dwight would get an amount that we hadn't determined yet."

"So, the four of you are hanging out like regular Joes having this meeting at a booth in a restaurant? And nobody suspected anything?"

"Why would they? Four guys hangin' out in a booth having a talk. Then Dwight had to get back to the clinic and me, Skippy, and Chuck decided to check out to see where MacDonald might go for lunch. There was two or three bars close to the bank that served food. But we didn't think a banker would eat at a bar, so we circled around a bit and then went back to the Blue Diamond Restaurant and found his car parked across the street at another restaurant. In a little while, he came out with a tall woman, who probably was a teller. They both got into his car and headed back to the bank."

"What did you do then?"

"All right, well, we went down a few blocks to another restaurant and talked over coffee. And Chuck said that maybe we should try to grab MacDonald when he came out of the restaurant after lunch one day. We began plannin' that angle, when some motorcycle cops came in to eat just then and sat in the next booth, so I thought that was a good time for us to split up. We made plans to get back together and follow up with MacDonald later in the afternoon. That's when we watched his car for quite a while from a restaurant across the street from the bank. There was no need to follow 'im home, because we already knew where he lived, so we decided we would meet up in the morning and watch 'im some more."

"And that would then be Friday, December 5th, when the snatch went down?"

"True."

"Did you and Chuck and Skip ever think to give up on MacDonald and just forget the whole thing?"

"No, man. Never. I was workin' a case for the Agency."

CHAPTER 9

September 1, 1976 – Licking County Jail
Three weeks before trial

"What happened here, Andy?" Larry asked the clearly frazzled jailhouse deputy with the big paunch and droopy graying mustache.

"All's I can tell you is I come on duty last night and Sheriff Rex says to me that the FBI has some undercover agent in the prison population for the night, and that I gotta try to keep an eye on him. But then Bill called in sick—food poisoning, he thinks—so we're down one already. How am I gonna give anybody special attention? Then the sheriff says to me that he thinks the Feds are trying to get to Rocky—"

"Get to?"

"Yeah. Like take 'im out."

"Nice," said Larry with disgust.

"So Rex says that Rocky has gotten wind of it. So, I says to Rex that if Rocky knows about this, so does the rest of the population. Rocky's a likeable guy, you know, so that Fed guy could be more screwed than Rocky. Which is just what happened. The inmates stayed on watch, and right before lock-down looks like the Fed guy got too close to Rocky. They pounced on him like an eight-point buck in an open field during deer season."

"Jesus! Is he okay?" winced Larry.

"Well, he'll live, but he's gonna hurt for awhile. They took him outta here on a stretcher."

"How about Rocky? Is he okay?"

"Not hurt much. His buddies moved in fast before much harm was done to 'im." Andy nodded toward the conference room. "He's waiting for you in there. Got your radio?"

Andy followed Larry into the tiny lawyer/prisoner inner sanctum, removed the shackle that kept Rocky in place, and left the room. Larry turned on the portable radio, amped the volume, and leaned in toward Rocky so they—and hopefully only they—could hear each other.

A lit, unfiltered Lucky Strike cigarette dangled between Rocky's lips. His clear blue eyes, open and direct, met Larry's.

"How's it going?" asked Larry.

"They tried to get me, buddy. I told ya they would. I been around them way too much not to know how they work," Rocky responded, shaking his head. Then he laughed. Not a raucous laughter, but gentler, easier. "That ol' boy actually thought he could just waltz in here and whack me. Imagine that."

"Rocky, you could have been killed."

"You see that, don't ya?" Rocky answered pointedly, but not frantically, touching three deep scratches on his left cheek right above the line of his recently grown beard. In spite of the special considerations he had been given as a result of his Friday-afternoon seminars on the inner workings of both bank robbery gangs and the FBI, the past eight months as a required guest of the Licking County jail had affected him. His hair had turned to serious gray; his weight dropped a good thirty pounds.

His voice calmed even more. "Yeah, man, they tried to get me dead-bang on. That's for sure. You're right, I could've been wasted. But the boys in here, they got my back. No, sir, I don't think they'll try that again. I got the setup down pretty good, and now I got all them other eyes with me."

Rocky paused, distracted by an oversized red ant crawling down the center of the pock-marked table. Larry observed curiously as Rocky, almost transfixed, followed the insect. *Maybe the guy's finally losing it,* thought Larry, but he remained silent as he watched Rocky watching. The ant, oblivious to anything but its own narrow world, made a hard right and headed toward Rocky's left hand.

"The FBI, they don't care nothin' about killin', as long as it suits 'em," said Rocky in a pleasant tone. "They actually think I'm somebody different and less than them. Thing about it is...we ain't so different."

The witless ant continued its journey to within inches of Rocky's hand. He looked up at Larry, and commented genially, as though he were shooting the breeze at a Friday night church supper, "You know, buddy, I could kill you just as easy as I could kill that ant."

"Then why don't you, Rocky?"

"Oh, I ain't gonna do that now. I need you, my friend. You stand between me and the electric chair. After the trial, well, we'll see...."

Holding Larry's gaze, Rocky raised his arm, and using the heel of his palm, dropped it down on the ant with the finality of a Mack truck running over a squirrel. With that, Larry saw no need to continue this meeting with Rocky and left without a word.

CHAPTER 10

Jury Selection
September 17, 1976

Larry paused outside the common pleas courtroom to straighten his blue silk tie—the one that set off his sparkling blue eyes. Not that he was into vanity or anything.

Well, maybe just a little....

He took a deep breath, knowing the claustrophobically small, dark oak-paneled courtroom with its mere fifteen or sixteen available spectator seats would already be jammed full. Press, of course, would be there, too, and however many standing room only folks the fire code would allow. Judge Abbot had informed him of the miniscule venue a few days ago. His Honor had originally planned to use the larger courtroom, but changed his mind when the county commissioners failed to provide him with a public address system. Big or little, it really made no difference. Either way, the first day of *voir dire* was about to be underway. In a few minutes the initial group of potential jurors would be brought in.

Let the games begin.

As far as Larry was concerned, it was showtime, as it was for him every time he stepped into a courtroom. He was born for the theater of trial law, and few things delighted him more than its opening act: jury selection. He was good at it, too, and he knew it. At the age of twenty-nine, after a mere four years in practice, he had been invited to be the keynote speaker at the American Bar Association's national convention in New York for 5,000 fellow barristers. His subject? What else? *Voir dire*. In New York it had been rock and roll time, and with one great speech, he had rocketed into stardom. Ever since, his career had been even more meteoric, like a bullet shooting up on a pop record chart.

Larry opened the door and walked in, striding confidently to the defense table. Low murmurs from the gallery filled the room, but he pretended not to notice. Instead, he removed his notes from his briefcase. He rarely referenced notes while he was actually talking to the jury, but he was meticulous in his pre-trial planning. He knew exactly what he was going to say and how he was going to say it well before the curtain opened. Surreptitiously, he would check and recheck his game plan, but like a good actor sneaking a peek at the cue cards, he never let his audience know.

He took a moment to quickly check out the spectators waiting for the action—mostly reporters—and then nodded at Prosecutor Lansing sitting at the opposing table, still shadowed by a government attorney whom Larry chose to completely ignore. He glanced up at the judge's elevated throne, void of any papers, which made the ever-present gavel more prominent, noted the empty jury box and the position of the lawyer's lectern, strategically placed an equal distance from the prosecution and the defense tables.

Welcome to his current home away from home.

The bailiff, a massive hulk of a man who could easily double for a very intimidating bouncer at night, was already in the courtroom. A clerk entered from a door left of the judge's bench and placed a large folder and fresh water there for him.

The door to the right of the witness stand opened and a uniformed guard, no lightweight himself, led the handcuffed Rocky Hamilton into the courtroom and deposited him in a chair to the left of Larry and to the right of Co-Counsel Gus Steinwell. Steinwell greeted Rocky with a nod. Larry had come to deeply respect this experienced trial lawyer that the State of Ohio had appointed to represent Rocky. His law firm had worked countless hours on pre-trial findings. Throughout the trial they would share the responsibility of questioning witnesses, but Larry, as Lead Chair, was totally in charge of choosing the jury he wanted. To him, *voir dire* was the lynchpin of a trial. He needed an intelligent jury who would understand the inconsistencies of the FBI conspiracy against Rocky and who could understand the charge levied against him.

Rocky was decked out in his best powder-blue leisure suit and a clean white shirt. Larry nodded approvingly at Rocky's newly shaven face, although he couldn't miss the fact that ten months in a sunless jail had left his client looking pretty sallow. But Larry didn't waver for a second on his decision about the beard. He and Rocky had held their debate on this the previous afternoon.

"Rocky," Larry had told him, "you look like you're trying to hide something and change the way you looked when you were arrested. The jury will notice, and they won't like it."

"But..." Rocky had begun his rebuttal.

"No buts," Larry had insisted. "Get rid of the damn beard." And mercifully, today the beard was gone. Larry waited patiently until the guard removed the cuffs before shaking Rocky's hand.

"Looks good, Rocky. Remember what I told you. Make eye contact with the potential jurors. Stay interested and alert. Do not bristle, no matter what is or isn't said."

Larry pointed to the yellow legal pad and pen he had set out for Rocky. "If you have any questions or thoughts, jot them down. If somebody comes up that you really don't feel good about, write it down and let me know. Don't interrupt me when I am talking; just write it down."

Rocky nodded.

Larry saw the bailiff take his position and asked Rocky if he was ready. Rocky stroked his chin as though the beard were still there. "I'm on board, man."

"All rise," intoned the bailiff, and court was in session.

Larry watched carefully as the first group of potential jurors was ushered into the jury box for examination. Earlier he had heard the prosecutor tell a reporter that he expected to seat a jury of twelve, plus four alternates, within two to three days. The guy was blowing smoke, or smoking dope—or whatever—but there was no way Larry was going to get the jury he wanted that quickly. He was trying a complicated conspiracy case where the good guys were often the bad guys and the bad guys were not necessarily such bad guys. At least, it was his job to show that his guy wasn't. Not an easy job. The only bright spot here was that the more people that were involved in a conspiracy, the more likely it was for inconsistencies to rear their ugly little heads, and Larry was planning to expose a nine-headed monster at a minimum. At the end of the day, conspiracy trials were about educating the jury to follow seemingly unrelated pieces of a puzzle into a connected whole. Just like any good jigsaw puzzle, he had to be able to show how individual pieces, with uneven and disconnected edges, actually interlocked to create a picture different and more comprehensive than one might conclude simply by looking at each piece as a separate entity. Larry was going to have to be content to be the glue that binds together the pieces of the puzzle for the jury, and they were going to have to be smart enough, and to trust him enough, to follow it.

Voir dire. Larry loved the sound of the words, which originate from the French language, meaning "to see/to speak." In actuality, it is the questioning of prospective jurors by a judge and attorneys in court. *Voir dire* is used to determine if any juror is biased and/or cannot deal with the issues fairly, or if there is cause not to allow a juror to serve, such as knowledge of the facts; acquaintanceship with parties, witnesses, or attorneys; occupation which might lead to bias; prejudice against the death penalty; or previous experiences such as having been sued in a similar case. One of the unspoken purposes of *voir dire* is for the attorneys to get a feel for the personalities and likely views of the people on the jury panel. In some courts, the judge asks most of the questions, while in others the lawyers are given substantial latitude and time to ask questions, such as in this trial. Some jurors may be dismissed for cause by the judge, and the attorneys may excuse others in "peremptory" challenges without stating any reason.

Larry began his quest in search of a very smart jury. He stood to address the man in juror number one's chair, but in fact he was addressing the entire jury pool. He deliberately stood behind Rocky, resting his hands on his shoulders for a second or two, and then moved to the lectern, adjusting it closer and more directly toward the jury box. He had six women and six men in this group. If he had his way, he would be talking to twelve women, not because he was anti-male, but because most women dug him instantly. And he capitalized on that—this playing of the seduction game—subtly flirting with eye contact and body language, just enough to draw them in and keep their attention. He really wasn't trying to add to his little black book—not that he had one—or get into their panties. Although it was alright with him if that's what they thought. Whatever it took to get them to be willing to really listen to what he had to say.

But this role as the seducer was a delicate one. Overplay his hand, come on too overtly or too strong, and it would be off-putting to the men. In order for them to trust him, they needed to relate to him as a man's man. In his approach of sensual with women and guy-stuff bonding with men, Larry endeavored to strike a pose that would be inviting for both genders. Sorta like a Robert Redford—good for the guys, good for the girls. That was his goal: to achieve the vibe of an extra-tall, less photogenic Robert Redford.

In the game of law, some smoke and mirrors were necessary because, contrary to public opinion, the law wasn't as much about innocence and guilt as it was about coming to a consensus on conflicting points of view. Larry had always thought they should add a few courses in law school: Settling Our Little Disputes 101, 102, and 103—because that's what the law is really all about. Rocky Hamilton had become immersed up to his ears in the current dispute, and it was Larry's job to get him disentangled. So, although he would never lie to a judge or jury—and he never did—he was certainly not opposed to a little staging.

"Mr. Sabo," began Larry in a conversational tone, addressing juror number one as though he were having a chat with the fellow in his own living room, "I don't want you to worry about anything. Relax and take a deep breath. I know it's not easy to come here, especially when you come in here and find that you're the first one up at bat. But this is not a test and there are no outs, because it's not about that. *You'll* know if you're a good juror for this case. I don't know. All that I can do is ask questions that might illuminate to you—that might hit a nerve for you—whereby we could both together decide if you would serve our society better by being on this case or another one. Mr. Sabo, tell me, sir, do you like mysteries?"

"Well, yes, I do."

"That's great. Because a mystery is what we have on our hands. I've got a mystery, a conspiracy mystery I'm going to prove. But like all good mysteries, it doesn't just present itself full blown; it has twists and turns like an intricate puzzle. And like a good puzzle, you put a piece in here and a piece in there, and to really be able to get the picture, you've got to be able to sit back and watch these pieces come together. And then, on top of all that, you'll have to be able to keep track of all these things."

The woman in juror number four's seat timidly raised her hand. Larry glanced quickly at his seating chart. Margaret Broyhill. The Court immediately addressed her. "Yes ma'am, what is it?"

"Your Honor, is it possible for us to get writing pads and pencils?"

Larry kept a genial smile on his face, but inside he was letting a big whoop! Already, Margaret Broyhill was following him and trusting him. He was educating her, and through her request, she was educating the others in the pool. Without ever asking her a question, he had his first juror. In another setting, he'd have done an "Amen!" to that.

Larry included several elements in *voir dire* which few attorneys bothered with. He made sure that as he went along, the jury pool became more and more familiar with the details and angle of his case. He wanted it patterned in their brain long before the full jury was seated. So he offered a lot of information, and he asked a lot of questions.

"Can you understand the distinction between someone doing a crime for themselves or doing a crime for the government? Would you be able to follow the instructions from the judge on that point? Could you recognize the innocence, by law, of somebody who did pull off a crime, but he was working for the government, so by that very same law he is not guilty? Would you believe that an FBI agent, simply because he was an FBI agent, would not lie under oath? If I prove this, would you rely on it?"

From the beginning, he wanted them conditioned to the idea that his guy was a high-paid agent working for the government. An agent freelancing, if you will, at the request and behest of the government of the United States of America. If the intent of a duly accepted agent's actions is to help his government, then folks, my boy is not guilty.

Larry wanted them to hear it in *voir dire*, hear it in his opening statement, hear it in the weeks of testimony yet to come, and hear it again in his closing arguments. So his internal barometer for who stayed and who went was three-fold: First, they had to be intelligent. He needed a smart jury. Second, the vibes of seduction and bonding had to be present—that's how he knew they were communicating. Third, they had to be indoctrinated to his defense, hear the story and all of its intricacies again and again and again, until it was as familiar to them as the names of their children. In another trial earlier last year, after a particularly drawn out *voir dire*, Old Judge Tarnack had called him up to the bench for a sidebar. "Strong," His Honor had said in a hushed tone with a twinkle in his eye, "are you sure you want to go forward with your opening statement? They already know everything you have to say."

Larry followed his tried and true plan and spent this first morning of jury selection alternating with the prosecutor in lengthy, personable, non-confrontational dialogue with the members of this jury pool, making certain that he kept humanizing Rocky for them with his touch and references. His intent with the potential jurors was, of course, to discriminate regarding whom he wanted on and whom he wanted off this jury. For whatever reason, it mattered not. If he didn't want them there, he didn't want them there, and it was his job to help them eliminate themselves whenever possible.

He had asked juror number six, Alex Moore, about the fact that he might see detailed pictures of a bloodied man stabbed thirty times. "Mr. Moore, could you look at that? Or would that be too upsetting for you? Because if it would, there are other cases that won't have this in it. You don't have to sit here for that."

Larry noticed a flash of controlled rage cross the man's face. Moore was gone; Larry would make sure of that. Preemptory challenges—which came at the end and basically were I don't want you here because I don't like you—were limited. But cause challenges were unlimited. He wouldn't waste a preemptory on Moore. He'd wheedle something out of him and find a way to dump him for cause. But behind Moore, juror number eleven, an elderly man with stooped shoulders, raised his hand.

"Yes, sir," addressed the Court.

"I don't want to see those pictures."

Juror number eleven had eliminated himself.

Gail Hall, a middle-aged homemaker, was in the number nine seat.

"Mrs. Hall," asked Larry standing directly behind Rocky who was looking directly at the prospective juror, as Larry had privately instructed him to do. "Can you look at this man…" He placed his left hand on Rocky's shoulder. "Please look into his eyes. Can you believe that this man is totally innocent until the prosecution proves every element, every point without a single doubt? Can you believe and understand that you must be able to allow for that, in order to give this man the righteous and fair trial of which he is so deserving—of which every one of us would be so deserving?" Larry, who always made Rocky the person, never the defendant, continued on that vein until Mrs. Hall was practically fighting back tears.

Well, Larry thought, *she just might make the cut.*

Two weeks and a lot of mumbo-jumbo later, after one hundred and twenty successful cause challenges and thirteen preemptory challenges, Larry had his jury. Seven women, five men, and four alternates split down the middle by gender. He was pleased. He had gotten people that he felt were intelligent, thoughtful, and conscientious, all of whom were productive, contributing individuals in their community.

And, he believed they would buy his story that the Federal Bureau of Investigation, which the late J. Edgar Hoover had run as his own personal fiefdom for forty-seven years until his death just four short years ago, was in many ways a polluted quagmire, filled with murky water, lofty words, phony reputation, and dirty tricks. He would educate them on the law and the criminal charges against Rocky as the trial progressed. He would expose the inconsistencies of the FBI conspiracy—one by one.

Good old Lord Acton, the English historian, had it right: Power tends to corrupt; absolute power corrupts absolutely.

CHAPTER 11

Friday, December 5, 1975
Afternoon

From an abyss deep within the drug-induced cavernous black hole of my passed-out body, I, Jamie MacDonald.... Wait a minute, why does my name feel so foreign... like some detached something or other.... It's a nightmare, isn't it? I am having one hell of a ferocious nightmare.

Suddenly, a red-eyed, fire-breathing dragon pops up out of some weird dark swamp and scares the bejesus out of me. He's screaming at me with terrifying vigor, but I can't make out what he's saying. I don't know what he wants from me. He comes close to me, and I try to force him away with my hands, kick him away with my feet. But my body won't respond to my brain's commands.

Panic overwhelms me. I cannot breathe. I cannot.

And then... oh no. Oh my God....

Through the painful, dense fog in my head I realize it isn't a nightmare. It is real. My gag reflex takes over and I begin to sputter and choke on my own spit.

A sharp, stinging whack crosses my mouth and cheeks, piercing the fog in my brain, as the adhesive tape is ripped off my face. I puke right there, barely turning my head in time to keep it from getting all over me. I can't stop coughing and my head is exploding from the two-ton drum that's pounding inside of it. Lord, please make it stop! A scream that feels like it is stoked from the pit of my bowels, surges upward like a convulsing volcano, louder and stronger than anything I've ever felt, until it spills out of my mouth.

Yet, somehow, I have barely uttered a sound.

"Okay, man, up we go," says a voice from this morning in a conversational tone. It must be the one with the blond sideburns. Hands from behind me prop me up into a sitting position and begin to undo the restraints on my wrists and ankles.

But my eyes are still bound.

A pause. A glass is placed by my mouth and tilted upwards. I drink a few swallows of the cool water and cough up even more crud.

Genial-voice helps me stand and leads me to the stairs. I cling to the banister as my unsteady, heavy legs trudge up the steps and into the bathroom. My mouth tastes like it has been drenched in cotton. And my head....

I use the toilet in the small bathroom. I feel my way to the sink and clumsily slap cold water on my face and rinse my mouth. Mr. Nice Guy places a glass in my hand and suggests that I drink it slowly. It's orangeade, or orange juice, or orange something. He places three tablets in my other hand and encourages me to take them. "Excedrin, extra-strength," he adds.

I swallow the pills.

"Smoke." One word is all that I can utter.

"Oh, sure." He puts a cigarette, I think it's one of my Tareytons, between my lips and lights it straightaway. I take a deep drag and, unbelievably, I almost feel grateful.

It's all too insane. It's all more than I can handle.

"Let's go, man," he says almost like we were buddies going out to grab a beer. "We got to get out of here now. We're gonna be in the car for a bit, so you're gonna have to lay down low in the backseat. Okay? I don't want you to try anything, 'cause I don't want to have to hurt you. Okay, man?"

I am led out to the car. I assume it's the same one from this morning. But then, no, it's different. The area in the back seat is narrower and as I follow instructions and lie down, the upholstery is scratchier than the other one. I try to get comfortable, which is impossible. Hold on, Jamie, hold on. After all, they promised they will release you after the 6:30 ransom drop tonight. I don't even know what time it is. Maybe it's not 6:30 yet, and I can still be home by 7:30. This will all be over. They will all be there. Mom, Dad, Sis and her husband, their kids. Their wonderful, crazy kids – they'll all be there. And Katie. Katie will definitely be there. Katie... Why have I never told her I love her? Tonight. Before this night is over, I will tell her that I have been in love with her since our second date last summer when we were laughing like little kids over a hot fudge sundae, top-heavy with whipped cream, and minced peanuts. One sundae, two spoons, and count 'em – two cherries!

Tonight is the night...

My coat is abruptly thrown over me, startling me out of the temporary escape of my reverie. "You drive, Skippy," says genial-voice.

Right. Right. I remember now. I heard his name this morning. Skippy wore the Arab mask. He mumbles something almost inaudible as he gets in the driver's seat. But I am able to pick up a few words, the last one being "Rocky."

Rocky?

That must be genial-voice. Rocky.

Then there's a third voice. The new guy – the one I've never seen, but who had all those ransom money questions – says something about taking off in his own car. He'll be making the ransom calls, while we'll be...what will ***we*** *be doing? The door next to me closes and is locked.*

The one I now think is Rocky climbs into the passenger side.

The ignition catches, and the car moves forward. In what seems like only seconds, my groggy, groggy head takes over and I drift off to sleep.

CHAPTER 12

Opening Statement – The Prosecution
October 6, 1976

The first thing the newly seated jury might have been tempted to notice as Prosecutor Gary Lansing rose to begin his opening statement was the consistency of his seriously conservative style. They'd seen it, of course, during *voir dire* and now on this bright, sunny morning that held a definite hint of the impending winter, they were witnessing it again: brown suit, plain white dress shirt offset by a too-narrow, muted brown-and-blue striped tie. Despite his conservative appearance, his slightly rotund shape and dark full-head of hair graying at the temples gave him an air of experience—not some young whippersnapper, but rather a man who knew his way around a courtroom. A guessing man would put his age at around forty-five years.

In court, at least, he was not a man of demonstrable humor. This morning he seemed more relaxed, quite different from the man who had fought Larry tooth and nail in pre-trial. Perhaps he thought he had nothing to lose, since he believed the defense argument in this case was a fantasy. Nonetheless, Larry knew he would not give an inch and respected that he was a tenacious lawyer not to be taken lightly.

Lansing walked the few steps to the lectern and placed

a healthy-sized sheaf of papers on it. Inwardly, Larry suppressed a yawn, holding his face in a respectful, interested pose. Ah, the theater....

"Ladies and gentlemen," began Gary, "the people of the State of Ohio expect to prove beyond a reasonable doubt that the defendant, Rocky Hamilton, did purposefully commit murder while he was in the act of committing another felony, to-wit: kidnapping. We expect the evidence to prove that it was decided there would be a kidnapping prior to December 5th, 1975, for the purpose of getting a large sum of money, and then this act was executed on the morning of the 5th, outside the Detroit National Bank. From there we expect the evidence to prove that Rocky Hamilton and his accomplice, Skip Nowalsky, took Mr. MacDonald to a residence where they held him bound and blindfolded on the basement floor. At this time, we expect the evidence to show that they also had their guns or weapons with them, which included a 12-gauge shotgun, a sawed-off shotgun, a carbine, and some handguns.

"Now, we expect the evidence to further prove that Rocky Hamilton was never an employee of the FBI. He was a paid informant and nothing more. He was paid money from time to time for information he had furnished that led to the arrest and conviction of people who had committed crimes."

Larry kept a watchful eye on the members of the jury during Lansing's monologue, taking careful note of when their eyes started to hood over. By his count, halfway through the prosecutor's opening, four jurors and two alternates were already losing focus. All those "expects" can really wear one out.

One hour and thirty-eight minutes later, Lansing was still at it. "Now, there are many more items of evidence that we expect will be involved and which we expect to prove, but I thank you for your attention to my opening statement. I want to again reiterate to you that Rocky Hamilton ran the show and he called the shots, and it was all from kidnapping for the sum of $250,000."

Gary gathered his notes and returned to his chair.

"Well, now," the Court said, "I think we had better give the jury a little rest, so we will recess for a few minutes. The Court cautions the jury to not discuss this case among yourselves or with anyone else. Do not form or express any opinions on this case until you are instructed to do so."

After the jury left the room, the Court addressed the attorneys. "I have some housekeeping chores here that should have been done before the opening statements. Let the record show that the motion for the change of venue has been overruled by the Court—did I do that yesterday?"

"No, sir," replied Larry, "I don't believe you did."

"Fine. You will prepare such an entry, Mr. Prosecutor… and also at the beginning of the case did I …well, let the record show that the defendant has been present in open court with counsel since the commencement of these proceedings this morning."

"Your Honor," spoke up Gary, "the prosecution has a stipulation before the Court in regard to the numbering of certain exhibits we will be using."

From the bench: "It was just filed at 8:51 this morning. I'll look at it later."

"I would also like to stipulate," continued Gary, "that I notice there is a potential witness here in the audience, but he is also a reporter, as I understand it, from Detroit."

"Your Honor," said Larry, "although we filed a motion at the beginning of *voir dire* for a separation of witnesses so that all witnesses would have to remain outside this court until their testimony, the defense has no objection to this exception."

"All right, fine. Let's bring the jury in."

CHAPTER 13

Opening Statement – The Defense
October 6, 1976

Larry took an unnoticeable deep breath. Exactly seven days ago he had gotten one final file number from Protectorate, and although neither man mentioned it, Larry knew that would be his last call. He was on his own now. Armed and ready.

Larry rose, empty-handed, but didn't go immediately to the lectern. He hovered behind Rocky for a few minutes as he spoke to the jury, neighbor to neighbor. "We talked in *voir dire* about how a trial is like a puzzle and that last piece, the last witness, is just as important as the first. We also talked about how you were going to hear two sides of the same story. When you have heard both the positions of the defense and the prosecution that will be shown in evidence, I am certain that you will firmly believe you have heard two entirely different stories with a common theme.

"But ladies and gentlemen, this is what you are going to find. You will find that since 1973 Rocky Hamilton has been working with the FBI. You will find that Rocky is an agent without a badge, because if he carried a badge, he could not be effective."

Larry removed his hand from Rocky's shoulder, where it

had been resting for some time, and moved easily to the lectern. He turned the lectern more toward the jurors and inched it forward, physically getting as close to them as possible.

"Rocky Hamilton did not go through the training that most of the FBI agents who will be testifying here have. He has not been to the FBI training schools, and he did not go to college. Rocky has been to the school of hard knocks. He has been to prisons and incarcerated and has been tried and convicted of bank robberies in the past. That is part of Rocky Hamilton's history. And he served his time and paid his debt to society.

"But in 1973, everything changed for Rocky when the FBI made him an offer he could not refuse. 'We're going to throw you in jail for as long as we possibly can on these parole violations, or you can walk out those doors.' Now, they didn't put it in exactly those words, but the message was unmistakably clear. What they did is they arranged for his release, dropped all the charges, gave him back his gun and said, 'Rocky, we'll pay you money if you will travel with these fellow criminals you have been traveling with, but instead of being on the wrong side of the law, now you are on the right side of the law.'

"And time after time, Rocky said to his FBI contacts, 'I can get this person or that person for you. Just don't blow my cover.' If Rocky's cover is blown, the obvious thing is he loses his effectiveness for the Agency, and last but not least, he gets killed by the criminals he is reporting on. Because these people are ruthless killers.

"And all during this time, Rocky was in close communication with his main FBI contact, Special Agent Ed Marshall. Remember that name. It's going to come up many times in this trial. Rocky was Ed Marshall's snitch—that's how Mr.

Marshall will refer to him. An FBI informant, especially a very effective one like Rocky, is a particularly unique item, and a special agent does not share his informant—not even with other FBI agents. So Marshall had his snitch *par excellence*, and this snitch was in a position to help the agent solve crimes single-handedly, which looks good on anyone's résumé, and as much as anything, helps position an agent for promotion. And that's important, because they have the same concerns that we all do. They have families and bills to pay, just like the rest of us.

"The FBI's focus in all of this, properly so, is to use the little guys to catch the big guys. That's what all these recent FBI stings and misconduct that have been in the news so much are all about."

"Objection!" barked Lansing.

"Sustained."

"So the FBI keeps working the very reliable Rocky Hamilton as a small fish to catch the bigger ones. In the summer of 1975 Chuck Wilson, a character out of Rocky's past, is released from prison and contacts Rocky with another boyhood chum named Dwight Fisher. Chuck Wilson says, 'Rocky, we're going to do a snatch. Are you in?' And the whole process starts. But by now Rocky has been transferred to a new FBI agent, Howard Bolton, whom he doesn't quite trust, so he keeps reporting more often than not to Ed Marshall, who is no longer with the FBI. But Ed Marshall is a good buddy of Howard Bolton and conveys the information to him.

"And when Rocky says that Chuck Wilson is offering up a kidnapping gig and asks if the FBI wants in on it, the agents are all over it, because they had lost Chuck Wilson on a kidnapping charge once before when they had grabbed everybody too soon, and Wilson got off with a lesser charge of receiving stolen goods. This time they said to Rocky, 'We want to catch that sleazy guy, so Rocky, you work it and play along with it, because we don't want to grab anybody too early this time. We'll grab him when the money is picked up, because we're not letting him slip out of our hands again.'

"The plans progress, and all along Rocky keeps Marshall or Bolton informed. Heck, on December 1st, just four days before they execute the kidnapping plan, Rocky even goes over to Ed Marshall's house and shows him the blue Monte Carlo he's driving and tells Marshall that the deal is coming down soon. It's very close. Maybe about a week away.

"Through all the evidence and testimony we will present, you will see that Rocky Hamilton is an innocent man. He did not cause a kidnapping and he did not cause a death. He was working as an agent without a badge for the Federal Bureau of Investigation. So you will have to take that into consideration when you are making your decision regarding a verdict. The law dictates that for one to be guilty of a crime, he or she must have *scienter*, which is guilty knowledge and intent. This is why insanity is a defense. If one is legally insane, they lack intent and knowledge of right and wrong. In this case, if one is doing a robbery or a kidnapping for the purpose of catching bad guys and assisting the government, the act of robbery lacks *scienter* and there is no crime.

"This is not going to be an easy trial. It involves a conspiracy by the FBI against Rocky Hamilton for a variety of reasons, which will be revealed during the course of this trial. As jurors, you have an obligation to listen closely to the testimony and determine the lies and inconsistencies you will hear from the many players from the FBI.

"It would certainly be easier, and maybe even more fun, if there could be a Perry Mason moment, when someone comes forward and tells us something that will confirm our theory, but that most likely will not happen in this trial. There will be no last minute histrionic break-down confessional by a witness on the stand, and no TV cameras standing by live to record it. Instead, there will be lies and obvious inconsistencies that the FBI has concocted to support their conspiracy.

"The burden is on the State to prove that Rocky Hamilton did cause, did commit this offense. We have no burden here; we are taking one on because I believe without a doubt, ladies and gentlemen, that when you are done with this trial, after the shock has worn off about how it did occur, and the conduct of the FBI, there will be no question in your mind that Rocky Hamilton is innocent of the offense as charged. Thank you."

CHAPTER 14

Second Day of Testimony
October 7, 1976

Larry watched the jury file back into the jury box after their stretch-your-legs and take-a-pee break. Quite frankly, he had abandoned his client to the care of the deputies, and done the exact same thing. They were only two days into the actual testimony of this trial—the tedious, tedious testimony—which the prosecutor was clearly going to drag out for God only knows how long. Larry was more than ever lamenting the circumstances that forced him to bring this to a jury trial in the first place. Trying it before a three-judge panel would certainly have been neater and quicker. But with the stonewalling of both the prosecution and the FBI, he couldn't take the chance of waiving the jury. How much evidence would he be able to bring to the surface—how many layers of subterfuge would he be able to uncover to prove his theory that in this case the FBI was blatantly full of shit? He didn't know. It was all a crapshoot. What he did know was that in law, when circumstances force you to take a shot in the dark, you take that shot with a jury.

Jason Bintner took the witness stand and was duly reminded that he was still under oath. He'd already spent the better part of two hours painfully explaining and re-explaining to the prosecutor the fifteen minutes he had spent in his home on the morning of December 5th, 1975—that morning when Rocky Hamilton came a-calling with his buddy, Skip, and his poor, unfortunate captive, Jamie MacDonald. Now it was Larry's turn to do the cross, and try not to further numb the jury with his own redundant questions.

"Mr. Bintner," said Larry, rising to his feet, "let's go over a couple of points with the jury again. Your testimony is that on the morning of December 5th, you were sleeping on your couch, pretty much passed out after a night of drinking, and you hear a knock on the door, and in walks Rocky Hamilton?"

Jason nodded.

"Mr. Bintner," said Larry, "the Court can't record a nod."

"Oh.... Uh, yes."

"And that was a surprise; you didn't expect him?"

"No, he just showed up."

"And there were three people altogether?"

"Yes... well, Rocky comes in and he comes over to me and says, 'Hey, I want to talk to you,' and I'm still sort of... Well, when you get up, you are still sort of drunk, you know. So, we talked for a few minutes and two other people went by in the hallway into the basement."

"And you recognized Skip Nowalsky, because you know him, but you couldn't see the third person very well?"

"All I could do was... well, Rocky comes up to me and we are headed to the couch and I barely notice Skip go in the hallway with the third man, 'cause I'm still out of it, I don't really get much of a glimpse of that guy, you know what I mean?"

"Did you recognize Skip right away?"

"At first, no. But later he came upstairs and wanted a cup of coffee and I told him to make it himself, so that's when I knew it was him. He's sort of weird, you know."

"No; I don't know Skip very well. Tell us about him."

"Well, as a matter of fact, Skip was sort of a dumb guy, you know what I mean, a babbling dummy. I saw him a couple of times, and when he drinks shots, he gets loud and crazy, you know what I mean, and Rocky told him to shut up."

"On the morning of December 5th, during the time that Skip and an unknown third man had disappeared into your basement, what did you and Rocky talk about?"

"He said, 'I would like to borrow your house for an hour or so. I have to make a delivery.' I told him to go ahead, and then he says, 'Why don't you take off for a while,' or something like that, and I said okay. So, I took off and went to a field where I usually go hunting in the fall."

"Did you call your home later that afternoon?"

"Yes."

"Where from?"

"A bar."

"What time was that?"

"Around 3:00 in the afternoon, sometime around there, and Rocky answered and said, 'Hey, I'm just going to use your house for a few more minutes,' and he chuckled and laughed. He was sort of friendly... Rocky is sort of a friendly individual."

"And all this time you didn't think anything was suspect?"

"No, not really."

"Did you hear anything about a kidnapping?"

"I must have, you know. Maybe Saturday or Sunday. In Detroit, kidnappings and murders and all this other stuff you hear on the radio all the time, and you don't pay much attention to it."

"Well, I doubt that you are questioned about every kidnapping."

"Well, no, not exactly."

"When did the FBI question you about this particular kidnapping?"

"I think it was three months later, I believe."

"Three months!" exclaimed Larry in a tone of incredulity.

"Right."

"Did they ever discuss charging you with any offense?"

"No."

"No discussion of any offense arising out of your gun possessions?"

"I don't have any illegal weapons."

"Really. You have permits for your handguns?"

"Right."

"How long have you had these permits?"

"Since about four months ago; that would make it sometime this summer."

"And so, at the time the FBI agents were out talking to you, you owned the guns but did not have any permits, did you?"

"I can't remember, but I don't think so."

"Tell the truth—you did not have permits, did you?"

"I did not have a permit."

"For any of your handguns. And that's a crime."

"That's correct. I always have a handgun. I believe with the gun laws in this country, a man has got to have a gun to protect himself."

"Oh, give us a break, Mr. Bintner. We are not interested in your speeches. You were in possession of illegal guns when, according to your testimony, the police and FBI finally got around to coming out and talking to you. And your testimony is that the FBI did not talk to you about that or anything else earlier, and you did not have any agreement with them to avoid prosecution for carrying and possessing that gun?"

"No."

"No further questions," said Larry using his best disgusted voice, which in this moment was not a stretch. He turned his back on the witness, then abruptly turned back to face him.

"No, excuse me," Larry said to the Court, "let me ask one more question before we excuse this person." To the witness, he said, "You say you have your handguns only for protection? Not for any other purpose?"

"In a city that is a jungle," responded Bintner still in his preachy mode, "you keep at least one for protection. Yes, I do."

"And you need a gun for protection?"

"Where I live, everybody has a weapon."

"Right, for protection?"

"Right."

"Isn't it true that you have a black belt in karate, and you don't need protection?"

"You can't karate-chop a bullet."

Touché! Larry sat down.

CHAPTER 15

Mid-October 1976

Good grief, thought Larry as he drove along one of the more rural routes on his commute to the Licking County Courthouse, *can it really be mid-October already*? But the clear crispness of what was setting up to become a near perfect Indian summer day confirmed that it was. He decided that if the weather held, he would return home the same way. It was just too pretty to resist, although it went against his current rule of not driving consecutive routes. In Rocky's words, "Don't give 'em a chance to set up a pattern."

Not that Larry was trying to be paranoid or anything. But ever since the attempted attack on Rocky in the jailhouse, Larry had taken his client's warnings to heart. He had listened to Rocky's ramblings of dire threats to come, doing his own sorting through the wheat and chaff of the man's well-endowed ego, but intuitively Larry felt that underneath the baloney lurked some serious kernels of truth.

Rocky had told Larry to watch his back. Since the FBI had failed to get rid of Rocky in the jailhouse attack to make this case go away, they just might come after Larry next. Rocky even explained in detail how it would happen. First, Larry would be followed, so the FBI could establish a pattern. They would find out which roads Larry would take to drive to and from Newark and Columbus each day. All of the routes were rural roads, so the FBI had the advantage of no witnesses. Most likely they would use aerial surveillance to find and track him until they could get cars in the area. Larry would round a curve and find the road blocked by a car, and then another car would come up behind him and hem him in. Then the car blocking the road would straighten out and come toward him. When it got alongside him, someone in the car would blast him away through the car window.

Heaven forbid, thought Larry, *could the FBI be so corrupt as to assassinate its own citizens?* That very day, he had gone to the sheriff and applied for and received a permit to carry a concealed weapon, and like it or not, he had committed to varying the beaten track to and from home as often as possible. Since he had never owned a firearm, he had gone down to a training area near where he lived on the following weekend and learned how to shoot.

The advantage to this route was that it was virtually empty, and he could let the engine on his sweet Trans-Am rip wide open. Before he knew it, he was pulling up in front of the historic landmark courthouse.

Rocky's aunt, Janet Peterson, all of three years Rocky's senior, was on the stand, and Gary Lansing was wresting the answers he wanted from her. So far, it was just boring stuff, and Larry wondered how long it would take until Lansing could get to the meat of what Aunt Janet would have to say that interested him.

"Now, let me ask you, at this point in time, do you have any relationship whatsoever to the defendant, Rocky Hamilton?" droned Gary.

"Yes, I am his aunt. His mother's sister."

"Now do you know a woman by the name of Shirley Stevens?"

"Yes, I do."

"How long have you known Shirley Stevens?"

"About two years."

"How did you become acquainted with her?"

"Well, she came over with my nephew."

"And that was whom?"

"Rocky Hamilton."

Good grief! was all Larry could think, as he suppressed an inner wince. How could anyone be this boring?

During the next half-hour—was it only a half hour?—Gary Lansing elicited from Aunt Janet that Shirley Stevens was Rocky's wife—no, excuse me, common-law wife—and that while the picture she had just been shown was Shirley, it was, shall we say, not the most photogenic shot. And, yes, Rocky and Chuck Wilson had been boyhood friends. Skip, too. And the two fellows had visited Rocky at Aunt Janet's house when he and Shirley and their two little kids were staying with her. Yes, as recently as November of 1975, she had seen them all together. Oh, and guess what? She had also rented the blue Monte Carlo Rocky was driving on the morning of December 5th, and he had been driving it for several weeks. At Rocky's request, she had returned same vehicle on Saturday, December 6th. But Rocky also had a place in Ohio connected to a guy whose name she couldn't recall, but he was tall and skinny.

"Did you ever hear the name Jerome Madison?" asked Lansing.

"Sir, I don't remember the name, but he stopped at my house once."

"He did?"

"Yes, and we had stuffed cabbage and he took it with him. That's the only time I ever met him, and we were having, you know, it's like rolled up cabbage, and Rocky told him to come to supper, and he came by, but he did not have time to eat. He was going back to Ohio. They were cabbage rolls, you know, and he took his with him. We call them stuffed cabbage."

At that point Larry realized he was wrong. It had been forty-five minutes, if it had been a second, or had time managed to just plain stop altogether? Janet Peterson's testimony went on and on until, at long last, the prosecutor got to the finer morsels.

"Did anybody ever call you between December 5th and December 11th, 1975, and ask you if you knew anybody, or if you knew anything about the kidnapping of Jamie MacDonald?"

"Yes, sir."

"Who?"

"The FBI."

"Are you sure that was between December 5th and December 11th?"

"Yes, sir."

"What date was that?"

"I don't recall the date, but they were at my house four times. I think the first time was on a Sunday."

"Did they ask if your nephew, Rocky Hamilton, ever drove the blue Monte Carlo you rented?"

"They had pictures."

"I repeat! Did they ask you that question?" demanded Gary Lansing.

"Well, I want to explain," responded Janet, matching him with her own petulance. "Before they asked me the questions, they showed me pictures, and that is what I was trying to explain to you. I am trying to be honest with you, sir." She threw Lansing a triumphant look.

Several more "Do you knows" and "No, I don't" responses later, and it was Larry's turn.

"Mrs. Peterson," queried Larry, "are you very certain that the visits from the FBI were between December the 5th and the 11th?"

"Let me see...."

"Well, let me refresh your memory. Was it before Rocky was arrested?"

"Yes."

"So, if he was arrested on the 10th—and, by the way, he was—then the FBI would have had to show up at your house before then?"

"Yes, sir."

"What pictures did the FBI show you when they came?"

"They showed me pictures of Rocky, the blue car, and Skip and Chuck."

"Besides identifying these pictures at least a few days before Rocky's arrest, what else did they ask you for?"

"They asked for phone numbers. They asked for Shirley's, and her sister's and her mother's, and my sister's, who is Rocky's mother. But she was sick, and I didn't want them to bother her. They were asking for so many numbers, I just gave them my book and they wrote them down. I did not."

"And was there one agent present for all four visits? A Mr. Morrison?"

"Yes, and he always had someone else with him, but he did most of the talking, and the last time he had three others with him."

"But he's the one who handled your book?"

"Yes."

"It would seem Special Agent Morrison had lots of ways to check up on ol' Rocky here."

Lansing was on his feet. "Objection!"

"Withdrawn. Thank you, Mrs. Peterson. That will be all."

The weather had held, and after completing one of the more tedious days of trial law, Larry was once again flying down his favorite route, all four windows open, the wind blowing in his face, renewing him. He breathed it in deep. Ah, yes, he would live to fight another day, or so he thought.

And that's when it happened. That's when the unmarked orange helicopter dropped out of the sky. That's when eight agents in two cars sandwiched him in, creating a front and back door gridlock. That's when Larry realized the abruptness of life. The abruptness of *his* life. He went from looking forward to tomorrow to facing the grim reaper—to never seeing his wife and children again—in little more than a heartbeat.

And that's also when his deepest, yet unspoken prayer got answered. Thank God he got the answer he had quickly become so desperate for. He was alive.

CHAPTER 16

Friday, December 5, 1975
Early evening

My head still feels like a sledgehammer is pounding in it, but I am awake now and not as out of it. It's dark. I can tell. I have managed to work my coat off my head without drawing their attention, and I can't see any light coming in from underneath the blindfold.

So, I know it's dark. Even if I couldn't know with my eyes, my stomach is telling me it's late. I'm hungry, which surprises me—with all this, the idea that I would think about food… What causes that? Empty stomach, fear, stress, whatever stinking drugs they gave me? I don't know…I just know that I haven't had anything to eat today.

But it's dark, and that's good. In fact, that's wonderful. It's the best news I've had since this whole bitch of a horror show began. Because they told me I am going home tonight. And, thank God, nightfall is here!

The thought takes my mind completely off my stomach.

The car is stopped, and there is only silence coming from the front seat. Well, silence except for Skippy's little wheeze, so I know I am not alone. I will not be able to escape. But they will let me go.

They will!

The car door opens and the person I believe to be Rocky roars in. It's like a raging bull suddenly entered the small space of the car. What the hell happened? Rocky's voice holds no hint of calm and buddy-buddy in it. "Damnit, damnit, damnit!"he explodes at Skippy while beating his fist against the dashboard. The hysteria blasting through his voice causes his pitch to go up a couple of levels.

A knot, like some giant Draconian fist, grips my gut.

"What the hell, man, what the hell happened...?" shrieks Skippy back at Rocky.

"Drive, just friggin' drive!"

Skippy throws the car in gear and takes off.

"What the hell's up, man?" asks Skippy, still shrieking.

"Shut up, Skippy. Can't you just shut up! I have to think. Go across town to that K-Mart. I'll try the freakin' phone there. Go! Go! What the hell are you waiting for?"

Silence, then. My heart is pounding. It's as though they're not even aware I'm back here. That cannot be a good thing. Please, just give them the damn money! I only want to go home. Please....

Rocky shouts, "Over there on the left." Tires squeal as the car jerks to the left, and I lurch into the back of the front seat.

"Pull up to the entrance, and I'll jump out. You circle and pick me up. Make it quick."

Three or four minutes later, he's back in the car, still shrieking. "I finally got ahold of Chuck at Dwight's house. Those pricks from the bank didn't show up with the money!"

And now he does notice me. "That's how much they care about your skinny ass!"

They didn't pay? That's impossible! Insurance will cover it. How could they not pay?

"Skippy, get your ass on the damn freeway to Ohio. We're going to my place."

"What the hell...?"

"We're going to hole up in my place down around Newark, ass-hole. Now get the fuck going before somebody spots us."

They are taking me out of the state....

I have no words or thoughts. I can't understand why the bank did not pay. They have the money; they have lots of money. I simply watch as a part of me dies. It actually dies. I can feel it. It dies, as any hope I had dies.

CHAPTER 17

Mid-October 1976

It was the morning after the night when Larry had come within a stone's throw of meeting his maker. *This* morning, Larry drove the most direct route with the most cars around him to the courthouse, nerves still jangled after a sleepless night in spite of the two double scotches he downed the minute he had arrived home. He told Letty the whole frightening story. With worry written all over her face she asked what he was going to do. Seven hours of tossing and turning had left him with the same answer that he had last night—not much he could do. He had no proof, no names, and clearly, he had no identifying marks or numbers on the helicopter. He had only a heart that was still beating too fast, and a body that was still over-adrenalized. Expunge his leftover trauma, and he didn't have a damn thing.

He had arranged to arrive at court a half-hour early, having already placed a call to Judge Abbot, requesting fifteen private minutes. Not *ex parte*, he had assured His Honor. It didn't directly affect the case being heard, but it affected defense counsel a lot. What if "they" tried again, only with an end result more advantageous to them? Larry wanted someone with an official standing to at least know about it. He needed a brief and private off-the-record conversation.

The judge, leaning back in his chair with hands folded across his broad belly, listened attentively without interrupting as Larry retold his experience. When he was done, Judge Abbot closed his eyes for a moment. Larry waited silently. Then Judge Abbot looked at Larry and said matter-of-factly, "All right, I have the information. I think it is a good idea for you to remain armed at all times. You can keep your handgun in your briefcase in the courtroom. Just make sure that no one sees it. Furthermore, I will request extra security in the courtroom." He stood and offered his hand. "Mind your back, Counselor."

"All rise!" announced the bailiff. His Honor, now robed in black, entered the courtroom, sat down on his throne, and court was in session.

After the prosecutor had called Mr. Vassallo to the witness stand and extracted information about the bank's position in paying the ransom, it was Larry's turn to cross-examine the tall, professorial-looking banker coolly sitting in the hot seat of the witness stand. "Mr. Vassallo, you have testified that you have been employed by the Detroit National Bank for some twenty-six years and, as I understand it, on December 5th of last year you were in the position of operations manager, which included responsibility for the branch that Mr. MacDonald worked at."

"Yes."

"And by the afternoon of that same day you had received the ransom demand and the bank had agreed to pay the $250,000?"

"Yes, that's right."

"What was your role in this difficult situation?"

"Well, basically, to be the courier, but first, there were some discussions back and forth with me about my willingness to deliver the money."

"Discussions with the FBI?"

"The FBI and my superiors at the bank."

"And did you have assurances from the FBI that every precaution was being taken to protect you?"

"That was conveyed to me after I made the decision. At first it was simply 'Will you do this, or will you not?' And then afterward, the FBI gave me assurances."

"About how long did this discussion take?"

"The decision thing on my part? Well, I had some forethought on it earlier in the day because of the position I was in, and I think I deliberated in the afternoon about fifteen minutes and then I indicated I would be willing to do it."

"Were you scared?"

"Absolutely."

"How many agents were present when you discussed security?"

"At least three or four."

"What happened next?"

"I had to go to the bank's main office downtown to pick up the money."

"It was getting late now though, wasn't it? Late to meet the ransom deadline?"

"Yes, it was probably around 4:45 p.m., or so."

"And you were anxious about this?"

"Very anxious."

"Where were you supposed to deliver the money?"

"To a telephone booth at a K-mart store on Telegraph Road in Taylor."

"Let me make sure I've got this straight. It's closing in on 5:00 by now, the drop is scheduled for 6:00 but at a location some forty minutes away from the downtown office, and you have to go there first in order to pick up the money? And it's Friday afternoon rush hour in Detroit?"

"Yes."

"And, assuming the traffic gods are with you—which is a pretty big assumptive prayer—how long would it take you to drive from the branch to downtown?"

"Well, maybe twenty-five or thirty minutes."

"Time-wise, did that worry you?"

"Yes, it did, very much so."

"And I'm sure it worried the FBI, too?"

From behind Larry, Lansing interrupted. "Your Honor, counsel can't really be expecting Mr. Vassallo to testify to the thoughts of the FBI!"

"Sustained."

"Well," said Larry, addressing the witness, "did the FBI give you a police escort? Whistles, bells, sirens? Anything to get you downtown faster?"

"Your Honor..." Lansing said again.

"Well, if he knows—" replied the Court.

"No," responded the banker. "I drove, and they followed behind me."

"What happened when you got to the main office?"

"It was very hectic, and there were numerous people involved, and people were moving about. The FBI put a microphone and transmitter on my clothing, and the money was brought into the room in a canvas bag. Then the FBI put it in a cardboard box and sealed it and tied it with twine. Then they measured it with a tape."

"And you were aware at this time that you were already past the time as far as the drop was concerned?"

"Yes."

"Did you communicate those concerns to the FBI agents?"

"Yes. I don't remember exactly what I said, but I told them to hurry. I think I made it evident I was impatient."

"You wanted to get on the road and get to the drop and get this thing over with?"

"Yes."

"So, the money is finally placed in the passenger's seat of your car, an FBI agent is sequestered under a blanket in the back seat, but you've still got a minimum of a forty-to-fifty-minute drive?"

"Yes."

"And on the road, there are still major remnants of Friday night traffic?"

"Yes."

"Did you have a police escort this time?"

"No, just an FBI car that I was told would be following, so I was aware of the car behind me."

"No assistance at all to at least speed your travel until you got within range of the drop?"

"No."

"What time did you arrive?"

"It was close to 7:30 when I got there."

"Once you got there, how long did you stay?"

"Until 9:30."

"And no one ever showed or tried to make contact with you on the pay phone you had been instructed to stand next to?"

"No."

"Just one more question, Mr. Vassallo. How many federal agents were working around the bank on that Friday?"

"I have no idea, maybe fifteen or twenty. Maybe more. They were in and out constantly."

"And ninety minutes late was the best that twenty-plus

agents could do? Well, ninety minutes is a heck of a long time to ask a crook to be a sitting duck."

"Your Hon…" Gary began his complaint. Larry, who had consciously snuck that one in, waved him off.

"Never mind. That's all, Mr. Vassallo."

Gary almost tripped himself, brushing past Larry in his rush to get to the lawyers' lectern.

"Mr. Vassallo, did you ever feel that the FBI was unreasonably delaying anything?"

"I saw nothing that I would construe as a deliberate delay."

"They did express concern for you in delivering this money, correct?"

"Yes."

"And they took precautions to ensure its delivery?"

"Yes."

"And, one more time, you were, in fact, instructed to turn over the $250,000 for the release of Jamie MacDonald?"

"Yes."

"Thank you; that's all."

CHAPTER 18

The Defense Gets a Break

Thirty-five minutes after arriving at the courthouse, Larry was once again in his car. Today was field trip day. Judge, jury, lawyers, court reporter, news reporters, alternates—everybody but his incarcerated defendant—was going out to the house in Licking County that Rocky had rented from Jerome Madison during the last four or five months of 1975. It was also the house where Rocky and Skip had taken Jamie MacDonald on the night of December 5th after the botched ransom. Talk about the tail wagging the dog. Over an hour late for a drop when a man's life is on the line? Dumb as a stump....

The jury—all white, of course, because that was the non-diverse reality of Licking County—carpooled to the hilly rural area near Newark. They trudged around the small, square, clapboard farmhouse with aging white paint. One story with two small bedrooms. There it was—home sweet home for Rocky, Shirley, their two kids, and a humongous Great Dane. When the jurors were shown the closet in which the prosecution alleged the victim had been bound, blind-folded, and dumped while he was being held, they literally shook their heads in dismay. Larry observed them closely, his own dismay mounting. Rarely were field trips a walk in the park for the defense.

After viewing the house, the jury was driven about three miles to Harmon Road. There they stumbled along a path through the thick woods, much as Jamie MacDonald had, down a steep embankment and along about a quarter of a mile of dirt road to the top of a hill where Mr. MacDonald fell dead on a pile of decayed tree branches.

When everyone was done prodding and clucking, His Honor gathered the jurors together in the middle of the road, reminded them not to discuss anything, no forming opinions, et cetera. He gave them a two-hour lunch break—time for travel—and, having left his gavel at the courthouse, dismissed them with a wave.

Four hours later, back in the courtroom, Larry noticed that an armed deputy stood in each corner of the small courtroom. Judge Abbot had kept his promise. On the stand a Mr. Peepers clone from the Newark Telephone Company was being led through his testimony by the prosecutor, trying to validate or invalidate telephone connections and corroborate testimony. Larry didn't think spotty records were going to make a whole hell of a lot of difference. Many phone records were destroyed after six months. The ones that weren't—and that would make a difference to Larry's case—were hard as hell for him to get his hands on. Right now, they were still on Aunt Janet's phone. Larry had to force his eyes not to roll back in his head with a pantomime sigh.

"Mr. Hartwell," inquired Lansing, "can you tell us from your records what calls were made from that pay phone on Sunday, December 7th, 1975?"

The prosecutor called him Hartwell, but Larry knew that was wrong. It was Wally Peepers from the TV sitcom of twenty years ago. Spitting image. Had to be; only possible explanation.

Having adjusted his glasses way down onto the tip of his nose and peering down at papers he held in his hands, Mr. Peepers recited, "On December 7th, 1975, I show a call to 866-6048 of one minute's duration at 0920 hours military time. At 1107 hours military time I show a call to 792-5588 of seven minutes' duration; at 1257 hours military time I show a call to 498-0217 of ten minutes' duration; at 1325 hours military time I show a call to 984-6054 of four minutes' duration; at 1626 hours military time I show a call to 836-1134 of one minute's duration; at 1824 hours military time I show a call to 866-6048 of seven minutes' duration; I show a call at 2033 hours military time to 263-6765 of one minute's duration; at 2100 hours I—oh...oh, my...."

Mr. Peepers' alarm was the result of dropping one page of his notes, and then dropping the rest of them as he bent over to retrieve the original offender. Tittering laughter spread softly throughout the gallery. His Honor gave them a stern look, but kept his gavel silent.

Larry, having noticed his client checking out during this latest testimony, took advantage of the distraction to nudge him and say *sotto voce*, "The jury can glaze out all they want, Rocky, but you stay focused."

"But man, this is so bor—"

Larry cut him off, "It doesn't matter, Rocky. What it **is**, is your life. Stay interested and alert. You always tell me how you play a role when you're undercover. There'll never be a more important role than this one."

Mr. Peepers rallied, got his papers and his act together, and resumed reciting phone calls made from the pay telephone at the Kroger grocery store in the Plaza Shopping Center on Vernon Road near Rocky's house on Pointer Run Road. It was the phone Rocky always used to call his handlers when he was in Newark. Obviously, other people used the phone as well, so Larry and Rocky were listening for any numbers familiar to Rocky. "On December 8th, I have a call at 0832 military hours to 984-6054 for a duration of twelve minutes...."

And on and on.

And then the first break in the case.

Mr. Peepers was telling the jury that a long-distance, collect call on Monday, December 8th, 1975 was made from that pay phone to Detroit to an Edward Marshall.

Larry's antenna shot up to the ceiling. Former Special Agent Ed Marshall, Rocky's most long-term and intimate contact at the FBI. And now Mr. Peepers was confirming exactly what Rocky had told him. Larry was certain Ed Marshall would deny this telephone call when he got him on the stand. According to the telephone company records, the call lasted five minutes.

Lansing, having been drawn into a place he didn't want to go, closed down the testimony as soon as he could. "Your witness," he said to Larry.

Larry rose. Now for the *coup de grâce.*

"Mr. Peep... uh, sorry sir," Larry stammered, more than mildly chagrined with himself. "Mr. Hartwell, going back to the last page of your telephone records, you have just testified that Edward Marshall received a long-distance, collect call on December 8th, 1975 from that pay phone at the Kroger grocery store on Vernon Road. Is that correct?"

"Yes, that is correct."

"What time was that phone call made?"

"At 10:59 in the morning."

"And, how long did that call last?"

"Five minutes, sir."

"Are you aware that Ed Marshall is a former FBI agent who was the primary contact for Mr. Hamilton?"

"No, sir, I am not familiar with that name."

"Nothing further. Thank you, sir."

And God bless you, Mr. Peepers, Larry added silently with a secret smile as he returned to the defense table.

Larry put Co-Counsel Steinwell in charge and sprinted from the courthouse and contacted his office to prepare a subpoena for Ma Bell Telephone Company in Detroit to furnish all telephone calls made to and from the unlisted telephone number of Edward Marshall for the time period of several months in 1975. Judge Abbot approved the subpoena, despite vehement objections from the prosecutor.

A couple of days later, Larry was contacted by Ma Bell Telephone Company in Michigan saying the records were now ready, and that they could have a representative from their company drive them to Newark the following day to be authenticated. Larry got permission from Judge Abbot to call the representative as a witness out of order, since the prosecution had not yet rested. As soon as Larry had the witness from the Detroit telephone company on the stand, he asked him to look at his records dated Monday, December 8th, 1975.

"Do you see any telephone calls to Mr. Edward Marshall on that date?"

"Yes, there is a long-distance, collect call from a pay phone in Ohio."

"Exactly where in Ohio?"

"The phone is located at the Kroger grocery store in the Plaza Shopping Center on Vernon Road in Newark, Ohio."

"And how long was that telephone call?"

"Five minutes."

"Are there any more telephone calls that day that were made from that telephone number subsequent to that call?"

"Yes. He made a long-distance call."

"Where was that call placed to?"

"Nebraska."

"What time?"

"Military time 1330 hours."

"That would be 1:30 p.m. And how long was that after the previous phone call that Mr. Marshall had received from Newark, Ohio?"

"Right around two and a half hours."

"Who was the number Agent Marshall called listed to?"

"The first name was Robert, middle is Patrick, and the last name is Wallace."

"Are you aware that Bob Wallace was a former FBI agent?" Larry already knew the man would not have the slightest clue, but was asking the question for the purpose of the jury making the link.

"No."

"Can you determine from your records as to the duration of the call from Special Agent Marshall to Special Agent Wallace on Monday, December 8th, 1975?"

"Yes, this is a ten-minute call."

Larry wanted to say aloud, *And can you guess what they were talking about?* Instead, he thanked the witness and said, "No further questions."

CHAPTER 19

Autopsy Report

The prosecutor called Dr. Lawrence Pennington as an expert witness. He asked the pathologist to give his autopsy report. Dr. Pennington began flashing pictures of Jamie MacDonald's slashed and battered body onto a screen in the darkened courtroom. Larry was glad he could not see the faces of the jurors.

"There were barbiturates, a fairly large dose, in him. I think one could sum it up and say it would have caused an intoxicated situation. He would not have been functioning normally, either mentally or physically, although it's possible that he could stay conscious, but his motor functions would not be terribly coordinated, even though he might not actually be, to put it in the vernacular, falling-down drunk. Nevertheless, it would have a significant effect on the individual.

"All the wounds were inflicted within minutes, rapidly, one immediately upon another. These pictures show the bruises on the cheek areas and the forehead. There are abrasions across the nose, and bruises on the chin region. His eyes show severe swelling and bruising. The lips are bruised, also. And there are multiple stab wounds, but the carotid artery in the neck was not severed, or he would have bled to death immediately. But the point of the instrument, which could be a three-inch pocket knife, did cut through soft tissue in the neck and ultimately ended up in one of the bones that make up the spinal column in the neck region. Then this picture shows a knife wound that went through the full thickness of the chest wall into the lung. There's one over here in the left shoulder blade, this one near the back of the right armpit, two in the abdomen. His left hand was slashed on four fingers. There were also cuts on his left wrist and forearm. Thirty stab wounds in all. All of them from a blade that had a cutting edge on it. Jamie MacDonald put up a hell of a fight," said the Coroner sympathetically, shaking his head.

After a brief pause, he continued, "In recreating the scene and following the blood trail, we found that Mr. MacDonald got up from where he was attacked, stumbled down through the woods, crossed the road, and somehow made it up an embankment where his body was found face up, lying in a pile of brush. He walked over a quarter of a mile, despite a collapsed lung. No one injury killed him; it was a combination of all of them. He lived probably two hours after he was attacked.

"The victim was taken into the woods and attacked around midnight on Tuesday, December the 9th. Around 2:00 a.m., on the 10th, give or take an hour, Jamie MacDonald died of exsanguination. He bled to death."

When the lights came back up, a somber mood hung gloomily over the courtroom. Larry glanced around the gallery and noted that Jamie MacDonald's family mercifully was absent. The prosecutor interrupted the awkward silence, "Your Honor, the prosecution rests."

CHAPTER 20

The Defense Asks for Dismissal

"Your Honor," began Larry, rising to stand before the bench, "while the jury is still out of the courtroom, and before the defense cross-examines Agent Bolton, we must bring this matter before the Court. On direct testimony, Agent Bolton is allowed to state certain things as fact, and then when we go to enter certain exhibits whose substance would put his statements in question, we get shot down with 'Oh, no, that's not possible; the federal government objects on the grounds that those documents involve national security'—or some such nonsense. Yet Howard Bolton has testified, and re-testified, that there were four telephone conversations. *Only* four. He insists on it.

"As the Court is aware from the telephone records that have already been submitted into evidence, there are more than four telephone calls. A lot more. So quite obviously, with our submission of certain documents and reports that reference the FBI's contact with Mr. Hamilton, we are laying the groundwork for further cross-examination of Agent Bolton to prove that he is lying when he states he did not have contact with Rocky Hamilton at any time other than these four times.

"And at each turn we are blocked. Now, I do not know if the divulging of the contents of these documents which simply involve testimony in this court referencing Mr. Hamilton would actually endanger the national security of the United States of America. I don't know, but would the revelations therein really send us all running back to our bomb shelters of the forties and fifties?"

Larry noticed Judge Abbot's scowl and pressed forward quickly. "The federal government is saying they don't want this information divulged. However, what we have in this case is the federal government as the principal mover. The FBI has prime witnesses sitting in Columbus and Washington, claiming privileges whenever it chooses to, and in effect hobbling the effectiveness of our cross-examination in this state court.

"The case we are trying here is the State of Ohio versus Rocky Hamilton. It is not captioned the US Government versus Rocky Hamilton. You do that sort of thing in federal court. But it is the State that has chosen to prosecute Rocky Hamilton for an offense against the State of Ohio, and we have a right to be able to examine the State witnesses. We can't continue to be caught on the horns of a dilemma where the State is saying, 'We'll put our evidence on in direct testimony, and then you cannot fully cross-examine our guys because of federal requirements and privileges.'

"If the federal government believes that they are putting the country in danger by divulging this corroborative material that is critical to our defense—if they believe that it should not be done under any circumstances—then they have the option of not permitting an agent to testify; and, therefore, that puts us in a position to be able to move for dismissal of this case. The government has that choice. But the Court can't have it both ways. Either we have the right to cross-examine with these documents, or you should grant our motion to dismiss."

Judge Abbot nodded thoughtfully and then said, "Well, Mr. Lansing, the Court has been concerned since the inception of this trial that the United States attorneys just seem to be popping up all over the place and shadowing you in some form throughout the entire trial. The other day we had a motion filed by the US District Attorney on behalf of the United States of America to modify certain subpoenas. The United States of America is not a party to this particular criminal trial and therefore, so far as this Court is concerned, they have no standing here.

"I am concerned about the federal government stating to a witness what they can testify to and what they cannot testify to. The Court does not intend to permit anything to impede justice in this case. I am going to suggest to you, Mr. Lansing, that you get in touch with the US District Attorney and if he wants to participate in this trial, he is to come in here and sit there next to you, because we are going to be bumping into these particular matters time and again.

"Also, it was interesting for the Court to observe that you introduced Exhibits 89 and 90 out of the FBI files contrary to the court order. So, if the State intends to introduce things, I don't intend to stand in the way of the defense doing the same. Now, I am not criticizing you, Mr. Lansing. I am saying I am tired of the US District Attorney peering over your shoulder and trying to direct this case not only by filing motions, but also by instructing witnesses. Make your call to them, and just get them over here now." Judge Abbot tapped his gavel. "We will continue this trial at 1:00 p.m."

By the time one o'clock rolled around, the fireworks had settled down, and all parties straggled in with a quirky little compromise: the FBI witnesses would review the documents handed to them while on the witness stand and then testify accordingly, but they could not read anything verbatim from the documents into the record. *Weird, and not very sexy,* thought Larry, but it was as good as he was going to get.

CHAPTER 21

Cross-Examination of Former FBI Agent Marshall – The Defense

Former Special Agent Ed Marshall sat straight-backed and defiant in the witness chair, his dark eyes aglow—but not in a good way. In return, Larry met Marshall's glare directly, but not defensively. There's an art to lawyering—a game, if you will. Keep your own emotions in check, and play off those of the witness; well, that might be worth three pawns and both rooks. Make that a hostile witness, and you just might take out the queen.

"Mr. Marshall," inquired Larry as he began his examination, "from 1973 to 1975 in your employ of the FBI, were you what is called the 'control agent' for Rocky Hamilton?"

"Yes."

"And Bob Wallace was basically the second in command as far as a contact person for Rocky?"

"You could say that."

"Well, actually, Mr. Marshall," said Larry, remaining congenial, "I'm not the one testifying, so I need you to say that. Yes or no?"

"Yes," snapped Marshall.

"Would it be accurate to say that after Rocky was recruited to the FBI, you developed a social as well as professional relationship with him?"

"No."

"It would not be?"

"No."

"Mr. Marshall, would it be true to say that your relationship was more than a traditional informant/agent relationship?"

"It was not what the Bureau would consider a strict agent/informant relationship."

"Okay, what was it then?"

"Well, Rocky is a personable man to sit down and talk with, and many informants are not. In retrospect, I can look back and see that because of his, for lack of a better word, winning personality...okay, well, I probably did become too friendly. I had many occasions when I talked to him, and I got along with him well. I talked to him about his dog, about his child, about the fact that he was repairing his car and situations like that. But I would not consider Rocky Hamilton a friend of mine. I realize now that, well, while it was not improper, I could have used better judgment in that respect."

"Did you have Rocky to your house on a number of occasions?"

"On occasion."

"Tell me, Mr. Marshall, does an informant work for you because he likes you, or because you are paying him money for the information?"

"I don't think... well... both. I don't think that you could—well, this is just a hypothetical guess, but I have never been in a situation where somebody gives you information if they don't like you. They've got to be able to talk with you, to just sit down and talk with you."

"So your relationship with Rocky Hamilton was not like you have with, let's say, Former Agent Bob Wallace or Agent Howard Bolton?"

"Bob is a friend of mine and Howard is a friend of mine. Rocky is not a friend."

"In the years that Rocky worked for you, he was giving you valid, helpful, and accurate information?"

"Generally, yes."

"And you apprehended plenty of bad guys as a result of Rocky's information?"

"Yes."

"Now, let me hand you State's Exhibits 45 and 46, which are two masks. Can you identify them?"

"These masks look very much like the ones Rocky brought to us; Bob Wallace took pictures of them for the purpose of identifying Rocky when he was working a case. They look like a real face until you get within a few feet. They look like the same masks, but I can't say positively."

"And in September of 1973 you paid Rocky $1,500 to travel with the notorious Ashton-Keely Gang of bank robbers, and you knew that Rocky would wear this disguise so that he could be identified by law enforcement and not arrested and not have his cover blown?"

"I didn't know that for sure."

"Well, wasn't that the purpose of taking the pictures of the masks?"

"Yes."

"How did you get authorization for the $1,500?"

"That amount is way over our limit, so the special agent in charge of the office has to request it from the Bureau in Washington."

"It goes all the way to the Director of the FBI, doesn't it?"

"I don't know who it went to in Washington, but it was addressed to the Director."

"According to your records, you got the money on

September 20th and paid Rocky to go on the road with these criminals. How often did Rocky keep in contact with you when he was on the road?"

"He did not."

"Really? No contact at all?"

"Not to my recollection."

"And you got no value for your unusually large investment of FBI funds—so large, in fact, that you had to go all the way to the Director's office to get the approval?"

"No value."

"Didn't that make you mad?"

"Yes."

"When was the next time you heard from Rocky?"

"About two months later."

"Now I'm confused. Maybe you can help me with that. If sometime in September of 1973 Rocky scammed you for the exorbitant amount of $1,500, and then disappeared for two months, why on October 12th, a mere three weeks later, did you authorize another payment to him?"

"I have no recollection of that."

"The verifying document has already been submitted to the Court, Mr. Marshall. Why would you pay a dead-beat scammer additional monies when, according to you, he wasn't even in town, and he already owed you $1,500 worth of solid scoops?"

"I don't remember it."

"Overall, would you say that Rocky's performance in terms of accuracy has been very high at getting arrests and convictions?"

"Yes, for the most part."

"Please review this record I am handing you, Mr. Marshall. According to it, on December 14th, 1973 Rocky gave you the name of Roy Ingall, a man who had just robbed a supermarket of $5,000. With that information, your case was made."

"Correct."

"At that time, Rocky told you that Ingall was planning to rob a bank near where he was raised in Ohio. With that information, you were in a position to find out through Ingall's prison records where he was raised and identify exactly where he planned to execute this crime?"

"I could have run the records and found out."

"And it is your statement that if you knew where something was going to take place, that was all you needed? If you had a leg up on it, you could intervene and stop the crime before it happened?"

"Correct."

"What was the next thing that Rocky stated to you when he gave up Ingall?"

"That Ingall and his unknown partner would be armed with a .45 handgun and a shotgun. His partner would stay in the bank manager's home keeping the wife hostage, while Ingall took the manager down to the bank. So, I advised someone of this, but I don't know who, because it is blocked out on the report."

"You would be advising so that an investigation could be made, and you could capture Ingall and stop the kidnapping and bank robbery. Is that correct?"

"Yes."

"According to that report in your hand, what happened at the Garrettsville Branch Bank, which was Ingall's hometown, on January 7th, 1974?"

"It states that a robbery occurred."

"And, in fact, the bank manager's wife was held hostage?"

"Well, somebody was."

"And the FBI either did not or was unable to stop the kidnapping before it took place?"

"I have no idea, but evidently, because the robbery occurred."

"So, you cannot testify as to whether a decision was made to let the kidnapping take place, or if it was just missed?"

"I don't know."

"Did Rocky ultimately give you information that permitted the arrest of the people involved? Two of them?"

"Yes."

"Were they arrested?"

"Yes."

"And convicted?"

"Yes."

"And did the bank put up any reward money?"

"Yes."

"Did Rocky get it?"

"Well, there were some complications. There were three people involved, but we only got two of them."

"Did you make an attempt to negotiate with the bank?"

"Yes."

"There is a rating system of informants within the FBI, and these ratings are compiled by a neutral third party based solely on evaluation of confidential reports. What was Rocky's rating?"

"Excellent."

"Let's move ahead to 1975 when you left the FBI and turned Rocky over to Howard Bolton. After you left the Bureau, how often did you continue to have contact with Rocky?"

"Sometimes not for two or three weeks, sometimes three times a week."

"Did Rocky talk with you about his discomfort with Bolton?"

"Not that I recall."

"Was Rocky giving you information or statements about things he was learning in his informant role?"

"No!"

"You sound very unequivocal in that."

"I certainly am," bristled Ed.

"How long was it after you left the FBI before Rocky called you?"

"A while. I have no idea."

"Yet, Rocky's phone bill shows that two days later he called long-distance from his home to yours five times."

"Five phone calls?"

Larry held out the phone records to Ed. "Here, look. Five, count 'em."

"I have no recollection of that."

"And you have no idea what you would have talked to him about, long-distance, five times in one day?"

"No."

"How about the calls that came in the next day and were picked up by you—we know that because you had no answering machine, no company, and nobody lived there but you?"

"I don't know."

"How about two days after that on March 2nd?"

"No recollection."

"Are you saying the phone calls did not take place?"

"You have the records!" Marshall fumed.

There go the rooks, thought Larry. The witness continued brashly, "I'm saying I have no recollection. Period."

Larry, deliberately looking down at the phone records, said, "Well, then, let's try the next day, March 3rd? Still nothing?"

"No recollection."

"Rocky called you regularly, came by your house fairly

often, but was not giving you information and was not your friend—what the heck *was* he doing?"

"I don't know."

"During the summer of 1975, did Rocky ever mention the name Chuck Wilson to you?"

"He mentioned the name, but I don't know when."

"Would it help to know that Wilson was in prison until early summer of 1975?"

"Well, yes, I do think it was a hot night, so summer."

"Was Wilson's criminal reputation known among the bank robbery squad in the Bureau?"

"I don't know, but yes, probably."

"Did Rocky ever talk with you about the fact that he was working with Chuck, and about the case they were planning?"

"Never."

"Not even once?"

"Never."

"Did you invite Rocky to your house around Thanksgiving of 1975?"

"He was there, but I did not invite him. He called me about 8:00 in the morning after I had had about three hours' sleep and said he was going to be in the neighborhood in about a half hour and he would stop by and have coffee. I did not say no, but I did not invite him."

"Did you say yes, come on over?"

"I said okay."

"And you were still close friends with Howard Bolton at that time?"

"Yes."

"How often did you talk to Howard?"

"Two or three times a week, but I did not get into anything about Rocky with him, because it was not my place."

"Let's go back to the morning shortly before Thanksgiving. What car was Rocky driving when he pulled up to your side door?"

"I didn't notice."

"But you came to that door to let him in, right?"

"Yes."

"And you opened your door, and then unlatched and opened your screen door for him. His blue Monte Carlo was maybe three feet directly in front of that door."

"I didn't notice."

"How long did Rocky stay?"

"Fifteen, twenty minutes."

"Forty-five minutes, Mr. Marshall? Could it have been forty-five minutes?"

"Possibly."

"During this forty-five minutes, what did you talk about?"

"I have no recollection."

"You can clearly recall that you had only three hours' sleep the night before, the time of day that he called you, but of this forty-five minute conversation you have absolutely no recollection?"

"Correct."

"Have you spoken to Rocky since this meeting?"

"Not that I recall."

"You are absolutely sure you have had no contact with Rocky after that November meeting?"

"I said I don't recall," snapped Ed.

"You have stated that you have remained good friends with your former fellow agent, Bob Wallace, and that he was second in line for Rocky as an FBI contact. So, Mr. Marshall, I am handing you what has been marked as Defense Exhibit K. If you will look at the date of December the eighth, 1975, you will see there is a collect long-distance phone call placed to your home telephone from a pay phone booth at the Kroger grocery store in Newark, Ohio. The document reflects the call lasted for five minutes. May I remind you this is a pay phone where a number of other calls were made relating to this kidnapping? Can you please tell us who that call was from and what was the content of that call?"

"I have no recollection of any such call."

"Your testimony is that you did not talk to Rocky for a full five minutes on December 8th, 1975?"

"I have no memory of such a call."

"And Rocky did not talk to you about the kidnapping and the location of Mr. MacDonald or other items relating to the kidnapping?"

"No, he did not."

"Now you have said that you have stayed close to Bob Wallace, even though he had relocated to Nebraska?"

"I talked to him regularly, yes."

"I want to hand you what has been marked as Defense Exhibit H, which is the toll records for your personal home telephone. Going back to October, 1975, the phone bill shows you spoke to Bob Wallace at his home in Nebraska on October 16th. Do you see any other phone calls on any other day in the month of October to Bob Wallace in Nebraska?"

"No."

"Moving on through the month of November, do you see any phone calls to Nebraska to Bob Wallace?"

"No."

"Nothing at all?"

"No."

"You're sure of that?"

Marshall barked an irritated, "Yes."

"Moving right along through the end of November and Thanksgiving and through the first week of December, do you see any phone calls to Nebraska to Bob Wallace?"

"No."

"When is the first call shown on this phone bill to Nebraska to your friend, Bob Wallace?"

"December the 8th."

"The same day that the other exhibit reflects a phone call from Newark, Ohio, to you?"

"It appears so."

"It shows a ten-minute phone call from you to Bob Wallace on the 8th, so I assume the two of you did speak."

"Okay."

"What did you talk about?"

"I have no recollection."

"Did you talk to Wallace about the phone call you had received earlier in the day from Rocky?"

"No."

"And it is your testimony that after going almost two full months without placing a call to Bob Wallace, that suddenly you couldn't resist calling him on the same day that you received a call from Rocky Hamilton in the midst of a notorious kidnapping that was being blasted all over the radio, television, and newspapers?"

"I do not recall the conversation."

Larry held a look of quiet contempt for an extra beat, mostly for the sake of the jury. If he hadn't taken out the queen, he had come damn close. "We're done here, Your Honor; this man has lost his memory!"

CHAPTER 22

Cross-Examination of FBI Agent Bolton – The Defense

The afternoon moved along with Larry's teeth-pulling questioning of Howard Bolton, who for the most part perfectly parroted Ed Marshall. Polly want a cracker; Howie want to tell a lie?

Except for the closeness of Ed's relationship with Rocky Hamilton, which Bolton clearly did not have, and the fact that Howard, if he stood real, real straight—which he always tried to do—was still under 5'8" tall, these agent buddies were witness clones. Two men sharing one script.

Larry spent the next day and a half doing round after round with Howard Bolton, saying in as many ways as humanly possible the legalese equivalent of "So, Mr. Bolton, Rocky Hamilton never talked to you about that nasty criminal Chuck Wilson's plan to pull off a kidnapping the minute he got sprung from prison? You know Mr. Wilson; he's the one to whom your team has given immunity so that he would testify against Rocky. Because, as you know, Wilson's not dangerous to the FBI. But Rocky is."

"I'm outraged!" shouted Bolton.

"And you never talked to Rocky about wanting to nail Wilson because he had weaseled out of a previous kidnapping and left the FBI with a little egg on their face?"

"Get real" was his surly answer.

"You say that Rocky, who was the highest-paid informant in the history of the FBI, was a lousy snitch?"

"Sucked."

"And he only contacted you four times between July and November, 1975?"

"Correct."

"May I remind you that phone records don't lie, Mr. Bolton?"

"I'm not lying."

"What about the nine phone calls he placed from his mother-in-law's house to you guys? Or all the other calls from pay phones?"

"I have no recollection."

"None at all?"

"I said I have no recollection!"

"Alzheimer's?"

"Objection!"

"Forget about it—no pun intended." Even several members of the jury snickered out loud. "Were you aware of the location of Rocky's residence near Newark in Licking County?"

"No."

"You are saying you had no idea of his residence in Ohio?"

"No, I did not."

"How about the location of his mother-in-law's house near Columbus? That's where he made most of his phone calls."

"No clue where she lived."

Larry was getting nowhere with this lying bastard and decided to change tactics.

"You a betting man, Mr. Bolton?"

"No."

"You're sure you're not just a man caught in the middle

of this thing, who has the information and just sits back and plays some cagey card game? A poker player keeping his cards back while he watches this thing come down? And he knows how it is all going to take place, so at the perfect moment he can charge in and solve it? Couldn't he—couldn't *you*—have done that? That would look mighty fine on your résumé, wouldn't it?"

"Your Honor, can he talk to me that way?"

"Watch it, Mr. Strong."

"Sorry, Your Honor."

"Mr. Bolton, was the confidential FBI phone number which Rocky had been instructed to use to contact you ever changed?"

"Once."

"In 1975?"

"Yes."

"Let me just take a wild guess here. Was it changed in December—like around the time of the kidnapping?"

"I don't know!"

"Could it be that was part of the problem Rocky might have had reaching you between December 5th and 10th when this whole thing was in progress? Can you see that perhaps it made it even more imperative for Rocky to rely on your good pal, Ed Marshall?"

"I can see nothing."

"Ah, at last the truth. Oh, just one more thing, Agent Bolton, this surprise diary of yours that you have miraculously produced here today—the one with the extra notations about Rocky Hamilton—have you noticed that you have maybe eight to ten references to him in it, but they are all in pencil—different days, different weeks, different months, but all in pencil?"

"Yeah, so?"

"Well, don't you think it's odd that every other entry in your little black book—and we're talkin' every single one—is in pen?"

"No, I think it's just the way that it is."

"Are you familiar with the legal term 'tampering with evidence'?"

"Objection!" barked Lansing.

"Got it," Larry waved him off. "Your Honor, I don't know how you or the jury feel, but defense counsel is exhausted, and I have to go home now."

CHAPTER 23

Subpoena for Director of the FBI

Larry had heard through the grapevine that Gary Lansing thought Larry's subpoena of the Director of the FBI, Clarence Kelley, was nothing more than egoistic grandstanding. Well, actually, what he had heard was that Gary had said that defense counsel was an arrogant asshole. All second-hand information, of course. Clearly hearsay.

Arrogant or not, they were here now, 3:30 on a Monday afternoon, arguing the subpoena before Judge Abbot. It wasn't Lansing that brought them here. More hearsay had it that Gary was quite willing for Larry to make a fool of himself. It was the United States of America Department of Justice that had gotten their hackles raised, and because they *were* the United States of America Department of Justice, they filed yet another motion to suppress.

The subpoena had very specific requests. The Director of the FBI must appear in person, not by nominee or agent. The Director was to bring with him all records pertaining to Rocky Hamilton, including: the confidential informant identification number assigned to Hamilton by the FBI; all files on Hamilton during his employment as an informant, including a summary of money paid to him and the reason for it; all items the FBI had either given to, provided or returned to Hamilton including weapons, fake identification, ammunition, broadcasting and receiving equipment, papers and letters of instruction or direction, and telephone numbers Hamilton was to use to contact FBI agents or intermediaries; all telephone numbers wiretapped by the FBI and transcripts of recordings of the telephone conversations; and investigative files in which Hamilton provided information.

This gathering today was called, in legalese, "making your appearance." There were at least four US attorneys from Washington, DC, and a group of at least five FBI agents crowded into this not-so-large courtroom. Every one of the nine visiting lawyers wore blue suits. Larry commented to Co-Counsel Steinwell that they looked like they were all from IBM.

The lead attorney for Justice, Phillip Wlodzimierzu, was tall, almost as tall as Larry, and Jimmy Stewart-ish in lankiness and attractiveness. But there wasn't an inch of "aw, shucks, ma'am" in him. The guy was a bulldog.

The hearing commenced with everyone introducing themselves. Mr. Wlodzimierzu introduced himself first. Judge Abbot asked him to pronounce his name at least three times. Then he asked him to spell it. W-l-o-d-z-i-m-i-e-r-z-u. It became comical. Larry noticed that even the prosecutor could not suppress a smile, and even some of the blue suits were smiling. Wlodzimierzu then introduced his co-counsel from Washington, DC.

Both sides had shot off a few volleys, when Bulldog rose, holding the offending subpoena in his long outstretched arm, shaking and pointing it at His Honor, forgetting that it's never a good idea to screw with Santa.

"This is not acceptable—*you* do not supersede the Justice Department, and *you* cannot do this!" exploded the lawyer.

Despite the increased flush of Judge Abbot's already rosy

cheeks, his demeanor and voice were calm, even, measured; and under the circumstances, a little scary.

"Mr. Wulody... Mr. Wuduzy... Mr. Lodzi." At this point smiles erupted into giggles all around. Judge Abbot threw up both hands in frustration and continued, "Mr. United States Attorney from Washington, DC, I'll tell you what I can and can't do. Take a look out that window. What do you see parked out there right in front?"

"A grouping of sheriff's cars."

"Yes, indeed. The State of Ohio has a very large fleet of those. So let me tell you what I am going to do. Mr. Clarence Kelley will either comply voluntarily with that subpoena you're waving around, or I will order thirty-five of those sheriff's vehicles over to Washington this Thursday to pick up Mr. Kelley and have him back here in my courtroom on Friday. But on Friday I will have already gone fishing for a long weekend, which I richly deserve. But before I take off, I will draw up and enforce a no-bail order for Mr. Kelley, which means he will have the privilege of spending the weekend in our county jail here. So this is what you are going to do, Mr. Washington Attorney. You will call Mr. Strong by tomorrow and let him know if Mr. Kelley is coming of his own accord, or if he prefers to be a guest of this county for a few days. And, sir, if you ever try to wag your finger at this Court again, you will have a first-hand relationship with my jail." The slam of the gavel ending this little get-together was the only sign of temper Judge Abbot allowed himself.

The call from Phillip Wlodzimierzu came into Larry on Tuesday afternoon, and, as expected, negotiations took place. Mr. Kelley was out of the country, but would Mr. Felix Falsom, Assistant Deputy Director of the FBI, be acceptable? Yes, he would arrive late Thursday afternoon, leaving time for Larry to talk with him before Friday's testimony. This ploy was not lost on Larry. Wlodzimierzu knew full well that if the witness is willing to cooperate with counsel ahead of time, it obliterates any chance of being declared a hostile witness. For the moment: advantage—Felix.

Larry knew that Rocky Hamilton, having an extraordinary amount of spare time on his hands these last ten months, and being mildly paranoid, had made a second career out of collecting every possible negative story about the FBI. If the headline screamed anything about another FBI sting gone bad, it was a sure bet Rocky had a copy of it, as well as any other articles intimating their shenanigans. Rocky may not have been an educated man, but he sure as hell was a man on a mission.

Larry instructed his paralegal to get Rocky's file of articles and then pad it by simply adding more bulk underneath. He asked her to go buy a couple of magazines and newspapers and clip many articles—as many as 200—of no consequence. Each stack would contain ten phony articles with a legit one on top. Growing up in New York, Larry remembered that this tactic was used by diamond merchants to make a seller believe you had a lot of money. They would wrap a $100 bill around fifty singles and secure it with a rubber band and flash it. The viewer would believe they had a large roll of $100's and be impressed and negotiate. Of course, it was used only for show. He instructed his paralegal to jam as many stacks as possible into his lawyer briefcase so that it would be overflowing with potential exhibits. Larry was dismayed that the defense had never had money to mount any kind of real detective work for discovery, so he was going to have to bluff Falsom into thinking that he was armed with a lot more evidence than he actually had.

The meeting began promptly at 10:00 p.m.—God forbid Larry should have time for a good night's sleep—in the Columbus US District Attorney's office headed by Bernard Murphy, a tried and true old friend of Larry's, who was present along with the rest of Falsom's entourage. The reason Bernard had offered Larry his office and assistance for a pre-testimony meeting was to determine if the witness was cooperative or not. If cooperative, an attorney can only take him on direct examination and not use leading questions. But if the witness is hostile, an attorney can cross-examine him even though he had been the one who called him as a witness. Larry knew that Bernard Murphy was an honorable man and would help determine the intention of the witness.

Larry began his examination of the fiftyish, high-ranking Falsom. He had a Marine bearing accompanied by a personable style, and, as Larry noted, a very good ability to twist the truth.

Upon the Q & A completion, Bernard asked Larry, "Are those the same questions you'll be asking Mr. Falsom tomorrow, or will there be others?"

"Yes, those are the questions, and there may be a couple more. But I will tell you this, if Mr. Falsom lies to me tomorrow the way he has tonight, there will definitely be more." Larry got up to leave, opening his brief case in such a way—inadvertently, of course—that Falsom couldn't miss that it was overflowing with apparent potential anti-FBI exhibits.

"Mr. Strong," inquired Felix Falsom, staring Larry straight in the eye, "is it your intention to besmirch the FBI?"

"No, sir, but if you lie on that witness stand tomorrow, it is my intention to destroy the FBI."

CHAPTER 24

Testimony of Assistant Deputy Director of the FBI

Friday morning. Judge Abbot's threatened fishing trip had gone the way of recalcitrant witnesses, and court had been called to order promptly at 9:00 a.m. Another day, another showtime, only this morning it was more literal. In addition to more press reporters than usual shoehorned into the small courtroom, the TV cameras were also rolling.

It was time to do the two-step with opposing lawyer/not-too-happy-to-be-a-witness Felix Falsom. "Mr. Falsom," Larry asked his witness, "we know you've been with the FBI for over twenty years, but can you help the jury better understand your role with them?"

"My title is Assistant Deputy Director of the Special Investigative Division."

"Starting with the Director on down, where do you rank in position?"

"In terms of hierarchy, there are two people between myself and the Director."

"Could you give the jury a little insight as to the training of an FBI agent in terms of informants?"

"All special agents receive an extensive training period in the academy at Quantico, Virginia, which lasts fourteen weeks. During the course of this curriculum they devote a period of time to handling of informants, and development of informants, etc."

"You made the statement earlier that you would not direct an informant to commit an offense, and then you put a qualifier on that. When would you direct an informant to commit a crime and when would you not?"

"A qualifier would be, for example, where you might put an informant into a gambling operation. He would get into the gambling operation for the furtherance of putting an undercover agent into the operation. And another example would be during a period of time that the informant is associating with individuals and furnishing us information about certain facts which could constitute a violation of federal law, but we would not go to the point of directing the individual to do bodily harm to anyone during that investigation."

"But you would instruct an informant to violate the law if it did not involve any violence or bodily harm to any individual?"

"To the point of furnishing us information, as I indicated."

"Mr. Falsom, then that would be a yes?"

"Yes."

"So you would permit the informant to violate the law and commit that crime with the permission of an undercover supervisor of the FBI?"

"Yes," he said reluctantly.

"But because the person is furnishing information and working under your guidance, so to speak, there is no prosecution. Is that correct?"

"It would be based on the intent of what the individual is doing."

"In other words, there is no intent to commit a crime when he is working for the government?"

"That he can obtain information for us for the furtherance of federal prosecution."

"So, your answer would be that he would not have the requisite intent, and therefore no prosecution?"

"Well...yes. The purpose of an informant is to furnish us information on a continuing basis, and in matters over which we have any jurisdiction, and in situations such as locating fugitives and different individuals we have warrants on, and arrest information, and items such as that."

"Now, if an informant is in the planning stage of a crime with a gang of individuals—like for instance, the Ashton-Keely bank robbery gang—or a group of individuals—like for instance, career criminals such as Chuck Wilson and Skip Nowalsky—how does the FBI direct the informant to operate under such circumstances?"

"We would see if we have enough for a warrant."

"My question is when an informant is involved in the planning of a crime, and he is furnishing information to the FBI, do you still direct the informant to stay in the planning stages and report to you, so you can abort the robbery or whatever?"

"Yes, we have done that in the past."

"And although planning a crime, whether it is committed or not, is against the law—it is a conspiracy—because of intent, your informant still would not be prosecuted?"

"Yes."

"Mr. Falsom, you have made a distinction in terms of using an informant as to how far an informant is supposed to go, and made that distinction in the area of violence and bodily harm. Short of these two areas, an informant can be used, and in fact is used, to stay on a case and appear to be committing the offense, but no prosecution will occur because there is no criminal intent, and he is working for the government. Correct?"

"We still would attempt to abort the offense, or the alleged offense."

"Whether that goal is achieved is another question, but that is the goal you try to attain within the informant system?"

"Positively."

"Isn't it true that on occasion, part of the work of an informant would be interactive? To make it real, he would have to play the role of a participant, so that you can nab the guys you want. Your informant can't just sit back at a table, arms folded, and listen."

"There are times when that is true."

"If an informant has given you information that has put people behind bars, sir, these are usually pretty bad folks, major criminal types of individuals, is that correct?"

"Yes."

"And if the information leaks out as to who the informant was, is the informant's life in danger?"

"It can be."

"Are you aware of such cases where an informant has been killed when his cover was blown?"

"Yes."

"In a case where you have a close-knit, long-term bank robbery gang such as the Ashton-Keely Gang and you get one of the members to flip, you are even more careful to protect him because of the ease to trace the source?"

"Yes, sir."

"So, an agent's interaction with his snitch, if you will, is very private, and other agents would have no way of knowing anything about that interaction of informant to agent?"

"That's true."

"Yes, that does seem to be true, Mr. Falsom. Are you familiar with the armored car robbery in Phoenix by the Ashton-Keely Gang?"

Mr. Falsom shifted uncomfortably in his chair, realizing that he was not prepared for this question to come up in his testimony. Larry had not mentioned this question the previous night when they had met. "Yes, I have seen the file on that."

"As I understand it, five members of the Gang showed up at a Phoenix bank precisely when the armored car arrived with a large amount of money it had collected from supermarkets that morning. The bank is located in a shopping center and there were five cars parked outside the bank, each from a different state, obviously FBI cars. Is that correct?"

"Yes, that is correct," said Falsom between gritted teeth.

"When the bank robbers emerged from the bank wearing masks and carrying the loot, the cars began to move, with not a single agent knowing that each of the other cars was driven by an FBI agent representing a different snitch. And then they started shooting at each other, thinking they were getaway cars for the Gang. Five snitches, five FBI agents, and no communication with each other. Does that about sum it up?"

Lansing loudly interjected, "Your Honor, Mr. Strong is testifying!"

No answer was necessary. He knew he had made his point by the slack-jawed, "can-you-believe-this" look displayed on the faces of the jury. But he decided to sum it up anyway. "So, my point is, Mr. Falsom, that Rocky Hamilton was totally correct when he insisted on talking only with his agent, Howard Bolton, when he was arrested."

"Move along, Mr. Strong," warned the judge.

"Yes, Your Honor. Now, in the case before us, Mr. Falsom, testimony has already established that Rocky Hamilton, working as an informant for the FBI, actually worked stakeouts with Agent Marshall and others. Are you aware of such activities for informants?"

"That they've been on surveillance with agents?"

"Yes, sir."

"I would have to answer your question that no facts come to my mind at the moment of an informant being on a stakeout."

"Well, it happened here."

"If that matter occurred, that would be an exceptional circumstance."

"Mr. Falsom, how do agents move up through the ranks? Is there an annual review, or how does the system work?"

"The FBI is not a civil service organization, and the opportunity for advancement is dependent upon the individual and on the merits, whether he deserves administrative advancement within the FBI."

"If an agent single-handedly, when 150 other agents have been working on a case, if he single-handedly solved a kidnapping, would that be something that might be reviewed in terms of his merits?"

"Certainly, that would constitute outstanding investigative potential, and would be one of the categories in which we would rate the individual. Yes."

"One more question, Mr. Falsom—when an agent is the control contact for an informant, is that agent supposed to have telephone contact numbers and addresses for his informant? This is his responsibility, is it not?"

"Yes."

"Actually, it's more than a responsibility; it's a significant mandate of his job, isn't it?"

"Yes."

"Thank you. That's all for now. Your witness," Larry said to Gary Lansing.

Gary strode purposefully to the lectern. "Mr. Falsom, an informant is not an agent without a badge, is that correct?"

"Yes, sir, it is."

"Is he an employee of the FBI?"

"No, sir, he is not."

"Does he have a license to commit a crime?"

"No, sir."

"Just by the fact that he is an informant?"

"No, sir."

"Now, let's take the situation then that you have had an informant that has been very, very valuable to you in breaking up what has been known as, let's say the Ashton-Keely Gang of bank robbers who have committed numerous robberies throughout the country, and this relationship between the FBI and the informant has gone on for over two years, and you have paid him well and even allowed him to travel along with the Gang to provide any other information that might be developed. Now, all at once, we have a situation where this informant in the company of two other individuals, not members of the Ashton-Keely Gang—well, where we have the informant utilizing his aunt's rented automobile and masks that were purportedly obtained as a member of this original bank robbery gang who had kidnapped an assistant bank manager, and they take him to a house belonging to a friend of the informant, and then subsequently transport him to a farmhouse in Licking County which is rented by the informant, where he is kept and where subsequently the victim of the kidnapping is required to make a tape recording to substantiate the demands that he is alive, so that the ransom of $250,000 is paid. And then—"

"Objection, Your Honor!" interrupted Larry with an extra edge of "can you believe this" in his tone. "Now, Mr. Lansing is testifying—and besides that, I have absolutely no idea if there is a question anywhere in our future."

"You are not to testify, Mr. Lansing," responded the Court. "Let's get to a question."

Gary continued, "I related a set of facts to you, Mr. Falsom, of some of the activities of the so-called informant...."

"Object to 'so-called.'"

"Rephrase, Mr. Lansing."

"I have related the activities of this informant who allegedly is acting fully with the knowledge and acceptance of the FBI. Would this be, in plain language, the role of an informant of the FBI?"

"No, sir, it would not. The whole purpose is to abort the commission of a crime based upon what the informant would furnish to us."

"Now, the situation that needs to be clarified here is this... is an informant permitted to go out and actively promote a crime? To induce it to begin?"

"No, sir."

"And you would not promote that or allow that?"

"No, sir."

Gary took his seat and Larry approached Falsom for redirect.

"Mr. Falsom, just to clarify, you do have informants playing along with a crime to furnish information and this is specifically done, correct?"

"Yes."

"Oh, and one more thing, should an agent ever keep information regarding an informant in a personal diary instead of the appropriate reporting system used within the Bureau?"

"No."

"In your extensive history with the FBI, have you ever heard of an agent doing such a thing?"

"No."

Well, thought Larry, *I have just gotten Howard Bolton fired.* "Thank you very much for coming out here to Ohio, sir," said Larry, wrapping up.

He caught Rocky's eye as he returned to the defense table and gave a slight nod. All in all, pondered Larry, was it worth it to drag this guy out here all the way from Washington, DC? It didn't hurt, but it didn't blow many holes into the prosecutor's case, either. On the one hand, Felix Falsom had for the most part played it straight today. Yep, he had definitely earned a quarter under his pillow from the Truth Fairy tonight.

CHAPTER 25

Monday, December 8, 1975
Early morning

Unbelievably, it is Monday morning and I am still here, unshaven, unbathed, and stiff from spending most of my time drugged out on the floor of that tiny closet. Last night, at least they gave me a couple of lumpy pillows and an extra blanket. That tan raincoat of mine, even though it has a zip-out lining, it wasn't enough. If I get…when… when I get out of here, I am moving to California or Florida or someplace where I never have to be cold again. Food has been sporadic, but I haven't been that hungry, so it's okay.

The last two days have mostly been a blur, like some kind of a tangled maze, so confusing and unfocused. I know it's because of those damn drugs they've been injecting in me, or making me swallow, so I understand the fog. Yesterday, they opened the closet door and let me out to eat something – a hamburger and fries from I think Burger King, and I got a couple of smokes in, too. There are only the two of them here with me, Rocky and Skip. They took the blindfold off my eyes. I don't know why. It was a relief to see, but really, is that a good thing? How can that be a good thing?

They had the radio on while I was chewing my burger, very, very slowly – I did not want to go back into that closet! Two men were talking on the radio, and then I recognized one of those voices.

Joel Gathiers, an exec in public relations at the bank, was saying that they were waiting for someone to contact them and give them "assurances that our man is okay."

Our man. It's stupid, but I almost cried. They're looking for me. They haven't forgotten me. I don't know why I would even think they would. My head is so scrambled, I'm not sure I can even hold a rational thought for more than a few seconds.

Joel was saying that they weren't sure that the person who made the first ransom call still had me. Joel, they do. Then I heard him say the bank was going to pay the ransom, but needed the kidnappers – my kidnappers – to call them again and make arrangements. It took every fiber of my being not to scream out to the two guys to go call them this minute and tell them I am okay.

For a moment, for one brief flash, I had hope. But I couldn't hold it.

And now, today, they are giving me water, juice, coffee, eggs. They are telling me they want me alert. Another man enters the room. This is Chuck. He looks groggier and more hung over than I feel. Can that be possible?

I keep my head down and eat, still very, very concerned about the fact that they are letting me see their faces. Yesterday, I asked Rocky why they were doing that. He said they had nothing to fear from me. They were going to let me go, but if I tried to identify them, they knew where I lived. And where my family lived. So, they had decided to trust me. I don't know. It sounded good.

I want to believe it....

This morning my three imprisoners are sounding off again about the FBI, how they're not really interested in my safety, they just want to capture the kidnappers. They keep saying the FBI is more than willing to let me go down, as long as they get the kudos for apprehending them. They tell me that is how the FBI works. It's not really so much "them" telling me anything. Rocky does most of the talking, and he is by far the friendliest of the lot. But the others are clearly in agreement.

They are even going to let me wash my face and brush my teeth this morning. Then I am to make an audio tape for them. They tell me what they want me to put on it, and that it will be addressed to my sister Jenny. I say okay. Maybe it will help.

The tape is rolling, and I speak into the microphone.

"Jenny, I am okay. I am frightened, but I am hanging on okay. Jenny, you have to make sure that no FBI people follow the person who picks up the ransom money. I am begging you; tell Mom and Dad the same thing. Everyone has to be sure the FBI stays away. I have been told the FBI cares nothing about my safety, and I believe them. All the FBI wants is to catch the kidnappers, so they look good. That's what the kidnappers tell me, and I believe them. They have told me that they will move me again when it is time to pick up the ransom, so that the man getting it will not know where I am and will not be able to help the FBI. You have to know that if the FBI picks up the person who gets the ransom money, my safety is at stake here. You will see me alive if these men get the money, okay? I know the bank is willing to pay the ransom; I heard it on the radio. So, Jenny, you have to make the FBI listen to you. Make them listen to Mom and Dad. I don't want these men to get caught. It will just make it harder on me.

"I do not like these men at all, but they will let me go after they get the money. I do not believe they will hurt me **if** *they get the money. This is a hard, hard time. I am trying to get out of this without getting hurt.*

"Don't worry, just don't let the FBI interfere with the pick-up. The capture of these men is not worth my life.

"Mom, I wish I had taken that job as a waiter in California instead of the bank position. The money wouldn't be as good, but at least I wouldn't be here.

"I miss you all so much. That's what keeps me going. Tell Katie how much I miss her, too. I miss Ganny and Die. I remember how much Mom missed them when we moved from Scotland. It's not easy to leave your parents; I am learning that. I feel them around me, Mom. I thought you would like to know that. Maybe I feel them because they are watching over me.

"We'll all spend Christmas together. I'll have a cup of tea and just sit with all of you for a few days. There is so much that I miss right now, but mostly I miss just being with you all. They're signaling me to stop now. Jenny, they will call you with instructions on where to pick this tape up, so then you can call the bank and tell them to go ahead with the ransom drop. I love all of you, and I'll be seeing you shortly."

CHAPTER 26

The FBI Did What?

Mrs. Beth Kempfer, clothed in her best church dress, navy blue, and solid black walking shoes, tottered nervously to the witness stand. She was not used to the spotlight. She fidgeted briefly with her fifties pin-curl hairdo, then folded her hands primly in her lap to keep them out of harm's way. She was everybody's grandmother.

"Mrs. Kempfer, you live out in the country on Pointer Run Road in Licking County, is that correct?"

"Yes, Mr. Strong, it is."

"Do you get a lot of people visiting out there?"

"No, sir, it's quite rural. There are only three houses in the immediate area where we live. My husband built all three of them," she said proudly. "One of them belongs to my husband and me, the one down a piece, but next to us, belongs to my husband's brother and his wife, and we sold the one across the road to Jerome Madison awhile back. He has been renting it to a couple with two children—I think there were two of them. I didn't see much of them; we just waved once in a while. And they had a huge black dog, which scared me, he was so big."

"Mrs. Kempfer, can you remember in December of last

year what kind of cars you saw parked at the house across the road?"

"Well, my husband is a car buff, so through the years I've learned to take notice of them, and I think at that time there was an old muddy-colored one, a Chrysler, I believe, but then for a few weeks or so, there was also a new blue one. I think a Chevrolet. Then on Saturday, December the 6th, there was an orange or red Pontiac parked in the driveway. I remember it was that day, because we had just put up our Christmas lights and we were out looking at them and admiring them, and my husband commented on the new flashy car. There was also a white Pontiac that came a couple days later, I believe. I had seen that one before."

"Did you have visitors stop by your house on Tuesday afternoon, December 9th?"

"Yes. Two FBI agents came by about 3:00 in the afternoon. And they never really told me what it was all about, but they said it was a matter of life and death. They wanted to know if there had been any unusual activities going on at the house across the road, but I didn't see anything that was really unusual. It was just the same as any other time."

"Did they show you any photographs, or give you any names or description of vehicles to identify?"

"No, they just stated that if there was any unusual activity, or cars, or people or anything to let them know."

"Did they make any phone calls while they were at your house?"

"No."

"They didn't call and check in with their FBI office for further instructions or anything like that?"

"Leading, Your Honor!" interjected Lansing in a booming voice.

Wow! Calm down fellow, thought Larry. *Do you think you're on Broadway or something?*

"Sustained," agreed the Court.

"How long did these agents stay at your house?"

"I would imagine about fifteen minutes would cover it. They just said it was a matter of life and death."

"A matter of life and death, and fifteen minutes was all they give it?"

"Well, I said if they wanted to know about the house and who was in it, and maybe even get a key, why didn't they just call Jerome Madison, because he was the owner."

"Did they give you any response to that?"

"I believe they said they did not want to talk to Jerome at that time. And it was really them talking to each other, and I overheard, and it was something about not wanting to tip their hand or something like that. They left two numbers for me to call if I saw anything."

"But even though there was a massive manhunt going on with at least fifty Ohio FBI agents and another one hundred and fifty Michigan agents involved, they never suggested that at least one of them stay and keep an eye on things themselves?"

That got Gary out of his chair again. "Objection. Counsel is editorializing!"

"Well," replied the Court, "if she knows... but rein it in, Mr. Strong."

"Mrs. Kempfer, when they left did they say something like, would you specifically watch this on a detailed basis? Or did they suggest one of them stay, or that they would bring another agent back forthwith?"

"No. They just said to check once in a while. I did not know what I was looking for, and that's about it, except that it was a matter of life and death, and if I saw any activity, I should call. They seemed real eager to know of any activity at that house."

"The timetable here is very important, so I want to make sure we have it correct. They arrived at your house, which was right across the road from the house of interest at 3:00 and had completely vacated your house by 3:15?"

"I believe so, yes."

"Did you have occasion to use either of those two numbers they left with you that day?"

"No, because around 4:00 my sister-in-law came over and asked if she and my husband's brother could stay with us for the night. She said that the FBI asked to borrow their house, which is next door to ours, to set up surveillance on the Madison house."

"Did you have any more contact with the FBI?"

"Not until the next morning. But around 11:30 that night, I heard a car drive up to the Madison house and got up out of bed to look. I noticed that the front porch light was on."

"Did you see anything else that might be of interest to the FBI?"

"Well, I could tell from the porch light that it was the older Chrysler car that we had seen at that house before. I think it belonged to the couple who lived there. It was parked odd. It was backed up real close to the garage door on the left-hand side, and the trunk was open. I watched a few minutes, but since nothing was happening, I decided to go back to bed. I figured that if I was seeing this activity, that the FBI next door was seeing it too."

"Mrs. Kempfer, did you see anything else going on at that house?"

"Yes—early the next morning, maybe around 6:30, I saw

a green station wagon leave from the Madison house. I'm not sure of the exact time, but I was up making coffee for everyone and just looked out the window. I didn't see a FBI car following it, so I went over to my brother-in-law's house next door to be sure the FBI was aware of it. I knocked on the door several times before one of the FBI men finally answered it. He looked like maybe I had woken him, and I looked over at the couch and there was a pillow and blanket all messed up, but I don't know for sure. I followed the agent through the house to the kitchen, and there were two other men and they were looking pretty tired and disheveled and making coffee, and I think, toast. I told them what I had seen, both last night and that morning, and at first they didn't believe me. They didn't because they hadn't seen the car last night or that morning and they had men who were supposed to be watching outside, and they hadn't seen them either. But it was a cold night, so who knows what they had to do to keep warm? Maybe they all fell asleep."

What a terrific witness, thought Larry, *surmising the scene for the jury.* He just let her ramble on without interruption, but could not believe that the prosecutor had not objected on the grounds of conjecture.

"So, at first they did not believe me, and then later, they did believe me. And then, of course, much later when their investigations proved that the green station wagon had really been there, there was no doubt to anyone that I was right," she said primly.

"On the morning when this happened, did the FBI re-interview you about what you had seen?"

"Yes, about a half-hour later they came over to my house. They looked better; their shirts were tucked in and all that. I hadn't really seen a lot, but there were maybe four or five people in the green station wagon that I could make out as it went under the street lamp. And then they asked me again what time it had left, and I told them. And they asked me more questions about the car I had seen during the night, the old Chrysler."

"Thank you, Mrs. Kempfer. No further questions."

CHAPTER 27

Tuesday, December 9, 1975
Late afternoon

It's strange how one adjusts to the impossible. I'm still captive, but I'm still alive, and somehow, I seem to be coping better. I have lost count of the days. I don't even know what day it is. It's very strange.

Skip is the only one here with me. He's been drinking or drugging or whatever the hell he's doing since at least noon, when he let me out of the closet to use the bathroom and eat something. He looked like he was already out of it then, though, so who knows how long he's been on this bender. He's a little scary, and getting more hyper with each swig he chugs out of the whiskey bottle. I am trying so hard to clear my head, because I think an opportunity could be coming my way, and I need to have my wits about me and my strength. That's why I ate that horrible bologna sandwich and drank the cold, stale coffee. Maybe today really will be my lucky day.

I think he's forgotten that I'm still out, so I purposefully try to blend into the sofa. He'll have to reach a point of passing out. It's almost dark outside. That's good. Even if he doesn't pass out, under the cover of darkness, I'll find my moment and make my escape. Just a little while longer, and I'll be free. I'm sure of it.

Somebody is banging on the front door. Oh my, I must have drifted off to sleep. It is pitch-black dark outside now.

Skip staggers over to the door. "What? Now? Clean what? Right now? It's almost midnight!"

His voice gets louder with each word. The other voice is that of a woman, but I can't make out what she is saying.

"Damn it. You have to help me. Back the car up to the garage, open the trunk, and wait."

Now his voice has taken on a terrible shrillness as he yells at her.

"Shut up! I know it's hard to see out there. Okay, okay. I'll put the damn light on. Right now, all right, damnit, I said I'd do it!"

He slams the door shut and glares over at me. He walks near the door and flips the switch for the porch light with a lot of pissing and moaning and one violent kick to the door. The sound of wood splintering sets every nerve in my body on fire. Something has happened, and something is very, very wrong.

He fumbles in his pocket and pulls out something. "Take these!" he demands, placing five capsules in my hand.

"No, man," I say in my most cajoling voice, "really, I have had too much already. I'll do whatever you say."

"Take 'em now, you little prick, or I'll shove them damn things down your freakin' throat myself!" His voice is still shrill and loud. I look at him and know that he damn well means it. I figure I can handle two, and try to palm the other three. He catches me and damn near breaks my fingers prying them open. I manage to slip one on the floor, but there are still another two in my hand. He shoves them in my mouth and pinches my cheeks together, hard, until I swallow. He's on a total rant, but also homed in on me. There's no escape. Not right now. I've got maybe fifteen minutes before those damn pills take effect. I know it, and he knows it, too.

And it looks to me like he's got enough fight in him to stare me down, or hold me down for the next fifteen minutes until I pass out. Which he does, he sits across from me and doesn't budge. My eyes are getting glassy and I'm getting woozy, but I've also built some tolerance for these friggin' things, whatever they are. I have fight in me, too, and I think I can beat this. I think I can make myself stay conscious. But I'm not going to let him know that. It will just make him crazier, so I'll fake it. Maybe, just maybe, he'll let his guard down.

I slump over on the couch, eyes closed, but force, absolutely force, myself to stay awake. Skip grabs my arm. It startles me, and I realize I had started to drift. He half carries, half drags me into the garage. He's totally crazy. His rant has started up again, and even in my messed-up state I can smell that he reeks of whiskey while he carries on like a schizophrenic accidentally released from a mental ward. I stay limp, which under the circumstances, isn't difficult. He opens the garage door and a blast of cold air hits me like a dagger and… and…and I'm confused. And then I get it. He has just tumbled me into the trunk and slammed it closed!

It is only a five-minute drive, or perhaps eternity, whichever way you look at it, when I feel the car brake, then pull to a stop. My heart is pounding, but from someplace far away, like some distant fog. That's how I feel. Out in a distant fog, but not.

The trunk opens, and I continue to play dead, hoping against hope that he will just toss me onto the road and leave me there. Maybe they've gotten their money, and this is how they are releasing me. I'll wander around for the night and then make my way to town in the morning. I hope….

Skip pulls me out of the trunk; I force myself to resist helping him. I hear him telling whoever is driving to be back here in exactly five minutes. Is that good news? I can see trees along side of the road. Will he just drag me into the woods a ways and then rush back to the car? The car that is now driving away.

He starts to pull me into the woods. It hurts, but he does not go very far, just barely off the road. I feel his knee on my chest, and I can't help it – I open my eyes in alarm!

He is plunging some kind of sharp blade toward me. I twist, but still feel the stinging plunge drive into my neck. The shock of my movement throws him off balance, and I am able to twist further out from under him. I try to swing. He comes back at me and stabs and stabs. The knife catches my hands as I swing, and then I feel it crease my forehead. It should hurt more, and it does, but it's distant, like everything else. He's five inches taller than me, probably fifty pounds heavier, so I focus with all my might and slam him in the groin with all my might. He howls, and I try to run, but then his knife rips into my back. I turn and his fist meets my left eye. I kick him hard and try to land another punch. This one connects, but not without me getting sliced some more. This one I feel the most. It's in my chest. His fist beats on my face and head like a battering ram, and he's still screaming unintelligibly. Constantly the screams and the blade cutting me and the fists hurting me. Constantly. I am out of breath. I try to jump on him, to leverage, to get his eyes, his Adam's apple, his anything… anything vulnerable. Anything at all that might save me.

Anything! Sticky stuff is running out of me from all over. I can feel it. It's…it's blood. My blood. I grab a stick – I think it's a stick – and go for his eyes. He howls. I have hit something, but I don't think I got his eye. Maybe his ear. And then the knife, that horrible, horrible blade… that drives into me again and again and again. And finally… finally… I fall to the ground…

The snow. I am lying in the snow. So dark and so quiet. No one's here. Skip, he's gone. The snow, so soft. Why isn't it cold? How odd. This is my chance. I have to get up. He might come back. I can see the shadow of a tree right near me in the moonlight. I crawl to it, and brace myself on it to get up. And I do. I do. I don't know how long I've been lying here, but I do think I should get the hell out of here now. But what's binding me? What is that? Oh, my coat. Okay. I'll just take it off. I'll get it later. Later, I'll get it. Yes, that's what I'll do.

Okay, now – okay, here we go. Straight ahead. Good. I'm making it, yes I am. Maybe I should cross the road. That way, if they come back, they'll look in the wrong place. Here we go, crossing the road. Oops. I didn't see that stump. Okay. Get up, Jamie. Come on, Bud, get up. There we go. Yes, this side of the road is much better. I'll go up over this embankment. I'm sure I can do that. If I get over it, then they really won't be able to find me again. Not ever, ever again. They will never have me again. No, not me. Because I'm free now.

Wow! This...this is steeper than I thought...but I'm almost... almost there. Ooh, ooh. It's... it's getting hard to breathe. Hard to keep up with myself. Hard to... breathe now.... Here we are. How long did that take? I'm all wet and sticky... my pants, they're all wet and sticky. Good God, did I pee on myself again? Okay. I'll take care of that later. But now... now I am so out of breath. Maybe I can just rest here in this nest of... of tree branches. Yes, yes, that's better. My sweet grandmother, Ganny, I can see you. I can.

Mom, I love you. Katie... Katie, did I tell you I love you....

CHAPTER 28

Direct Examination of the Defendant – The Defense
November 10, 1976

Rocky Hamilton, hair neatly combed, dressed impeccably in a suit, albeit a size too large, approached the witness chair with a spring in his step, as if this were the moment he had been waiting for all his life. His ego was now in control, and what no one knew was Rocky's intention of driving a spike into the heart of the FBI. But Larry suspected it. His pleading with Rocky about not taking the witness stand had gone unheeded. Larry was confident he had already won the jury over to their side. The case was as good as won. He worried that situations not related to this case of Rocky Hamilton's sordid past and association with bad people would be exposed in cross-examination by the State. It was risky and unnecessary. Nevertheless, after questioning him about testifying against the wishes of his counsel, Judge Abbot allowed Rocky to take the stand.

During the months of trial preparation, Larry had met with Rocky numerous times in the county jail. He had heard enough stories about FBI antics to convince the jury how irresponsible the FBI had been in this kidnapping case, and how they had abandoned Rocky when things had turned ugly. He would make it appear that it was the FBI that was on trial.

When Rocky insisted on testifying, Larry practically screamed at him. "Rocky, for God's sake, it is not necessary. It is dangerous. I have the jury on my side; I can feel it. You have to trust me!"

"Look, all them FBI agents have lied through their teeth on that stand, and I want the jury to know what really happened."

"Rocky, I have already told the jury what happened, in my opening statement, and I will drive it home in closing. That is my job!"

Larry left the jail that day in frustration. Nestled comfortably in his Trans Am, windows open so he could enjoy the rushing breeze and the sound of the purring of its magnificent engine, Larry thought with dismay, *Why can't Rocky admire and appreciate the job I am doing for him? Why does he second-guess my strategy? Where is the trust?* Larry knew it was futile to convince Rocky not to testify. A criminal's world was painted in different colors. People like Rocky lived on the periphery of society, never contributing to its goodness, rather sucking whatever they could from good, hard-working people for their own survival and greed.

The following morning Larry warned Rocky, "No grandstanding! A jury hates that. They will see right through you. No rambling in cross-examination! Make your answers short and to the point. Answer with 'yes' or 'no' whenever you can. When you hear me make an objection, it is really a message to you to be careful what you are saying. Sometimes, I do it as a distraction to the prosecutor, and sometimes I do it to slow you down, to change the way you are thinking. Know the difference!"

Rocky was upbeat as he took the stand, but Larry could sense the stress of the trial from Rocky's weight loss. After Rocky was sworn in, Larry approached him and asked him to state his name.

"Rocky Lee Hamilton, Jr."

"Rocky, how old are you?"

"I just turned forty years old on October 16th."

"And for the last eleven months, where have you been residing?"

"The Licking County jail."

Larry continued, asking Rocky about his childhood, and the jury learned that Rocky committed his first burglary in the fifth grade at the age of twelve and had quit school at fourteen. Rocky testified he had grown up with members of the Ashton-Keely Gang, and rattled off now-familiar names to the jury, namely Skip Nowalsky and Chuck Wilson.

Larry knew from his research that the Ashton-Keely Gang was by far the most effective bank and armored car robbery gang in the United States. They would take weeks to pull off a job, initially sending one or two members to a city to evaluate the target. Then a couple of days before the crime, the part of the Gang who would do the scheduled heist came into town for a dress rehearsal. They rarely got caught. The FBI was stymied.

Rocky had already gone to federal prison twice and when he was arrested in Albuquerque, he was facing the "three-time loser" statute, known as the "big bitch" statute in the underworld. If you are caught a third time, you face life imprisonment, regardless of the crime. So the FBI gave Rocky a choice: life imprisonment or work as a snitch in the Ashton-Keely Gang and help the FBI break it up and capture its members. Larry had no choice but to expose Rocky's life of crime that had resulted in three arrests. Only then could the jury understand the underlying reasons why Rocky had accepted the FBI's offer to become a snitch for them rather than spend the next thirty years in the penitentiary.

Larry asked Rocky to tell the jury about the Pataskala Bank robbery in Detroit. Rocky said the Gang had hatched a plan to rob the bank, and assigned him and Scotty to *work* the bank, which he sometimes called *sitting* on the bank. For at least a month, the two sat in a car near the bank each day at different locations and watched for patterns to develop. Every detail had to be observed, and Rocky even jotted down notes in a journal. The two found out who the manager was, who the assistant manager was, and where they lived. They wrote down the times each arrived and left their offices, even for lunch. They followed them to see where they ate lunch. They followed them home at night and found out if they had families. They checked all the roads around the bank to plan the best escape route. They checked the density of traffic at all times of day.

They paid particular attention to armored trucks that delivered and picked up money. Which day of the week did the armored truck come to the bank? Was it the same day each week? Was it there to deliver or pick up? What time of day? How many guards were in the truck? Did they carry two bags or one bag each? Could they reach quickly for their gun without dropping the bag? If delivering, what was the method of hand-over once they were inside the bank? Occasionally, Rocky would go inside the bank pretending to be a customer, just to observe the hand-over. Often, the guards just threw the bags into a pile in the lobby, leaving them for the bank staff to move into the vault later.

Within a month, they knew the very heartbeat of the Pataskala Bank. When the Gang felt the moment was right, the robbery would take place. Rocky explained that he never knew the exact date; Don Ashton, one of the leaders of the Gang, usually called the shots as to the timing of a robbery. Rocky was almost always in charge of the get-away plan.

It was never a good idea to just leave the bank in your own car and make your way out to Highway 70 and drive towards Columbus. Stolen cars were the way to go. Drive a couple of blocks and switch to another car, and eventually wind up at a gang member's house. In the old days, stealing a car was easy by using tinfoil in the ignition, but all the new cars today had cylinder locks, and Rocky and Scotty were no longer capable of stealing a car. Rocky came up with the idea of how to steal a car in a parking lot across the street from the bank. They would tie up the lot manager and car boy and get the keys to two cars, drive across the street, and rob the bank. Then they would ditch the stolen cars.

Rocky explained that Scotty decided he did not want to drive one of the getaway cars, so the Gang called Jimmy Wilson in Detroit to do so. Jimmy Wilson was Chuck Wilson's cousin. On the morning of the robbery day, Rocky drove by the bank for one last look and noticed that there were only two cars in the parking lot, which normally held twenty to twenty-five cars.

"I rode back to the office and told the guys, 'something's wrong; there should be more cars in that lot.' Later, I learned that the FBI was set up on this. It was a *fi-sur*."

Larry seemed astonished that Rocky would know such a sophisticated legal term and asked, "Rocky, can you please tell us what is *fi-sur*?"

"It's a FBI term. It means like if I was to tell, to give information that a bank was to be robbed and give 'em the details and tell who is gonna do it, they would not want the bank to be robbed, so they'd try to stop it, and try to make sure that nobody got hurt. That don't mean they could stop it, but they'd try in a number of ways. They can be inside the bank themselves waitin', or they can be sittin' in cars across the street from the bank. In this case, they was probably in the car lot; they was set up so the bank robbery would never take place. Sometimes they notify the employees, not all the time, but sometimes, and if so, they put a lot of manpower inside the bank, pretending to be customers. I mean they're already there when you show up. If you come out with the stuff in your hands, and they are parked across the street, they'd be sure to have a clear line of fire. You either put your hands up, or not, but you ain't goin' no further. That's it. It's over."

Larry summed up Rocky's explanation with a question, "So *fi-sur* simply means a FBI stakeout?" Not waiting for Rocky to answer, Larry continued, "Getting back to the Pataskala Bank, what happened next?"

"We just blew it off. Gerry Nader and me went to Pittsburgh, then Indianapolis, where we met up with some members of the Ashton-Keely Gang. We heard they was working an armored car in Phoenix and a bank in Albuquerque. So we went first to Phoenix and then to Albuquerque. There was a lot of us; it don't take seven or eight people to rob a bank, but the Gang always had two or three things goin' at once."

The jury had already heard in detail what had happened in Phoenix from FBI Assistant Deputy Director Felix Falsom, so Larry moved on. "What happened between your arrival in Albuquerque and the time you wound up in the Albuquerque jail?"

"All right, that would be possibly three or four weeks. I'm not sure. We all met up at Jacks & Queens Doll House, a nightclub in Albuquerque, where we met Buddy Harrison and Lee Merritt. We wound up stayin' at Harrison's apartment and immediately begun workin' banks in Albuquerque. I drove my own car those days with a twenty-day tag that Lucas Scott gave me. My car plates was hot in Michigan, and the police was lookin' for me because of a parole violation and suspicion of the robbery in the Bay City area."

Too much information, Larry thought, but he let Rocky continue. "While I was in Albuquerque the tag ran out of time, so Scotty mailed me another twenty-day tag and some money. He was financin' me. We worked about seven or eight banks in Albuquerque, but only robbed two."

Larry interrupted, "Are those the two banks that FBI Agent Jones mentioned in his testimony?"

"Yes."

"You used the term, 'Scotty was financing me.' What did you mean by that?"

"When I went to Albuquerque, I didn't have much money. I was sent there to rob a bank, but I needed money to live on, so Scotty was the supply man for the Gang. He gave us money to live on, bought the guns and the things we needed."

"Does the man financing it get a portion of the loot?"

"Yes, a kickback, actually Ashton, one of the leaders of the Ashton-Keely Gang, always took the position of being a ten-percenter, and I'll try to explain this and enlighten you a little bit."

Enlighten me a bit. He sounds so damn pompous, Larry thought.

"A ten-percenter is somebody who sets the job up. He's not always directly involved, but he's the one who gave the information that led to the robbery, like if he was in a bank cashin' a check and he seen a drop, it's his. We always kept our eyes and ears wide open in bars. People talk about all sorts of stuff when they are drinkin'. Anybody who gives you reliable information that pays off is a ten-percenter. But that information has to be checked out. You don't never take nothin' at face value. You go sit on that bank, sometimes for several weeks. If the hit is a really big amount, some get greedy and ask for more, maybe twenty percent. But the Ashton-Keely Gang ain't givin' up that much."

Larry then turned his questioning back to the bank robbery in Albuquerque, asking Rocky to go ahead with his testimony.

"Well, I guess my value to the Ashton-Keely Gang was to put together the details of the getaway. Anybody can rob a bank—well, I mean, if there's enough robbers, the bank will give you the money. But it's not easy to get away with it. The second you leave the bank, they are hittin' the alarm button. I had this one all worked out. I had maps, and I had run the streets, seein' how long it took to get to this place and that place. In the getaway, the most important thing is to ditch the car you are in as soon as possible. We all had police scanners, so we knew exactly when the police went into action. They could be at the bank in minutes, so in those few precious minutes, we had to be as far away as possible and changin' to a new vehicle. I had a plan all worked out for three ripe banks."

Larry asked, "What is a ripe bank?"

"An easy one. It could be hit, had a good means of escape, and the car could be switched and you could get away in a matter of seconds with almost no chance of gittin' caught, unless there was a fluke."

"Give us an example of a fluke."

"Well, one time it started with a misunderstandin' between Gerry Nader and myself. We was workin' the bank every day. Buddy Harrison had got tired of us all stayin' at his apartment, eatin' everything out of his ice box and not payin' our way. He was pressurin' us to rob a bank as soon as possible so we could have some money. Nader agreed with him, but I didn't. I knew the exact days the banks was loaded with cash. That would be on Thursdays and Fridays. But Nader wanted to go on Wednesday to hit the armored truck. I told 'em they'd get only checks mostly and very little cash, probably under $10,000. I told 'em, 'Crap, so what if we have to wait a couple more days 'til Friday?' But they wouldn't listen, so I refused to go with 'em. I finally agreed to monitor the radios for 'em. So, when the armored car made the drop, Nader went into the bank right behind 'em and leaped up on the counter and fired a shot in the ceiling, like a cowboy. He then grabbed the bag and ran out to a U-Haul where Lee Merritt was waitin'. They used my getaway plan, switchin' cars about two blocks from the bank. We gathered back at Buddy Harrison's apartment and opened the bag. There was maybe $25,000 of checks made out to the Daisy Dairy Company and only $900 in cash. That fool robbed a bank for $900, and I said, 'I told you so.' After that, Buddy Harrison threw all of us out of his apartment."

Larry glanced at the jury box. They were paying attention to every word Rocky said. Some were taking notes. This was a good sign. Larry told Rocky to continue.

"Merritt and Nader left Albuquerque. I would liked to have left too, but I went out and rented an apartment that very day, 'cause the next day four members of the Ashton-Keely Gang was stoppin' on their way to Phoenix for the armored car thing, and I had to meet 'em. Kevin Earls and Bob Keely and the burning bar man was in that group."

Larry raised his hand to stop Rocky from going any further and asked, "What is a burning bar man?"

Rocky took a deep breath, as if he were pondering how to answer. "Well, technically, I can't explain it, but I'll try to give you an idea. They used to burn into vaults with acetylene and oxygen; it's like weldin' and cuttin'. Well, now they use what is called magnesium rods and these things burn at maybe

2,000 up to 10,000 degrees. If they can get into the building next to the vault, even by tunnelin', they can burn right through concrete and steel with these hot rods. Just like that," Rocky said with the snap of his fingers. "Once you get inside the vault, you can clean it out, even the safety deposit boxes. You don't have to work so hard or so fast 'cause you have bypassed the alarm system. Of course, somebody's monitorin' the radios and alarm system."

Larry prodded, "Go on."

"We met at the Jacks & Queens nightclub. Keely pulls up in his big white Mark Four." He glanced over at Larry and said, "He drives a Mark Four, you know."

What an idiot, Larry thought. *Here he is on trial for murder, possibly facing a life sentence or the electric chair, and who in the hell is he trying to impress? Me? The jury?*

Rocky continued without skipping a beat, "We all go into a back room and I tell 'em, 'Hey, this town is on fire, a bank robbery just went down, and I heard on the scanner the cops are looking for out-of-state license tags, mainly Ohio and Massachusetts.' For that reason, I had took the Ohio tags off my car and put on the Michigan tag. Keely and the others decided they'd stay overnight at the apartment I just rented and leave the next mornin' for Phoenix. When we left the nightclub, we immediately picked up surveillance. I later learned it was Officer Hennley of Vice. We lost 'im, but soon another car was on our tail. We managed to shake that one too, but they had made both of our tags.

"Once we was inside my apartment, the discussion turned to whether they should stay overnight or go. They'd been drivin' all day and was tired. Keely was furious about the surveillance. He said, 'I'm damned sure I did not bring it with me from Michigan.' He acted like it was my fault. Eventually they decided to leave. In the meantime, FBI Agent Miller runs an intelligence report, reaching all the way to Michigan. The report said, 'If you've got Hamilton and you got Keely, you also got Jake Holt and Jay Moss and they're all there, so watch out. If they are pulled over for a traffic ticket, they'll shoot.' The next day when I went out, the cops was all over me, so I pulled into a gas station, got out of the car, and put my hands on top of the car, and they was all goin' for their guns. They arrested me and took me down to the Albuquerque city jail."

After a recess, the Court reconvened and Larry stated, "Rocky, we just arrived at the point when you were arrested in June of 1973 and taken to the Albuquerque city jail. Did the interrogation begin that day?"

"Yeah. I wasn't the only one who got arrested. They also arrested Buddy Harrison, Kevin Earls, and Kevin's girlfriend. First they questioned Buddy and Kevin, and then me. They took me to another buildin'. I guess it was a squad room where the vice cops was. The only people present was the six officers that took me into the interrogation room."

"Did they tell you what you were charged with at that time?"

"I was charged with a federal firearms violation for carryin' a concealed weapon by the ATF, and carryin' a deadly weapon by the Albuquerque Police Department. I was also charged with armed robbery in Michigan and parole violation from armed robbery."

"OK, now, did they tell you they had outstanding warrants for your arrest?"

"I already knew that at the time of my arrest. They found my ID in the glove compartment. The cop said, 'Rocky Hamilton, we got you now. You're wanted in Michigan for armed robbery.' There was two federal agents who interrogated me,

Agents Benchley and Jones. Jones did most of the questionin'. It was intense; felt like the third degree."

"Are these the same two agents who have already testified in this court?"

"Yeah."

"What kind of information did you give them during that interrogation?"

"Not much, except after about forty-five minutes of being moved around the room, I finally admitted to possessin' guns. They had an intelligence report with 'em and they kept lookin' at it and askin' me questions."

"When you say 'moving around the room,' what do you mean?"

"They kept pushin' me around the room and sometimes smackin' me on my head."

"They did *what*?" Larry said in a disbelieving tone, seizing the opportunity to paint the FBI with a tainted brush.

"You know, hittin' me on the head."

"How? Show me."

"With their hands. Like this." Rocky slapped his right temple with his open hand.

Larry heard an audible gasp from a female juror. He had made his point. But to beat a dead horse a bit more, he said, "Okay. With this treatment, did you confess to anything?" as if to say, "Did they beat a confession out of you?"

"I admitted just to the guns. I kinda said, 'Well, I'm supplyin' guns to the Gang,' since them FBI agents was so hell bent that I admit to somethin'."

Larry was firing the questions more quickly now. "Was there any discussion about you being shipped back to Michigan?"

"There was discussions of me being charged with bank

robbery and deadly weapons violations, and goin' back to Michigan for armed robbery and parole violation, unless I agreed to talk."

"Was there a discussion about how much time you would spend in jail?"

"The rest of my life, or many, many years, which to me meant the rest of my life. I kept refusin' to admit to any participation in almost anythin'. Finally, they took me back downstairs and put me in a cell in the back of the jail. I hollered to Kevin and told 'im, 'Watch out for them; if they get you in that room, they'll beat your head in', or something like that. I was hopin' he could hear me. I tried to get a bondsman but wasn't successful in that. I sat in that cell day after day. On the fifth day, they allowed me to use the telephone. I began callin' everybody to get me out. A lot of promises, but nobody came with bond. I had a lot of time to think about what was gonna happen to me now. I'd just finished doin' nine and a half years, and I was lookin' at possibly twenty years for bank robbery, five years for federal firearms for an ex-felon carryin' a gun, plus four years left on the parole violation, so I was lookin' at probably thirty to forty years.

"I thought a lot about the interrogation and the promises they made durin' the third degree. They played the Mutt and Jeff game; you know, like good cop, bad cop. One of the federal agents was the heavy and one was the lightweight. One would whip me around and the other one would be the nice guy."

"What do you mean in terms of promises?"

"Of bein' able to walk free if I'd cooperate. See, I didn't give 'em the names of the Ashton-Keely Gang. They already knew who everybody was, anyway. They knew who Bob Keely was, who Dan Ashton was, and Earls and Harrison.

They had all the names in the intelligence report. It took me several days to come to a decision to flip. It wasn't an easy decision. These was people I grew up with, robbed banks with, and spent time in jail with. I saw my decision as a weakness in me."

Larry wondered how that statement played for the jury. Did they have empathy for a guy in a tough spot, who was now confessing a weakness of character, or were they disgusted by Rocky's loyalty to his criminal compatriots? Regardless, they were seeing a more human side of Rocky.

Rocky continued, "On the eighth day, I asked to see Agent Jones. I told 'im of my decision to tell the truth and cooperate with 'em, but I was deeply worried about how he would handle it, 'cause the Gang was well connected with state senators and judges and people of the underworld. Information has a way of leakin' back, and I was deathly afraid of when I cooperated, it might bounce back on me."

"Rocky," Larry's voice was a little softer now, showing sympathy for a guy who wanted to do the right thing, hoping the jury would pick up on this nuance, "you had served a number of years in jail prior to that time. What happens to a person who is cooperating with the Feds, in your position, if the information leaks out?"

"He ain't around too much longer. Somethin' has to happen to 'im. He has to get hurt or killed. If I woulda been discovered in the Ashton-Keely Gang as being workin' for the federal government, I would not be in this seat today. I don't know exactly what woulda happened to me. Most likely I would be dead."

"What about if you're in jail and it leaks out?"

"Pretty close to the same thing. The prison will try to give you protective custody, like put you in a solitary cell. But even that ain't always enough. People have been burned up in their solitary cells in the pen. They throw lighter fluid on a guy and then throw in a lit match. The door is locked and the person can't get out, so he burns to death."

Larry noticed some of the jurors cringing at Rocky's statement. He continued, "Okay, we see how frightened you were."

"Yeah, it was fear for my life, man, and fear of my safety. I didn't want to go back to jail, but I was as much in fear of my life for cooperatin' as I was of goin' back to jail. So I went ahead and told Agent Jones everythin' about the bank robbery in Albuquerque. There happened to be a second bank robbery while I was in jail. It was a bank that I'd cased, so I also told all the details of that robbery to 'im, and the names of the people who did it. In a way, that second bank robbery was a blessin' for me. I gave Agent Jones valuable intel that could prove to be correct. To further show 'im what I could do for 'im, I threw out the fact that there was gonna be a armored truck robbery in Phoenix."

"What other information did you give him?"

"Agent Jones wanted names of union officials who was financin' the Gang, and connections we had with judges and the top political people in Detroit. He wanted them names bad. And that was the thing I was most afraid of—givin''im names. A state senator in Michigan furnished us money, and he had access to police records and could easily check up on me."

"Were you released from jail?"

"Yeah. But first they made me talk to FBI Agents Ed Marshall and Bob Wallace in Michigan on the telephone. They was the agents in Detroit who was in charge of the Ashton-Keely Gang. I told 'em the same stuff I told Agent Jones. After that, I went before a judge and got released. I was amazed at the power them FBI guys have. All the power in the world, I guess. They gave back my 357 Magnum gun and I was told to return to Detroit. They knew how important it was for me to get the gun back. If I showed up in Detroit without equipment, like my gun and radios, the Gang would wonder what was wrong and I'd have some explainin' to do."

"So the FBI gave you back your gun?" Larry wanted to make sure the jury had digested this piece of the puzzle, since Agent Jones had blatantly lied about this on the witness stand.

"Yeah. And from then on the FBI always made sure that I had hot loads for my gun. That's what we call the ammunition. The agents used mostly Magnums, but lately they've got down to usin' .38s."

"Who specifically in the FBI gave you ammunition?"

"Ed Marshall, Bob Wallace, and Howard Bolton all gave me hot loads for the Magnum."

"Did you have more equipment than just the one gun, the Magnum?"

"Oh yeah. When the Ashton-Keely Gang robs a bank, they go in heavy, with carbines and shotguns, to match the equipment the police have. You see, it works this way. The robbers never want a shootout. This heavy equipment is used more as intimidation of the people in the bank and there is less chance that anybody will rebel. Usually nobody in the bank has ever been robbed before and they just go into shock. Nobody believes it is happenin'—it's like a movie; everybody just stares at you and nobody puts their hands up, until you wave around a carbine or a shotgun. Everybody knows that if that shotgun is fired, everybody is gonna get hit. That's when they start followin' orders."

Rocky then testified about fake car registrations and fake

IDs, which he pointed out was done for the FBI by the same man who made fake IDs for the Gang. *Unbelievable*, thought Larry.

Rocky went on to describe his first meeting in Detroit with FBI agents Ed Marshall and Bob Wallace. "We met at Michigan and Junction Streets, across the street from the National Bank of Detroit. I got in their car and they took me for a ride, askin' me thousands of questions as we rode around. I gave 'em information about bank robberies that had happened and gave names and what jobs each person did, like who did the vault, who had the carbines, and who the getaway driver was. Then they started askin' me about people who had disappeared."

"What do you mean about people disappearing?"

"You know, killed. I told them that Earls put out a contract on Jeremy Wheaton. They done a robbery together, which ended up with hard feelings with each other. Wheaton had shot up a police car, which could've got everybody killed. He was just sloppy. They parted company, but Earls tracked Wheaton down through a bad cop. He was hangin' out at a motel. The agents told me they knew about this and was set up on it."

"What else did you talk about?"

"We had to get the story straight on how I was gonna go back into the Ashton-Keely Gang without anybody gittin' suspicious. The only way was if nobody got arrested. If they was, then the Gang would suspect that I told on 'em. My cover story of how I got out of Albuquerque was that I jumped bond. Although the Albuquerque cops really wanted Nader, the Detroit FBI would keep 'im from gittin' arrested. My deal with the FBI was that I was supposed to report all activities, and all planned robberies, and I was supposed to remain a member of the Gang. At no time did they tell me to deliberately rob a bank, but I was supposed to go along with the planning and keep 'em informed so they could stop it before it happened. We musta drove around three or four hours."

Larry was a bit surprised by Rocky's total honesty and keen memory. Hopefully, he came across to the jury and the reporters in the audience as totally believable, although it was a bit uncanny to hear a career criminal talk so matter-of-factly about his past, like he was only relating a job description. So far, his ego seemed in check. Up to this point, he had certainly revealed all the ways to rob a bank. Everyone present was now schooled in Bank Robbery 101.

Rocky continued, "So I got back into the Gang, and they was lookin' hard at a couple of banks, and there was still that armored truck thing in Phoenix goin' on. The Gang wanted more masks, guns, and crystals—and they assigned that job to me. There was no stores in our area that had good disguises or good hair, like mustaches and goatees, so I had to go to Fort Wayne, Indiana to get 'em."

Larry held up a couple of masks and hairpieces and said, "Ladies and gentlemen of the jury, these masks are marked Exhibits 45 and 46. Rocky, are these the masks that you bought?"

"Those are the exact masks that Claude Haggard and me bought in Fort Wayne. We stopped by and showed 'em to Nader, and then came back to Detroit. Before I delivered 'em to the Ashton-Keely Gang, I contacted Agents Marshall and Wallace, and they came down a back stairs and through the alley to where I was in a parkin' lot across the street from the FBI office and got into my car. They laid all the disguises out on the back seat and took pictures of 'em with a Polaroid."

And then things began to get ugly for Rocky. The FBI told him it was time for them to arrest Nader. Rocky told them that it made him nervous. But if they were going to do it, they should break a tail light at the time of the stop so that they could say they had a reason to stop him. They promised to make it appear like a traffic stop, but that wasn't the way it came down. Gerry Nader was following Rocky on a six-lane highway, when all of a sudden his car was surrounded by cops. Rocky sped up and got away. Gerry Nader's arrest caused a lot of problems. It was clearly not a traffic stop. Word on the street was that Rocky set up Nader to get arrested, and Rocky was worried that the FBI was not protecting him.

To protect his cover, Rocky hired a lawyer for Gerry Nader and took care of his girlfriend and her three children, who had been living with Gerry. But he could tell that the girlfriend was suspicious. She was telling people that it had to be Rocky, because he was the only one that made a phone call that day. Soon thereafter, Rocky called Ed Marshall and told him he was going to California to take the heat off. Rocky confirmed Ed Marshall's testimony that Ed gave him $1,500 for the trip to Sacramento to reconnect with the Ashton-Keely Gang.

When Rocky returned to Detroit, he was once again in a lot of trouble with the gang members. The FBI had approached Jeremy Wheaton and told him that there was a hit on him. Kevin Earls got wind of this and accused Rocky of revealing this information.

"How did you explain this to Kevin Earls?" Larry asked.

"Well, he lit into me sayin', 'What the fuck! You and Claude Haggard are the only two I told!' I reminded him how Claude was always running his mouth about what he was going to do, and convinced him it had to be Claude who told the FBI."

Larry interjected, "Rocky, you have been speaking for

four or five hours now, and you have not used that kind of foul language before. Do you normally speak the way you are speaking in this courtroom?"

"With the Gang I use street talk, you know, foul language, but not with my family. I used a lot of four-letter words with the agents too. They talked the same way to me. Really filthy."

"When you called Ed Marshall about the conflicting things that were happening that were pointing to you, what did you say?"

"My own words?"

"Yes."

"It was my street talk. Do you want me to say what I said in front of the jury?"

Larry reconsidered; there was no need to add any more ugliness to this case. "No, there's no need for that. But you do have two ways of talking depending on the circumstances, right?"

"Yeah, sure."

"Were you excited when you talked to Marshall or Wallace?"

"Hell, yes—my life was in jeopardy. They'd promised me over and over again that they was gonna protect me, but when they go and do things like that, that's no protection for me."

To ease Rocky's fears a bit, they came up with a plan where Ed Marshall would write up the reports using slightly inaccurate information that could not be traced back to Rocky. Marshall assured Rocky there was a "flash" on Rocky's FBI sheet, which was useful if he ever got picked up by local law enforcement. Rocky was counseled by the FBI never to talk with a patrolman, but instead to always ask for the shift commander. When an inquiry was made on Rocky Hamilton, it would go to the Bureau, and they could intercede with local law enforcement and confirm that Rocky was working with them.

Rocky next told the Court about breaking into a cigarette warehouse, which actually amused the jury. The hapless burglars had inadequate equipment for breaking through cinder block of the outer walls. A twenty-minute job turned into a seven-hour job. Once inside, they ran into a steel-plated door that prevented them from getting into the warehouse where thousands of cases of cigarettes were stored. They had brought along a 22-foot U-Haul truck. Instead of leaving empty-handed, they loaded the truck with furniture from the offices, which they sold for $400—just enough to cover the cost of the truck rental.

Larry asked Rocky if he had discussed with Agent Marshall what would happen if he had gotten caught at the cigarette warehouse.

"Yeah, a lot. He said that I'd have to testify, but promised I'd never get prosecuted. Instead they'd give me a new ID and relocate me and find me a job."

"Now let's move on to the Garrettsville Bank. Tell us about the planning for that robbery."

"Well, a couple of the guys involved in the cigarette warehouse robbery was involved in that bank robbery, too. Roy Ingall had went to robbin' supermarkets, but he was also in on the plannin' of the kidnappin' of the Garrettsville Bank manager and his wife. Roy and a fella by the name Allan Phelps and one other, his brother or brother-in-law, went to the bank manager's house in the early mornin' hours. They took the wife to the woods and held her as a hostage and took the manager to the bank and cleaned $164,000 out of the vault. The three of them split up the money, $54,000 each."

"Did you go with them?"

"No. I didn't feel safe, since I didn't know nobody down there. All I did was give 'em masks to wear. Since I was givin' the FBI the details, they'd try to stop it from happenin', but if it did happen and you come outta the door, they open up on you, meanin' they start pullin' triggers. I didn't want this traced back to me, so I hinted to Marshall that if they'd question the sister-in-law, she was weak and she would give 'em the names. Sure enough, she cracked that same day and that was the way the report was written, givin' me the cover I needed. Marshall and me had this understandin' that the FBI would never come kickin' down my door when the Gang was stayin' at my house, or pull me over when they was in the car with me. If I got arrested, my usefulness to the FBI would be over, 'cause it couldn't be explained."

"What happened next?"

"I took Allan Phelps down to Florida to get 'im out of town, since the police was lookin' for him."

"When you were in Florida, what funds were you functioning on?"

"A couple of thousand was from Allan from the bank robbery and the rest from my federal funds, from Ed Marshall. I still had some of that $1,500 for information I gave 'im, and there was always a lot of smaller amounts all along he was givin' me for livin' expenses."

"Okay, Rocky, we are now at April 1974, right?"

"Right."

"What happened next?"

"Well, both Ed Marshall and Bob Wallace had been moved to the Organized Crime Unit. Instead of just gittin' a bank robber here and there, they wanted large-scale arrests. They wanted information on a cigarette semi-trailer truck that was hijacked. They wanted their names and the names of the fences, so they could round 'em all up. They wanted me to connect with the LCN, the La Cosa Nostra, as the Italian Mafia was called, and the old Jewish syndicate called The Purple Gang. I knew the top two people in the Jewish syndicate, Melvin Sachs and Leonard Feinberg, and they was plannin' to rob a rich doctor who kept a lot of money in his house. But the FBI seemed more interested in union activities than anythin' else, mainly the Teamsters and the Riggers. I knew Frankie Sacco, who was big in the unions. He had told me of a plan to rip off a coin collection of a rich man. I passed the information to the FBI, who warned the man, but the robbery took place anyhow. The Mafia and the unions was tight with each other. I passed a lot of info to the FBI, especially on people who was marked, that was supposed to be dumped or found in the drink. That activity was handled by two top Mafia officials, brothers Mickey and Tony Jacconelli. There was a lot of violence among them union officials."

"When you say dumped, are you referring to being dead?"

"Yeah—gotten rid of, shot or killed. Sometimes you find the bodies, and sometimes you don't. It was about this time, late in 1974, that Jimmy Hoffa wanted to come back to run his home Local 299 in Detroit. There was a power struggle between the outgoin' president, Dave Johnson, and those who was to take over the leadership. Johnson supported Hoffa, but then his boat got blew up and he backed off. Everybody knows Hoffa disappeared, but nobody really don't know what happened to 'im. Then there was information I passed on a politician who got his hands on a bankrupt skatin' rink that was bein' built. He got a sweetheart deal from the bank. The union workers used substandard buildin' materials and everythin' just crumbled."

"Okay, let's move on to January of 1975, to the question of drugs and stakeouts."

"Yeah, that's a strange one. Ed Marshall called me one night around 9:00 and asked me to come over to Detroit and help 'em on surveillance. This didn't seem right to me, but I told Shirley that I had to go to Detroit."

"Shirley is your wife, right?"

"Yes. Shirley Stevens."

"Did Shirley know who Ed Marshall was?"

"Yes, I had to tell her in case he called when I wasn't home. She spoke with 'im on the phone several times, takin' messages. He always identified himself as Pete in case some of the gang members might be present. Ed had interrogated all the gang members at one time or another, and they'd recognize the name Ed."

Larry felt he needed to expose a softer side of Rocky Hamilton as a family man, and this seemed the best opportunity. By now, the jury must have been drawing a conclusion that this hardened criminal lived and breathed only for his next criminal activity. "Let's divert for a moment. Tell us when you first met Shirley."

"It would be at the Vegas Club in 1973. In the beginnin' she was just a girlfriend, nothing heavy. I wasn't attached to her. But after I came back from each trip, I dated her a few times and then she moved in with me. At some point I just fell in love with her."

"Did anybody besides Shirley, outside the FBI, know about your involvement with the FBI?"

"Nobody. Not even my mother."

"How much did you tell Shirley?"

"I never told her specifics, because that stuff has no place in a woman's head. But she was always worried that somethin' would happen to me. I assured her that if anythin' ever happened, like she was in the car with me when we might get stopped or arrested by the police, that she just be quiet and wait for Eddy until he came to talk with her. I trusted that Ed would come and take care of everythin'."

"Okay, back to the stakeout that Ed wanted you to participate in. Did you go?"

"Yeah. I took two guns with me. Although Ed and me and Wallace was pretty close friends by this time, I still thought the phone call was really strange, so I was a bit nervous. I figured the only reason they wanted me involved was because I'd given them the tip that $85,000 worth of Mexican brown would be comin' into Detroit the followin' day. When I got there, they took me to a phone booth and had me call the TIP line. That's a line that goes to the Michigan State Police to 'turn in a pusher.' I gave 'em the license plate number of the car and the address where the drugs would be delivered. They was carryin' about eleven pounds of heroin. It cost 'em around $85,000, but the street value was eight to ten times that much.

"We got into four separate cars and headed for the stakeout. Ed and me was in one car; Bob Wallace and Calhoun in another; and the other two was CBI cars. That's the Criminal Intelligence Bureau, a function of the Detroit Police. We sat watchin' the house where the drugs was supposed to be delivered to most of the night. Then about ten minutes to seven the next morning, a car pulled up and beeped four times. Nobody came out of the house, and no one went in. I think the guy in the car spotted us, 'cause we was too close. He kicked the car in reverse and got outta there fast. One of our cars followed, tryin' to make the license plates, but wasn't successful. So we never got the drugs or even found out if they was delivered."

"So that was a wasted effort?"

"Yeah. It's too bad, 'cause if they had caught 'em, I woulda got a big paycheck from that one. The FBI promised me thousands of dollars. So, I had this idea if I could get some listenin' devices into the house through Skip, who was a drug user, we might hear 'em talkin' about the delivery. I shared my idea with Ed, and he gave me a down payment of $200, which I used to buy a receiver, which is called a bug. I was able to get two bugs in that house through Skip. Most bugs run off of a FM radio frequency. You can listen in on your car radio within a two-or three-block area."

Larry interrupted, "Rocky, let me hand you what is marked as Defense Exhibit E, this little green box. Can you tell the jury what this is?"

"Yes. This is a more sophisticated bug. It runs off a mercury battery and is received on the aircraft band. It is set to 110.5 and can be received on a multiple band radio, both AM and FM. The police can access those channels. It can run sixty hours continuously off the battery."

"Where did you get this device?"

"From a man named Gregg Lancaster. His company is called National Electronics Company. They used to be located in the US, but then it became illegal to sell buggin' and debuggin' equipment, so he moved his operation to Canada."

Larry handed Rocky a document. "Let me show you here what is marked Defense Exhibit KK. What is that?"

"It's National Electronics Company's brochure showing the price list of equipment, such as telephone taps, eavesdroppin' bugs, and stuff like that. This green box receiver is shown right here for $155."

"Did Ed Marshall or Bob Wallace know where you got the bugging equipment?"

"Sure they did. They gave me the money to buy it. I showed

'em the brochure and Bob even copied it on a Xerox machine. Ed told me it was better than their equipment, which could not run as long as sixty hours."

"How did you get Skip to cooperate in getting a listening device into that house?"

"I told Skip we was gonna case this house and rob them of the drugs. So he goes in to make a drug buy and slips the receiver under the couch. Of course, Skip don't know this is for the FBI. After it was planted, I'd listen for information. I told Skip, 'Don't plant it near a radio, or near a fan, or anythin' that makes noise. Put it where you think they'd have confidential conversations.' It'd be best if he could put it in a bedroom where they go to whisper, so this is what he did the second time. When the battery ran down, he went back in and planted a new one. We picked up a lot of talk, but we wasn't successful in findin' out where the shipment went."

"How did this listening device wind up in the hands of the police?"

"It and the brochure was in my car when they arrested me."

At this point, Judge Abbot banged his gavel and adjourned for the weekend.

Ah, a weekend. Prior to this trial, Larry looked forward to spending weekends with his wife and kids. They would unwind doing fun things, like going on camping trips. Letty would prepare food ahead of time, and on Saturday mornings they would load the car and head in a different direction, exploring the state parks of Ohio. The boys loved it. Unfortunately, there had been no camping trips for almost a year. In a trial of this magnitude and intensity, there is never a break. Larry spent every waking hour of weekends preparing, adjusting, and modifying areas of inquiry based upon what had or had not been proven in the previous week's testimony.

On Monday morning, Larry reminded Rocky that he was still under oath. "Rocky, something important happened with your relationship to the FBI in February of 1975. Can you please tell the jury what happened?"

"On February 25th, I got a call from Ed Marshall to come out to his house. I was livin' at the time in Fred Bunker's house in Monroe, Michigan on Lake Erie. Me and Shirley bundled up the two boys and dropped 'em off at my aunt's house in Detroit to babysit, and her and me went to Ed's house. I could smell trouble. Ed had warned me a week earlier that he was in hot water with the FBI. When we arrived, Bob Wallace and Howard Bolton was also there. Shirley waited in the TV room. The guys had been drinkin' beer and whisky and we all sat down goin' over the past, about how Ed and Bob and me had worked together almost daily on the streets for over two years. I learned that Ed and Bob was being fired from the FBI and they was turnin' me over to Howard Bolton. That throwed me for a loop. I felt like Ed and Bob and I was good friends, although I've learned through this trial that they didn't feel the same way."

"Why were they being fired?"

"It seems they got fired, or was forced to resign, over nothin'. They'd failed to report an accident they covered. They'd expected a thirty-day suspension and was stunned when they got fired. To be fired over such a trivial thing was shockin'. They'd loved, lived, and breathed as FBI agents most of their lives. It's the only thing they wanted to do. Now their problem became my problem. What would happen to me? They'd promised they'd take care of me. If ever I got caught in the middle of somethin', they'd give me immunity as long as I would testify. Ed now confessed to me that he never did get my parole lifted, since that was my cover, and now it was too late. If I was to get arrested and checked out on the NCIC, they'd find out that I was still wanted.

"I was upset and worried about my safety. At the time, I felt I wanted out also. I didn't trust a new handler. We talked for hours fillin' Howard in on everythin' that had taken place in the past and what we expected of the criminal element in Detroit in the future. We talked about the Ashton-Keely Gang, about organized crime, and so on. Ed and Bob assured me I could trust Howard Bolton. They whispered to me when Howard was outta the room that he, too, was in a bit of trouble for coverin' up for another agent who was in an accident in a FBI vehicle while doin' personal business. They'd put 'im on desk duty as a result, so he was flyin' straight as an arrow now and wouldn't let me down. Durin' the conversation, they mentioned FBI Agent Calhoun's name. He was the agent who had been on the stakeout with us. I could tell they didn't think very highly of Mr. Calhoun, so I refused to agree to report to him. When Howard Bolton left that night, his last words to me was to keep workin' through Ed and Bob until we got to know each other. It had been pounded into my head over and over again not to give any information to anybody but your contact agent, for your own safety."

"Did you continue contacting Ed after this time?"

"Yes, I did. Ed was present at the first two meetings I had with Howard Bolton, even though he no longer worked for the FBI. Actually, we met at Ed's new office. Him and Bob both had gone to polygraph school and was now workin' at that."

"How did you pass messages to Howard Bolton through Ed Marshall?"

"By phone." Rocky was looking at the phone records that

Larry had handed him. "Here's five calls I made to Ed on February 27th telling 'im that Jerry Jacoby, who was wanted by the FBI and the DEA, was in possession of a stolen 45-caliber revolver. I told Ed where Jacoby could be found."

What an amazing, razor-sharp memory this guy has, to remember what he discussed in a phone call almost two years earlier, thought Larry.

Larry handed Rocky a document labeled Defense Exhibit NN. "Do you know if Ed, although he was no longer working for the FBI, passed on that message to Howard Bolton?"

"Yes he did, because it is listed right here in Howard's FBI report dated February 27th as being received telephonically."

"You did not give this information directly to Howard Bolton?"

"No. I only talked to Ed about this. I can see all the calls to Ed's number listed on my telephone records all the way through March. These calls was made from the phone under my alias name, Rocco Edwards, when I was living at Fred Bunker's house on the lake."

The phone records were discussed at length. Rocky testified on each long-distance phone call, saying that as he moved around, he would always call in and keep the FBI informed of his whereabouts. At all times. Most of the calls were made from pay phones at rest stops.

"Rocky, we have heard your testimony on how you kept in touch at all times with the FBI, mainly through Ed Marshall. Yet, in this courtroom, both Mr. Marshall and Mr. Bolton testified that they could never find you. What do you have to say about that?"

"They always knew where I was. At all times!"

"At what time did you start dealing directly with Howard Bolton?"

"After a couple of months, I felt we'd established a relationship, but nothin' like I had with Ed Marshall. Ed understood the streets and the importance of bein' able to reach 'im at any time. He always kept me informed of his whereabouts, even when he went outta town for weekends; he always left me a phone number where he could be reached. I only telephoned Howard Bolton in his office between 8:00 and 5:00, but I didn't have a phone number where I could reach 'im on weekends. Howard didn't have no understandin' of the streets and how things worked, like he always wanted to know the exact date somethin' was gonna come down. Even I didn't know exact dates! Plans was often scratched at the last minute for a variety of reasons. Howard would ask questions like, 'What day is the bank robbery gonna take place?'"

"What were some of the specific cases you discussed with Howard Bolton?"

"Howard told me about a truckload of tires that was hijacked in Detroit and some was sold to a gas station in Indiana by Arthur Lennane's son-in-law. When the guy came back with the second load, they caught him. But the FBI wanted to know where the rest of the tires was and wanted me to infiltrate that group to see if I could find out where they could find the tires. And then they wanted me to infiltrate an organized crime establishment run by Fred Bunker to get information on two Wayne County prosecutors that appeared to be involved with Bunker. So I became buddy-buddy with Fred Bunker, and this is how I wound up living rent-free in his house on Lake Erie.

"Another time I called Howard when I got worried when Vice Officer Dexter Sawyer saw me at the Vegas Club in Columbus. In the meetin' back on February 25th with Ed and Bob and Howard, they'd warned me to stay away from

Dexter Sawyer, 'cause he had it in for me. They didn't tell me what, but now that Sawyer had seen me, I didn't know what to do and called Howard Bolton to tell 'im in case somethin' happened to me."

There was a lot of interaction back and forth between Larry and Rocky, with Larry trying to pinpoint the subject of each phone call. Rocky had become confused about which phone call hooked up with each incident, and Larry kept correcting him. Finally, Prosecutor Lansing jumped to his feet and loudly stated, "Your Honor, I think counsel is doing the testifying."

"Yes, he's doing a good job of it," responded Judge Abbot. Larry took it as a good-natured compliment and turned back to the witness box, "Okay, Rocky, let's move on. What else did you tell Howard Bolton?"

"I told 'im about Chuck Wilson gittin' out of a halfway house and gittin' in touch with me. Chuck and several others had been indicted for stealin' half a million dollars' worth of stock a few years back. They all wound up in the pen, but Chuck was now out and still fumin' about it. We met on a Sunday mornin' and Chuck said he'd found out who the informant was, Landon Steinbeck, and that he intended to kill 'im. Chuck was all wound up. He had the bad habit of wantin' to kidnap anybody who had money. He ranted on about kidnappin' a rich lawyer named Nathan Schuler, or his daughter, to get money. Then he talked about kidnappin' his cousin Jimmy Wilson's daughter to even an old score. The whole Wilson family is kidnappers and extortionists. They think this is the best way to get a lot of money."

"Why were you telling Agent Howard Bolton about Chuck Wilson?"

"The FBI has wanted to git Chuck Wilson for a long time; they have a long memory. So Howard told me to stay close to 'im. I was really hesitant to do so, 'cause when you get outta jail, you are kept under surveillance for the first thirty days by the Detroit Police Department or by the Feds. They want to know what he's doin' and who he's hangin' with. I told Howard about my fears and he told me he would take care of it. He said, 'You stay with 'im, and we want to know exactly where and when he snatches anybody or robs a bank, or when and where he does anythin'.' So for the next four or five months, I was with Chuck almost daily and we worked a lot of areas."

"So you told all of this to Howard Bolton?"

"Yes, and to Ed Marshall, too."

"How often did you talk to Ed Marshall during the spring and summer of 1975?"

"About once a week. Ed never stopped livin' the FBI. I guess it was somethin' he couldn't turn off very easy. Ed and me had nothin' in common but the FBI and the underworld. That was the only thing we ever talked about."

"What next?"

"Well, it was about this time that Jimmy Hoffa disappeared, and Howard wanted me to dig around and try to find out what happened to 'im. Also, the FBI wanted me to steer Chuck to bank robberies instead of kidnappings. But Chuck was just too difficult to handle. Dwight Fisher was also involved in the kidnappin' schemes, as was Skip Nowalsky. They especially wanted to kidnap lawyer Nathan Schuler."

"In early fall of 1975, did you move your residence?"

"Yeah, Detroit was on fire and I felt I had to get outta there. So, I moved here to Newark, Ohio, mainly so that Shirley could be close to her mother. That would be about the first week of August. I rented a house from Jerome Madison out on Pointer Run Road, out in the country."

"Did Chuck come to Newark also?"

"He never moved here. He only came a couple of times to visit."

"Rocky, tell us more about your dealings with Chuck Wilson."

"Well, although I'd moved to Newark, I was goin' back up to Detroit often and was stayin' close to Chuck like Howard told me to, and I was reportin' everythin' back to Howard."

"What kind of things was Chuck Wilson involved in?"

"Chuck told me that him and Dwight Fisher had robbed the Farmington Pavilion Pharmacy in Detroit and was gonna sell the drugs in a penitentiary in Atlanta. They pulled off this heist on a Sunday by goin' into the medical center, and usin' a key that Dwight had to git into the doctor's office, and then gittin' into the pharmacy through a false ceilin'. Chuck asked me to hold on to some of the drugs until they made the trip to Atlanta. They had connections with somebody in the Atlanta pen to sell the drugs. It was very lucrative. You could sell these pills on the street for twenty or thirty cents a pill, but in the pen you got from $5 to $10 a pill. I went with Chuck to Atlanta to deliver the drugs. Well, as luck would have it, the guy who was supposed to sell the pills in the pen for us got a new trial and left just after we delivered the pills to 'im. So we had to make a second trip to Atlanta to pick up the unsold pills. Later, Chuck tried to sell 'em in the pen in Jackson, Michigan."

"Rocky, I see two telephone calls on the list from Jackson, Michigan, one on October 6th and one on November 7th. Did you go to the Jackson Prison on those dates with Chuck?"

"I did go to Jackson Prison, but not with Chuck. I went with my wife Shirley. You see, I'd served time at Jackson and had an old buddy there by the name of Dean Falco. When I wanted information about what was comin' out of that prison, I'd contact Dean. I personally couldn't go into the prison because of my parole violation, so I'd send Shirley and she'd give 'im a phone number where he could call me so we could talk. He didn't know I was working for the FBI. Those two phone calls was to Howard Bolton, tellin' 'im the circumstances and that Chuck was tryin' to put dope in Jackson Prison. But Howard didn't seem to care about the dope heist. The FBI really wanted to catch Chuck in a bank robbery. They wanted that really bad."

Larry turned to the judge. "Your Honor, the prosecutor and I have a stipulation in regard to that. We have verified the trips to Jackson, Michigan on October the 6th and November 7th, that on these two dates Shirley Stevens does show on the records as having gone into the prison to see this person there. That has been verified through the FBI, so the jury can accept that as a fact."

Mr. Lansing agreed, "That is correct."

Judge Abbot requested the stipulation be entered into the record.

Larry felt he had gained real credibility for his client. He now pressed on about the questionable credibility of Chuck Wilson. "Rocky, in your opinion you have stated that Chuck had a desire to kidnap rather than to rob banks. Did he ever say to you that he was against bank robbery?"

"Objection; that's hearsay," insisted Prosecutor Lansing.

Put a sock in it! Larry would have loved to say that out loud. Instead, and in the same tone, Larry addressed the judge. "Your Honor, if it pleases the Court, Chuck Wilson testified in this courtroom that he made no such statement, and I think I have a right to explore this to determine his credibility. The question was, did Chuck say he was against bank robbery, and why he would rather do a snatch or a kidnapping?"

"Well, he may answer. You can always put Mr. Wilson back on the witness stand again."

Rocky started talking at Larry's nod. "Well, Chuck and his whole family was kidnappers. They'd done it their whole life. He preferred not to go in on bank robberies. I kept tr-yin' to lead 'im that way, which Howard had suggested. I was always tryin' to keep 'im clean and away from violence. Always tryin' to keep 'im from grabbin' somebody's wife or daughter. Anythin' can happen in a kidnappin'. People can get blew up or hurt. It's hard to control. Almost any hint at money set a kidnappin' in motion for Chuck. Like one day we was having lunch with Jerome Madison at a little restaurant on Mt. Vernon Road, sittin' by the window. A man came in to get an order of food, and as he walked outta the restaurant, Jerome made the offhand remark, 'Look at Mr. Von Vickery's old car and bald tires. I'd guess that guy's probably got the most money in this town.' Chuck started to pump 'im immediately for information, like 'Where does he live; where does he work?' Finally, Jerome told Chuck to leave that man alone."

"Okay, Rocky. Did you and Chuck have any more conversations concerning potential kidnapping victims or bank employees during the month of November?"

"Yes, there was an incident involvin' Fred Bunker in Detroit. He had had a run-in with a man named Lonnie who lived in Fred Bunker's house on Lake Erie—the same house I had lived in. I can't remember Lonnie's last name, somethin' like Geohagen. He was a heavy money lender, nothin' small like five or ten grand, more like anywhere from $200,000 to $400,000. Fred had borrowed some money and Lonnie was puttin' the squeeze on 'im to pay, but Fred had money problems and couldn't pay. They had a scuffle. Fred wound up slappin'

Lonnie. He regretted it immediately and became deathly scared of what Lonnie was gonna do to him. It was widely known that if you crossed Lonnie, you wound up in the drink. Even union bosses was afraid of 'im. Fred got ahold of Chuck and me to ask our advice on what to do. We looked around for someone who could act as a body guard for a couple of weeks at Fred's bar, but when we couldn't find nobody willin' to do it, Chuck was convinced to do it. But when Chuck heard the whole story, about how Lonnie is sittin' on top of a lot of money, he was no longer interested in protectin' Fred Bunker. Instead, he wanted to kidnap Lonnie for some money. Fred would have none of that and forced 'im off of Lonnie. So Chuck turned again to plannin' to kidnap Nathan Schuler."

Upon more questioning, the jury learned that Nathan Schuler was an attorney who had represented members of the Ashton-Keely Gang. One case had involved Jimmy Wilson and the kidnapping of the wife of an organized crime person. She was never found. Jimmy extorted $50,000 from the woman's family to tell where her body was, and Nathan Schuler was the go-between. The money was delivered to Nathan Schuler, but Jimmy did not know where the body was after all, so he never got the money. Chuck planned to kidnap Nathan Schuler's sixteen-year-old daughter for money. "I talked 'im outta that, so he was gonna go directly after Nathan himself. Dwight Fisher was in on it, too. After watchin' Nathan's house and the courthouse where he spent a lot of time and all the other places he went, they couldn't establish a pattern, so they finally gave up."

"Did you report any of this to Howard Bolton?"

"Yeah, all of it. And to Ed Marshall, too."

"In checking the FBI file on yourself, did you see any reports on this incident?"

"No, they musta took it out of the file."

"What happened next?"

"Well, we was still in Detroit at the time, and we started workin' the Bank of the Commonwealth, which was where Dwight Fisher banked. It was the Monday of Thanksgivin' week. Chuck had already found out the manager's name. Chuck and me began sittin' on the bank and checkin' out the car lot across the street where bank employees parked. Dwight knew a guy who worked for an auto recovery place, and he knew where to call to check car plates. So Dwight and Chuck wrote down all the car plates in that lot and got the addresses where them cars belonged. We then began goin' to those addresses at night to see who lived there, but the cars was never at those addresses. This seemed strange to Chuck and Dwight, but I knew what was happenin' since I had already told Howard that we was workin' that bank. Those was FBI bank security plates. I played along like I was puzzled too."

Good testimony, thought Larry. Rocky had emphasized both his role playing and keeping his FBI agent informed. "So, now it is late November and you are planning to rob the Commonwealth Bank in Detroit?"

"Yeah. On Thanksgivin' morning I drove to Columbus, Ohio to be with Shirley and the family, but Chuck wanted me right back in Detroit that night. He was callin' the shots. On that Friday mornin', we went to the parkin' lot again to re-check some of the plates, and found that they'd all been changed from 1975 to 1976 plates. Now Chuck and Dwight knew somethin' was up and they got really scared and said, 'We gotta get off that bank.' It was just too hot. Looks like the FBI had the last laugh on that one. At that point I went back to Columbus to be with my family."

Larry glanced at his watch and asked for a lunch recess

before they moved into the critical first week of December. Judge Abbot admonished the jury not to discuss the trial and noted that court would reconvene at 1:10 p.m.

Over lunch, Larry recapped Rocky's testimony in his mind. He felt he had successfully established Chuck as a kidnapper, established Rocky's credibility as a witness, and challenged the credibility of the FBI witnesses. Around 1:00, he went back to where Rocky was being held and told him he was doing a great job and to just continue telling the truth. Then he made a quick stop in the men's room on the way to the courtroom, feeling that he could most likely wrap up his direct examination with Rocky this afternoon. Hell, he hoped so. He was exhausted.

"Okay, Rocky, we left off where on the day after Thanksgiving you went back down to Columbus, Ohio. When did you go back up to Detroit?"

"That would be early Monday mornin', December 1st. When I was coming in on I-75 around 7:00, I stopped at Telegraph Road and called Ed Marshall. He said to come on over to his house in Grosse Point."

"What car were you driving?"

"The blue Monte Carlo."

"Did Ed see the blue Monte Carlo?"

Mr. Lansing interjected, "Objection. Hearsay."

He was overruled, and Rocky answered, "He couldn't help but see it. It was only a few feet away in the driveway and I was standin' right in front of it."

"What discussion did you have with Ed Marshall that morning?"

"I told 'im about all that we had done the previous week at the Bank of Commonwealth and told 'im that now we was switchin' to workin' the National Bank of Detroit, that very day. He said he would relay the information to Howard."

After more questions, Rocky reiterated that whatever he told Ed, he always told Howard the same thing, and vice-versa. Always. And Howard would verify that Ed Marshall always relayed the information to him. This was Rocky's way of making sure the FBI was always fully informed. If he could not catch Howard by phone, he could always catch Ed. Rocky explained, "It was easier to just go to Ed's house and lay things out than jumpin' in and out of phone booths to call Howard and try to explain everythin' to 'im. That mornin' I told Ed all about our plans to work the National Bank of Detroit. In the past we had considered burnin' into it, but now we was talkin' about a robbery or a kidnap-robbery, which Chuck preferred."

Larry asked Rocky, "Now, at that time had you talked to Ed or to Howard about—when you were talking about a possible kidnapping—any more details about how long a kidnap victim would be held, or where a person would be taken, or that kind of thing?"

Mr. Lansing jumped to his feet. "Objection to counsel constantly leading the witness. He is telling the story and asking the witness to simply confirm it!"

Judge Abbot responded with a shrug and a hint of impatience, "Yes, this is the direct examination."

Larry chimed in, "I'm asking if he talked about any of these areas, and he can say whether he did or did not."

The judge admonished Larry, "Well, I am just warning you, please."

Larry apologized by saying, "I beg your pardon, Your Honor, but I am trying to move this along a little faster so we don't spend another day or two on it. Now I ask the witness once again, did you have discussions about what the plan was going to be if a person was kidnapped?"

"Yeah, sure. I had this discussion with Ed on Monday mornin' at his house. I laid it all out in heavy detail, and then I later told the same plan to Howard on the phone. In a kidnappin' they need exact details so that it can be aborted. You don't just say that he's gonna be took in front of the bank on a given day. You say where you plan to grab him, and where you'll be takin' 'im if it isn't aborted. You always have to have a plan in place in kidnappings. Like when they had planned to kidnap Nathan Schuler, he was gonna be took to the basement of the Farmington Medical Center."

"Rocky, could you please tell the Court the plan you had in place for the National Bank of Detroit kidnapping?"

"Well, the idea was that the bank employee was to be took for only one day for ransom. Dwight Fisher was a maintenance man at the Farmington Medical Center, and he had keys to a maintenance building where he'd be held. After the ransom was paid, they was gonna let 'im go."

"Did you at any time discuss with Ed and Howard about what you were supposed to do if a kidnapping was not aborted?"

"Yes. My instructions was always to try to stop it. I was never told to go ahead and commit a kidnappin' or a bank robbery. I was supposed to report every detail and I questioned 'em many times on what would happen to me if the kidnappin' jumped and I was caught in the car—what would happen to me? My instructions was always to follow through and try to keep everythin' under control, to try to see that no harm came to anybody and to report everythin' that happened."

"Okay, Rocky, let's move along more quickly. Tell us what happened during the first week of December."

"Chuck already had found out who the assistant manager was, and he became our target. We didn't know his name at that time. On that Monday night, Chuck and me followed Mr. MacDonald in separate cars as far as St. Simon Street and then dropped off. The followin' night we picked 'im up again at St. Simon Street and followed 'im some more until we found out where he lived. That is how it is done so that someone won't notice that they're bein' followed for several miles. Skippy helped with the surveillance, too. All day Tuesday we circled the area watchin' the nearby restaurants to try to find out where MacDonald ate lunch, but we didn't see 'im all day. So Skip and me decided to follow 'im home from St. Simon Street, but he hadn't came by that way by 6:00, so we left. It turns out that Chuck was waitin' at the bank and saw 'im leave late, around 5:45, and followed 'im home. On foot, Chuck tried to scope out the house to see if we could make an entry, but there was a noisy barking dog next door."

"Rocky, during this week that you are talking about, were there any discussions between yourself and Dwight, Skip, or Chuck about when this thing would come down, when it would be done?"

"There wasn't yet a set date. It was in the early stages of bein' worked. At this point it was just a casin' operation. We needed to establish routines and those such things first. I thought we was about a week away."

"Okay, what did you do the next day, on Wednesday?"

"We circled MacDonald's house and found a police station just around the corner from the house, so we knew we couldn't grab 'im at his house. We kept circlin' the bank and lookin' at the restaurants in the area."

"What happened on Thursday, December 4th?"

"We spent most of the day takin' turns in the parkin' lot across the street from the bank, still tryin' to establish a routine. MacDonald was finally spotted at lunch at the Blue Diamond

Restaurant with a woman. We figured she was a teller. Chuck felt he had a good chance to grab 'im right then, but a police car drove by at that very moment. We also checked out all the side streets to see if that was how he entered the bank parkin' lot. We had a plan to pull out in front of his car before he entered the parkin' lot and then have another car pull in behind 'im and git 'im that way, where nobody would see us.

"That afternoon we had a meetin' out at Dwight Fisher's house to discuss the case. We realized we couldn't grab MacDonald at his house because of the barkin' dog. Nathan Schuler's name came up again. Chuck was hell bent on gittin' Nathan Schuler. We even drove by Nathan's place of business on our way back over to the bank. It was late afternoon and dark. I was assigned to stay in the parkin' lot across from the bank where nobody could see me. Skippy was parked elsewhere in the lot, also. Then a lot of cars begun comin' into the lot at that odd hour when most of the cars should've been leaving. It looked suspicious, so I suggested to Skip that we leave the lot."

"During this week, are you having any contact at all with either Bolton or Marshall?"

"Yes, I kept 'em wired up on the situation and told 'em we wasn't ready to jump yet, but that we was followin' the banker. I couldn't give 'em a definite date yet."

"Rocky, let's move to the day of the kidnapping, Friday, December 5th. What happened that day?"

"Well, Skip Nowalsky and me was in my blue Monte Carlo. Skip was drivin'. We was sittin' up on the street just above the bank to see if he came in that way. We was still tryin' to establish a routine on what streets he took to the bank each mornin'. Chuck did not show up, and neither did the bank manager. So we decided to blow off this surveillance and Skip said we should make one more drive around. We cut through the alley and saw MacDonald just pullin' into the bank parkin' lot and Skip shot in there and said, 'I'm gonna git 'im.' Skip put on his rubber mask, which we kept on the car seat right beside us. I had no choice but to put mine on, also. Skip grabbed a gun and jumped out of the car. I was hollerin' for 'im not to do it, sayin' 'Chuck ain't here yet.' But he went to MacDonald's car and grabbed 'im anyway. I stayed in the car durin' all this, kind of frantic, but did get out and open the door when he brought MacDonald over to the car and slipped 'im into the front seat between us."

"Had any of this action been planned for Friday morning beforehand?"

"No, not at all. It was all spur of the moment. I seen numerous people around in the parkin' lot, and I felt sure they'd seen us take MacDonald in the blue car. It was a stupid act to do it in the parkin' lot where there was a lot of people to see us. If Skip hadn't interfered and the plannin' was complete, MacDonald would never have got taken. The FBI would have stopped it from happenin'."

"What happened then?"

"Skip shot through the alley and up into the Livernoise area. We stopped at a pay phone and I called Chuck and said, 'We got 'im; he's in the car.' He told me to take 'im to where we had planned. I told 'im a lot of people seen the car so we needed to get off the street as soon as possible, which meant that the Farmington Medical Center was too far away. I told Chuck we was gonna take 'im to Jason Bintner's house, which was close by."

"So you were in the blue Monte Carlo. Do you own that car?"

"No, it was rented for me by my aunt."

"And that was the same car you have testified that you showed to Ed Marshall? Did Howard ever see that car?"

"I told Howard I was drivin' a blue Monte Carlo twice in that two-week period of time."

"And the masks you were wearing, were they the same masks that the FBI had pictures of?"

"Yes, they was the same masks."

"What happened when you got to the Bintner house?"

"Skip took MacDonald down to the basement. I waited upstairs for Chuck to arrive. The minute Chuck got there, he got Dwight Fisher on the phone and told 'im we needed to transfer the MacDonald kid to the Farmington Medical Center, but Dwight disagreed and told 'im not to bring 'im there."

"And that had been your plan from the beginning, to take him to the Farmington Medical Center maintenance building?"

"Yeah. But now Dwight has changed his mind. Sayin' it was too risky to bring 'im there."

"Well, did Dwight stay involved now that the kidnapping had taken place?"

"Yeah, Chuck told Dwight to go rent a car for us since we now had to ditch the blue Monte Carlo. He rented us a red Firebird."

"What happened next?"

"Chuck, he questioned MacDonald on who to call at the bank to arrange a ransom. The plan was just to hold MacDonald all day 'til the money was dropped off at 6:30 or 7:00 that same day. Chuck told me to put MacDonald in the red Firebird and keep 'im there. We sat most of the day in a shoppin' center parkin' lot waitin' for the money to be dropped off. Around 7:15 that evening, I finally reached Chuck by phone and he told me they didn't drop off the money as requested. I asked 'im what I should do with the kid. Chuck said, 'Put 'im in the trunk or just get rid of 'im. I don't care either way.' I told 'im that was crazy, that if he had any hopes of gittin' the money, he needed MacDonald to be alive. Chuck said, 'I don't know where to take him; just get rid of him; we don't need him.' I told Chuck I'd take 'im to my house in Ohio, and he told me I was crazy."

"Is that what you did? Take him to Ohio?"

"Yeah. It was a terrible drive, about four hours, rainy and sleety, but Skip and me got to my house on Pointer Run Road just outside of Newark here late at night. On the way, I stopped off to see Shirley at her mother's house and told her I'd be gittin' a lot of phone calls. I told her that if Howard called to tell 'im I had what he wanted at my house."

"Okay, now, did both Ed and Howard know where you were living in Licking County?"

"Yes, they did."

"At this point, did Chuck say anything to you that caused you to be concerned about the safety of Mr. MacDonald?"

"Oh yeah, Chuck was always talkin' about killin'. He's got no emotion. His exact words to me was to put 'im in the trunk or get rid of 'im. I had plenty of concern about MacDonald's safety."

"Did you make any attempt in terms of staying with MacDonald?"

"Yes, I stayed at the house constantly over the weekend. I wasn't always in the same room with 'im. Skip was with 'im alone a lot of the time, but I never let 'im be alone with Chuck except for the tapin'."

Handing Rocky several sheets of paper stapled together, Larry asked him, "On Sunday, December 7th, did you make any of these phone calls reflected in the record?"

"Yes, about fifty or sixty calls to Ed and Howard and Chuck, all relatin' to what was goin' on. I was tryin' to pin down Chuck as to when he was to git the money so that I could tell Ed and Howard the location. Chuck kept tellin' me he'd have it within the next couple of hours."

"What else happened on Sunday?"

"Late Sunday night, Chuck came down to Ohio for a tapin' session and slept for a while. He actually did the tapin' on Monday mornin' while I went to Burger King to get us all somethin' to eat."

"The tape you heard in the courtroom—were you present during that taping session?"

"No. Like I said, I went to get us somethin' to eat. Chuck and Skip was there at the house. Chuck wrote out what he wanted MacDonald to say. When I came back from the Burger King, the tapin' was finished. We all three listened to the last part of the tape. Then Chuck left with the tape, headin' back to Detroit. I told 'im to drive slow and not get caught, to not get any traffic tickets.

"I realize now, I shoulda never left Chuck and Skip alone with MacDonald. I'm pretty sure that was when they hatched a plot to kill MacDonald without my knowledge. When Chuck left, I went over to the Kroger store and called Ed Marshall and told 'im that Chuck was on his way to Detroit with the tape."

"What did Ed tell you in terms of what the FBI was doing?"

"He said he was relatin' everythin' to Howard and to watch out for the kid's safety. That's all."

"Now tell us what else happened on Monday, December 8th."

"That afternoon, I called Chuck to see if he'd delivered the tape and when he was gonna pick up the ransom money.

He tells me that Dwight Fisher has got scared and backed off and he needs me to come up to Detroit to help 'im pick up the money. Since I am pressurin' 'im for information that I can relay to the FBI, I agreed to come up there early the next day, on Tuesday the 9th, to help 'im. I was ready for this to end."

"Go on," Larry prodded.

"I got there around noon and Chuck and me, we drove around aimlessly tryin' to find a drop site. The final extortion call was scheduled for 4:00 that afternoon. We decided to go to a restaurant in separate cars, at which time a FBI surveillance car got in between us and followed us to the restaurant. Chuck noticed it and mentioned it in the restaurant, but I sloughed it off sayin' it was probably nothin'. Afterwards, we went down to a large shoppin' center and there was the same surveillance car, with the same man watchin' us. I could see that the FBI was closin' in, but they should've had thirty or forty cars doing the surveillance, not the same man and the same car you can recognize. Chuck started hollerin' and tried to chase the man down, but he got away. Man, I wanted no part of that and wanted to get away from Chuck as soon as I could. Chuck wanted to know why I didn't pull the car over to confront the agent, and I told 'im, 'Look, I'm wanted by the police and don't want to get arrested.' I'd been playin' along to this point, but I refused to help 'im chase down that FBI car and told 'im I was gonna go to Jason Bintner's house."

"Why did you want to put distance between you and Chuck?"

"Why? Cause I knew the FBI was closin' in and when it came time to take Chuck down, they'd consider 'im armed and dangerous and would take no chances in missin' 'im. If I was there, I could get blew up too."

"So you went to Jason Bintner's house. Did you make any phone calls there and to whom?"

"On the way, I stopped and called Ed Marshall and told 'im to back off a little bit. I told 'im his men was all over me, and Chuck had now been alerted. After I got to Jason's house, I called Dwight Fisher and tried to put 'im at ease. I didn't want everybody panickin'. Then I drove over to the Presidential Inn about a mile from Jason's house to call Howard. I kept gittin' a busy signal. So I called the main FBI switchboard and they told me that Howard wasn't in. So I called Ed again and he assured me he was passin' all of my messages to Howard and that Howard was worried that I wasn't callin' 'im directly. I told 'im I was always gittin' a busy signal and that I still didn't have a definite time that the money would be dropped. Chuck was hard to pin down. I also told 'im that I was gonna go back down to Newark tonight to move MacDonald to a motel tomorrow mornin' so that we could release 'im after the money was picked up. I was in hopes the FBI would intercept and get MacDonald durin' the transfer to the motel."

"What time was that when you called Ed Marshall?"

"That was around 5:00 or 6:00. By that time, Chuck had arrived at Jason's house and he wanted to go check out some more drop places. We drove around for a couple of hours in Jason's station wagon with a lot of weapons in a duffel bag. There was one place out by the airport, and another one here and there. I told 'im to stop so I could make a phone call. I tried to call Howard, but never did get through to the Bureau that night. Just kept gittin' a busy signal. So I had no idea what the FBI was doin' with the information I was passin' to 'em.

"Finally, we went back to Jason's house and I called Shirley around 10:30 p.m. and told her to go out to the Pointer Run house and give a message to Skip. My exact words was,

'Don't go in the house. Just pull in the driveway and blow the horn or go knock on the door and tell Skip to clean up the house and then leave. Don't stay; don't go in the house; just take 'im that message.' I wanted the house clean by the time I got there the next day to move MacDonald to a motel. Shirley complained that it was awfully late to drive out to the house. I told her to do as I told her and that I'd be home later that night, in about four hours.

"I told Chuck I was goin' back to Newark to move MacDonald to a motel. Afterwards, I would call 'im and let 'im know how to reach me, so he could let me know when he had the ransom money in hand and I could release MacDonald. He said he would keep lookin' for a place to have the money dropped. Dwight Fisher was back on board to help Chuck pick up the money. Chuck wanted to keep the red Firebird, 'cause he felt sure that FBI agent he chased down had made his tag number. I asked Jason if I could borrow his station wagon for a couple of days, and I headed out for Columbus."

"Did the trip go uneventfully for you?"

"No, man, it didn't," said Rocky shaking his head. "When I left Bintner's house, he told me that the gas gauge in the station wagon didn't work but that the gas tank was full. It was a stormy night and sleetin'. I saw one gas station along the way, but it was closed. Before I could find another one, I ran out of gas on the highway. I had to hoof it for a few miles to a rest stop in freezin' rain. Somebody there took me to get some gas for the car."

"What time did you arrive in Columbus?"

"With this delay, it was 4:30 in the mornin' when I arrived at my mother-in-law's house. Shirley was up waitin' up for me, which surprised me. She seemed upset and told me that Skippy was there at her mother's house. I was shocked. He was supposed to be out at the farmhouse with MacDonald. Skip was asleep in the front room on a roll-out bed. I woke 'im up and demanded to know what had happened. I asked 'im where was MacDonald and what happened to 'im, and he blurted out somethin' about stabbin'. He sounded confused and muddled and too groggy to tell me anythin'—still too drugged up. I was in total shock. My head was spinnin' and I was confused and deeply upset at the idea that somethin' bad had happened to Mr. MacDonald. I made Skip git up and said, 'We're goin' back out to the farmhouse,' 'cause I wanted to know what had happened. I wanted to know if the kid was still alive. I told Shirley to get the kids up, and we all got in the station wagon to go to the farmhouse. It is hard to explain what I felt at that moment."

Rocky had become emotional, like he was reliving the moment. Larry said, "Well, you'll have to explain it to us, Rocky."

In an excited tone, an agitated Rocky said, "I told Skip, if you've hurt that banker kid, I'll do the same damn thing to you that you did to him. This didn't seem to bother 'im at all; he was too groggy to even know what I was sayin' to 'im."

Larry asked for a five-minute recess so that Rocky could compose himself for the remainder of the testimony. After the recess, Larry picked up the questioning. "What time did you arrive at the farmhouse on Pointer Run Road?"

"Around 5:30 in the morning."

"What was going through your mind on that drive out to the house?"

Lansing was on his feet in an instant. "Objection! That is not a proper question. What was going through your mind?"

"Rephrase your question, Mr. Strong," admonished Judge Abbot.

"Okay, Rocky, in terms of what you talked about with the

agents, was everything going the way it was supposed to be going?"

"No, ya know, everythin' was confused. I'd gave all the information to both Ed and Howard. They knew which house he was in. I couldn't understand how Skip wound up at my mother-in-law's house. None of it made sense to me. Not only the man gittin' hurt, but how did he get past the FBI when they knew exactly where he was? My head was in a turmoil. I was heavily confused."

Rocky was still visibly upset, but Larry thought it played well to the jury and let him continue.

"I went to the house to try to find out what had happened. Skip still hadn't said what had happened. I looked for MacDonald, but he wasn't there. I told Skip he had better clean up the place, to pick up all the stuff and put it in a bag. Shirley washed down the wall in the closet. Then we vacuumed. I made sure that everythin' was put in the plastic bag and took it to the car. We loaded up, and I told Skip to take me where he last saw MacDonald."

"How long did you stay at the farmhouse?"

"About an hour."

"Was the plastic bag with all the stuff in it the same green plastic bag that was found in the car when you were arrested?"

"Yes."

"Did you have an opportunity to dispose of the bag before the arrest?"

"Yeah, sure. But I was confused and agitated and didn't think to do so. I wasn't concerned about the bag; I just wanted to find MacDonald."

"Did you find him?"

"No. He wasn't where Skip took me down in the woods. I really cussed Skip out. I called 'im a lot of bad names. Shirley didn't hear it; her and the boys was up on the road waitin' for us back at the car."

"What did you do then?"

"We all got back in the car—Shirley, Skip, the kids, and me—and drove to a gas station where I called my brother-in-law and asked if he'd come and meet us at a certain truck stop and pick up my wife and kids and take 'em to his house. Shirley decided she wanted to stay with me and Skip, but she wanted to go home and pack a few things and come back. We waited for her at a shoppin' center. Skip wanted to split at this point, but I told 'im we was goin' to Indianapolis and would be there by the next mornin' and we could drop 'im off at the bus station. I also made a couple of calls to Chuck, and he was still lookin' for a place where the bank could drop off the money. I told Chuck that Skip had done somethin' with MacDonald, but I didn't know what had happened, but that I thought MacDonald may be dead or hurt bad. Chuck responded with no emotion whatsoever, 'That is the best thin' that could've happened.' I cussed 'im out and hung up."

"Did you notice any surveillance since you left the farmhouse?"

"No, not until we reached Interstate 70. They mighta followed us to the woods and to the shoppin' center, but I didn't see 'em. I didn't try to do anythin' to avoid 'em. But on I-70, they was everywhere, like a caravan. They was all over me and I was confused. They had the information that I was workin' with the FBI, so I couldn't understand why they was after me. I pulled off at a gas station and they did also, not to gas up but just to linger and watch me, and buy maps and things like that 'til I left and they left right behind me. They could've captured me right then, but they didn't. I was still so confused at what was happenin'."

Rocky still hadn't calmed down, but Larry let him continue. "Go on," he prodded.

"Further down the road, when they seen I didn't make the turn to go to Detroit, they began to hem me in, gittin' closer and closer. I was watchin' all this in my rear view and side mirrors. Then I seen two of their cars comin' alongside of me and seen what I thought was a rifle or a shotgun pointin' out the window of the second car. I seen the man in the knee position, and I knew they was about to blow us off that highway."

"What did you do?" asked Larry, perhaps a little too anxiously, remembering when he had found himself in a similar situation just a few weeks earlier when the FBI had tried to assassinate him in a similar manner.

"I made a sharp left turn across the grassy median and broke into the traffic goin' in the opposite direction and stopped the car, jumped out, and put my hands in the air. All of the traffic behind me came to a screechin' stop. I know it created a lot of chaos, but I had hundreds of witnesses and felt the FBI couldn't shoot me now to cover up what had happened."

"Were you trying to make a run for it? To get away?"

"No, no. I just wanted to get away from that shotgun."

"What happened then?"

"Agents surrounded the car. They took me into custody."

"Did you have any discussions with the agents in the car on the way back to Columbus?"

"Yes. As soon as I got in the car I asked them not to use the radio, not to notify the press, and to put me in touch with Agent Howard Bolton in the FBI's Detroit Office. The agent from Cincinnati said he knew Howard Bolton. And they did request radio silence and checked in and requested no publicity. They told me there was a warrant for my arrest, but they didn't say what it was for. They wanted to know where the kid was, and I told 'em I wanted to talk to Detroit, and they said okay and caravaned me to Columbus. All the time I was wonderin' what happened to Shirley. When they arrested me, I could hear her hollerin' and cryin' in the car. I didn't care about what was happenin' to Skip."

"What happened when you got to Columbus?"

"They took me to an office. I don't know whether it was a FBI office or not. They started shootin' questions at me, and I insisted on talkin' only with Howard Bolton in Detroit. But the questions kept comin'. They kept playin' the 'if and but' game. If he was hurt, could he be found? If he was dead, could he be found? I told 'em I would speak only to my contact agent. They told me there was no need to talk to Detroit, that I could talk to them. When they realized after about half an hour that I wasn't gonna talk to 'em, they put me on the phone with Agent Jerry Calhoun in the Detroit FBI office."

"Did you ask to speak with Jerry Calhoun?"

"No. I asked to speak with Howard Bolton."

"How many times did you speak with FBI Agent Jerry Calhoun?"

"Two times."

"Tell us about those conversations."

"My openin' words on the first call, 'What the hell's wrong with you guys up there? Why didn't you do anything to stop this thing? Are you all crazy?' He tried to calm me down by saying, 'What's goin' on, Rocky?' And I asked him, 'Where's Howard?' He said, 'We're trying to locate him Rocky, and we'll have 'im here in a couple of minutes.' I'm really agitated and confused and asked, 'What are they tryin' to do to me, dump me? I've been feedin' you all from day one everythin' about Chuck. I laid it all out. Howard knows the whole set-up. And then I laid it all out for Calhoun again in that phone call. Then he said he would get back to me in a little bit and hung up."

"And what about the second phone call?"

"Well, it was about two hours before he called me back. Durin' that time, the agents was going back and forth from room to room, and about fifteen minutes after my phone call with Calhoun, they came in my room and told me that they'd arrested Chuck and cracked him. Chuck was sayin' I was the ring leader, that I had planned everythin', that I ordered the guy killed and they was chargin' me with murder. It became clear to me that they'd taped the phone conversation I had with Jerry Calhoun and had played it to Chuck, because everythin' Chuck was sayin' about me was the exact things I had said about Chuck."

"Okay now, you have heard testimony in this courtroom that there was no tape of the first phone call."

"Yes, but they tape all phone calls. I've been in their office when they taped each other. They use the tapes for stenography. They tape everythin', everythin'! That's part of their equipment in the Detroit office." Rocky was visibly upset again and practically shouting.

"You stated that you thought you were getting dumped. Explain that."

"I just felt everythin' was closin' in on me, that the case was too hot, and I was takin' the fall for it. They was settin' me up. They told me I was a defendant. They processed me and took me to the Franklin County jail."

"Did Howard Bolton ever call you?"

"No. I tried to get through to 'im the next day, but they wouldn't put me through."

"Did you ultimately see him?"

"Yeah. He showed up the next day with three people, but he talked to me alone. Just the two of us. He sat on one side of the table and me on the other side. I lit into 'im, 'What are you doin', Howard, and why?' He told me the case was too hot and that the Strike Force was in on it now, and there was nothin' he could do. It was out of his control. If I'd just keep the FBI out of it and testify, I'd go to prison for only a few years, that the FBI could work that out for me. Otherwise, he said, both me and Shirley would burn and the most that would happen to him was he would lose his job. I told 'im that I wouldn't do both—testify and go to prison—and that I had lost trust in the FBI."

"I have no further questions," Larry pronounced. Most attorneys would have exhaled a sigh of relief now that this phase of the trial was in the bag. But not Larry. He never allowed himself, not once, not even on weekends, to stop thinking about the trial from the moment it started to the second it ended with the final gavel blow. He was dominated by an omnipresent adrenaline, driving him toward the finish line.

CHAPTER 29

Cross-Examination of the Defendant – The Prosecution
November 16, 1976

The Prosecutor, Gary Lansing, Esquire, strode straight up to the witness box, where Rocky sat. Larry had never seen the prosecutor dressed in anything other than a conservative gray, brown, or dark-blue suit, white shirt, and nondescript tie. Yet, today, he looked rather dapper, despite his rotund shape. Lansing was wearing a powder-blue suit with a white shirt and a peach-colored silk tie with little light-blue polka dots, and a matching handkerchief tucked in his pocket, no less. *How odd,* thought Larry. *Looks like the esquire dug really deep into his closet this morning and found a suit more appropriate for a spring day instead of this chilly November day. Looks like he's dressed for a date. Yeah, a date with Rocky!*

Mr. Lansing re-established Rocky's name and age and then immediately asked Rocky how many years he had been a free man—meaning out of prison—since the age of eighteen. Rocky admitted to three or four years. Whoosh! In one sentence, he had reminded the jury that Rocky was a career criminal.

Then the prosecutor established a link to Chuck Wilson. Rocky told how he and Chuck had committed robberies together and were caught, and had served sentences at the same time, but in different penitentiaries. Rocky related how he once escaped from Jackson prison in Michigan, but was soon recaptured and returned to prison, which extended his time to nine years. When Chuck got out of prison, they linked up again and began working together. Mr. Lansing pressed for details, and Rocky did not disappoint with his keen memory. Rocky unloaded on Chuck, reiterating that he preferred kidnappings to robberies. Usually ransom money was much more lucrative than a bank heist, he explained. And Chuck always seemed willing to kill his hostages. He had even bragged about killing a man back in 1968 over some stolen bonds.

The questions kept coming, and Rocky kept affirming Chuck's criminal history of constantly committing breaking and entering, transporting and selling drugs across state lines, carrying a gun while on probation, and on and on. Rocky went into substantial detail when telling about the drugs Chuck stole and later took to Jackson, Michigan to peddle in the penitentiary there. A new detail surfaced that Larry found amusing. So did the jury. The drugs had been left with a man who had access to the prison and could smuggle in small quantities at a time. At one point he left the duffel bag full of pills in the pathway of a tractor, which ran over the bag and crushed most of the pills. Chuck had bought his new car on the promise of selling the pills for a lot of money, and now most of those pills were just a pile of powder that could have blown away in a slight breeze. Rocky ended by saying, "Of course, if the drugs would've got sold, he would've give me a cut. That's how we live in the underworld."

Larry chuckled inwardly as he thought, *They sound like the Keystone Cops. At least they take care of each other. They almost seem like good guys.*

The prosecutor moved on to Rocky's association with Skip

Nowalsky. Rocky told the Court that he met Skip in the mid-1960s, but then Rocky went off to prison until 1973. He met up again with Skip in late 1974.

"What type of person was Skip Nowalsky?" asked the Prosecutor.

"At the time I saw 'im, he was a drug addict, but I didn't consider 'im to be violent, or nothin'. I even left my son with 'im to look after when I took my wife to the hospital when our second boy was born last year."

In an incredulous tone, the prosecutor asked, "You left your child in the care of this violent criminal—this murderer?"

"He didn't seem violent at the time," Rocky insisted.

Treading the same chronological path that the defense had, Lansing turned his attention to Rocky's arrest in Albuquerque in June of 1973 and his first contact with the FBI. He started by asking Rocky why he kept moving around to different locations with the Ashton-Keely Gang to plan and carry out robberies.

"Why did I keep movin' around? You might say I was always on the run, 'cause I was always bein' hunted by the police."

"Under what circumstances did you go to Albuquerque?"

"After I got released from Marquette Penitentiary in Michigan, I jumped parole and went to Albuquerque, 'cause the Ashton-Keely Gang was workin' a bank there and they wanted me in on it."

"Rocky, after you became an informant for the FBI, did your lifestyle increase?"

"Did my lifestyle increase? In the beginnin' it did because they let me keep most of the money that was stolen from banks, but after awhile that changed and it actually went down."

"How so?"

"They only paid me from time to time for information that

I gave 'em. Usually in small amounts. Ed would ask me sometimes if I needed money. And they promised me reward money of $2,500 for the Garrettsville bank robbery, and $10,000 for an Indianapolis bank robbery that the Ashton-Keely Gang did, but the FBI never delivered."

"Did the FBI pay you for information about the drug heist?"

"No."

"Why not?"

"Because they didn't make an arrest."

"Where else did you get money to live on?"

"Where did I get money to live on? Well, when I needed money, I asked Fred Bunker or Jerome Madison. They was the money men for the Gang at that time."

"So, Rocky, how did your lifestyle change when you worked for the FBI?"

"How did my lifestyle change? Well, up until that time, I'd always drove new cars or one-year-old cars, but for the last couple of years I had two old cars. Chryslers. I bought the first one, a '66, for around $200 and the last one for $50. They was old clunkers, but I learned how to fix 'em using parts from one car to repair the other one."

"Rocky, if you were not with the FBI for money, why were you doing what you were doing?"

"I was in it to stay free, to keep from goin' back to prison. I wanted to be with my wife and kids."

Larry could tell that the prosecutor did not want to go down that path any farther. Larry also noticed that Rocky was repeating every single question before he answered. It was a delaying tactic that he felt sure the jury also noticed. Larry sensed that Rocky was either tired or confused. He wanted somehow to signal Rocky to stop doing it, but the prosecutor gave him no opportunity to object.

Changing the direction of questioning, the prosecutor asked Rocky, "Prior to December 4th, when was the last communication you had with FBI Agent Howard Bolton?"

"When was the last time? That would be the week prior, on Thanksgivin' weekend, I called 'im from Jackson, Michigan. I also stopped by Ed Marshall's house and fed 'im information to pass on to Howard about us casin' the bank and plannin' to kidnap a bank employee. They both knew about the blue Monte Carlo rental car and that I would be usin' it."

"Now, Rocky, in your own words, tell us exactly what happened on December 4th, 1975."

This was the day before the kidnapping. The prosecutor had expertly branded Rocky as a career criminal and confirmed his associations with other criminals. Up until this moment, there had been no surprises. Rocky was sticking to his testimony and emphasizing that Chuck Wilson was capable of kidnapping and murder. But Larry knew this was no time to relax; this trial was far from being over. The cross-examination would drone on for another full day.

"Do you want the whole week?" Rocky asked.

"I said December the 4th. You heard me. I said just December 4th!" Mr. Lansing's irritated voice grabbed everybody's full attention, especially the jury, several of whom sat up a bit straighter or leaned slightly forward to make sure they did not miss a single word.

Rocky, himself, sat up a bit straighter and recapped the day's events exactly as he had in direct examination. Almost verbatim.

"How long were you planning to hold him?" the prosecutor asked, as the questions of that day's activities wound down.

"I was never plannin' to hold 'im. My plan was for it to never get that far. I'd always hoped the FBI would stop it from happenin'."

"What about the rest of the plan? Like where the money would be dropped?"

"That was Chuck's responsibility. He was gonna arrange for the money to be picked up. There was no real location decided upon. It would be from phone booth to phone booth. He was thinkin' about an area near the airport, so I could never give the FBI a definite location."

"All right, let's move to Friday morning, December 5th. What happened?"

Almost word for word, Rocky told how he and Skip arrived at the bank in the blue Monte Carlo around 8:00 in the morning to case out the surrounding streets. Chuck did not show up. But around 8:30, they saw Mr. MacDonald getting out of his car in the parking lot and Skip nabbed him.

"I tried to stop Skip. I didn't get out of the car until Skip brought Mr. MacDonald to the car. I got out of the passenger side and held the door open and Mr. MacDonald slid in between us in the front seat. I wanted to run; I didn't want to be in that car."

"Rocky, you heard the testimony of two bank employees who said there were two men shouldering Mr. MacDonald to the blue Monte Carlo?"

"Yes, and I also heard another one say that the driver stayed in the car. None of that was true."

"What happened next?"

Rocky gave the same details as he had in direct examination by Larry. "We took 'im to Jason Bintner's house. First, I got permission from Jason. You don't just bring somebody in without askin', and then I went out to the car and I told Skip, 'Make the guy keep his head down so he don't recognize you,' and Skip brought the man in and took 'im to the basement. As I remember it, he had a coat coverin' his head as he went down the stairs, so Bintner could not see 'im either. Bintner decided to leave. He said he was goin' huntin', so he grabbed a couple of guns, rounded up two or three dogs, got into his truck and left. I went to work cleanin' out the Monte Carlo so I could return it."

"Why would you return the car that day?"

Rocky greeted the question with incredulity. "Why?" Rocky went on to school the prosecutor on criminal procedure. "That's a big part of the criminal plan. You follow the same procedure that you always would. You get rid of the hot car as soon as you can, and get another one that the cops won't recognize. The police would be lookin' for a blue Monte Carlo. I was always playing a part in the overall plan when I was with gang members. If they found out I'm a FBI informant, man, I'd be dead."

Rocky then recounted that Mr. MacDonald was being cooperative and how Chuck left in the Monte Carlo and came back with a red Firebird. After the prosecutor asked if Rocky had called the FBI yet, he answered no, that there had not been an opportunity to call the FBI from Jason Bintner's house because either Skip or Chuck was always within earshot.

"Later that day when you had been driving around for hours while hiding Mr. MacDonald in the car, why had you not called the FBI by this time?"

"I felt sure by now that the FBI was on the kidnappin' case and they'd be contactin' me for details on where MacDonald was. When I took 'im to Ohio, I told my wife that when Howard called, to tell 'im I had what he was lookin' for at my house. I'd already told 'em everythin' ahead of time except the date it would happen. Now that it had happened, they already had all the details. They knew exactly who all was involved."

Mr. Lansing reminded Rocky of the testimony of the three

FBI agents—Ed Marshall, Bob Wallace and Howard Bolton—where they had each stated that they never knew Rocky's permanent address or how he could be located at any time.

Rocky rebutted, "It is true that I mainly called them, either from my mother-in-law's house, or my aunt's house, or a pay phone when I was on the road. But every time I moved to a different location, such as from Fred Bunker's house on the lake to Jerome Madison's house on Pointer Run Road in Newark, Ohio, I told 'em the exact address and location. They always knew which city I was in. I kept them informed, even from the road, callin' 'em sometimes several times a day with details."

"Can you give me any logical explanation why that information would specifically be excluded from your FBI files then?" asked the prosecutor.

"I have no idea why they took it outta my file, except that it would prove my story right."

"Then are you saying that they deliberately lied relative to that particular question?"

"Yes, they lied about that and about a lot of other things, like when they said they don't know how to get ahold of me when they knew at all times exactly where I was. And how they said I wasn't callin' 'em with information about the kidnappin'. And how they couldn't remember what we talked about in those hundreds of phone calls."

"Did you finally call the FBI, since they were not contacting you?" intoned Mr. Lansing.

"Yes, I believe it was on Sunday the 7th, I contacted Ed Marshall from a public phone somewhere on the road from Columbus to Newark, and I told 'im exactly where Jamie MacDonald was being held and exactly what had happened, and what the plans was."

"Why didn't you call Howard Bolton?"

"Ed and Howard, they was one and the same to me. Ed assured me he was relayin' all my information to Howard."

"You have stated that you did not see any surveillance around the house where you were holding Mr. MacDonald. Didn't you find that surprising, especially since you say you were convinced that the FBI knew where both you and MacDonald were? Wouldn't you think they would be trying to get MacDonald out of that house?"

"I would expect the FBI to protect his safety. I would imagine they wouldn't bust into a house shooting."

"Had you discussed with Skip what the next step in your plans was?"

"Yes, I told 'im that when the money was dropped, we was gonna drop off MacDonald at a motel."

"What motel?"

"Any motel in the Columbus area. I would've been right there to supervise the move and make sure that nothin' happened to Mr. MacDonald."

Sarcastically, Mr. Lansing replied, "Oh, you would have made sure nothing happened. I see...okay."

Mr. Lansing proceeded with the same line of questioning that Larry had on what had happened on Monday morning, December the 8th. Rocky gave the exact same answers, never wavering from his testimony. They moved on to the activities of Tuesday, the 9th of December. Once again, the jury heard the same details that Rocky had stated earlier.

Wrapping up, Mr. Lansing asked, "What time did you arrive in Columbus on the morning of December the 10th?"

"Well, because I ran out of gas along the way, that held me up at least a couple of hours, so it musta been around 4:30 in the morning."

"What happened when you got there?" prodded Lansing.

"Shirley was up; she answered the door. She told me that Skip was there and that really surprised me. Skip was asleep, so I shook 'im awake and tried to talk with 'im about what happened. I cussed 'im out and asked 'im what he had done to the MacDonald kid. He was too groggy to make any sense. Then we woke up the kids and dressed 'em, and we all got in the car to go look for Mr. MacDonald."

"You got the kids up, too, at 4:30 in the morning? Why did you need to take the kids with you to go look for Mr. MacDonald?"

"Why? The kids are part of my family, and I couldn't leave them with Shirley's mother 'cause she had to go to work in the mornin'. I wanted Shirley along to help me 'cause Skip was too drugged out."

"Why didn't you just drop the kids off at your sister-in-law's house, which was just a few blocks away?"

"It was 4:30 in the mornin'!" Rocky was shouting. "I was going out lookin' for Mr. MacDonald, not out lookin' for a babysitter."

Larry was glad that Rocky's exasperation was on display for the jury.

"Where did you go first?" asked the prosecutor in an even tone, obviously trying to calm Rocky.

"We drove out to the house on Pointer Run Road that I was rentin' from Jerome Madison, where we'd been holdin' Mr. MacDonald."

"Why didn't you just go to where Skip had left Mr. MacDonald?"

"I don't know where that was. At that time, I was really upset with Skip. But Skip hadn't said if the kid was dead or alive. So we got to the house around 5:30 in the mornin' and I searched the two bedrooms, the closets, and the attic, but Mr. MacDonald was not there."

"How long did you stay there?"

"How long? About an hour. I told Shirley and Skip to clean up the place and that I was gonna lay down and sleep for half an hour. I hadn't had any sleep for two days, and I'd run down the highway with that gas can for two miles, and had drove for more than four hours and I was completely exhausted and could barely move my feet. My head was spinnin' and I was confused as to what had happened."

"You have stated earlier that you told Shirley to wash down the walls for Skip's sake. Why did you think it necessary to clean the house so thoroughly?"

"There was stuff layin' all over the place. I was playin' a part in front of Skip. I am always playin' a part when a gang member is present. I wasn't havin' the walls washed down to protect him, but because it was the normal thing to do. I didn't want 'im to think somethin' was wrong, especially since he was carryin' a .38 revolver and actin' real strange."

"When did you leave the house and where did you go next?"

"We left just as it was gittin' light, at dawn. Skip directed me to a country road. He said he had took Mr. MacDonald into the woods. I told Skip I wanted to see the MacDonald kid. We both looked around, but we couldn't find 'im. I cussed Skip out. I called 'im a dumb Pollock and a rotten bastard."

The prosecutor told the judge that he would like to break for the day. Agreeably, the judge gave the jury the standard warning not to discuss the case with anyone and that court would resume the next morning at nine o'clock. With a light tap of the gavel, another day of the trial was in the can.

November 17, 1976

The judge called order in the courtroom and asked Mr. Lansing to resume cross-examination. Picking up the thread, the prosecutor questioned Rocky about leaving the woods and then calling his brother-in-law to meet him at a truck stop to pick up the children. Rocky told how Shirley wanted to come with him but wanted to pack some clothes first. There followed a long exchange about the suitcases, and Mr. Lansing kept pointing to the two suitcases in the courtroom. He then asked Rocky why he wanted Shirley to stay with him, when he knew he was in trouble.

"I already told you I only half thought I was in trouble, 'cause everythin' had gone wrong. A man was missin' and my job was to keep 'im alive. But I knew I'd told the FBI where the man was, and it wasn't my fault. If somethin' happened to Mr. MacDonald, their communications got crossed up somehow."

"So at this point in time you are worried and thinking only about Rocky Hamilton. You are not thinking about whether MacDonald is dead or alive, are you?"

"That's not true. I'm thinkin' of us both."

Mr. Lansing continued nipping at Rocky like a mosquito at a Bayou picnic. "You are worried because you could not prove whether Mr. MacDonald was dead or alive and whether he can ID you or not. Isn't that right?" the heated exchange continued.

"That's not true, Mr. Lansing!"

"You also knew that by Sunday, December 7th, that the FBI was on the case, because your aunt, Janet Peterson, told you that the FBI had paid her a visit asking about the blue Monte Carlo she had rented for you. Is that correct?"

"That's true."

"And isn't that the real reason you called Ed Marshall on Monday, just to have a friendly chat to feel him out as to what he might know about the kidnapping? Not to feed him information to relay to Howard Bolton?"

"Mr. Lansing, that's not true!" Rocky said, almost shouting.

"Up until this time, you have stated that your wife did not know anything about what had happened. Is that right?"

"To my knowledge, she doesn't. She may have overheard somethin' when we was outside the car, but neither me or nobody else would talk in front of her in my presence."

"Well, your brother-in-law testified that Shirley was hysterical. If she knew nothing, why was she hysterical?"

"I didn't consider her hysterical. She had tears comin' from her eyes, 'cause she had saw tears comin' from my eyes, and she didn't want to be away from the children."

"Did Shirley want to go with you? Why did you insist on it?"

"Shirley is my wife. She came with me 'cause I asked her to, and she wanted to be with me."

"So the three of you—Skip, Shirley and yourself—left the shopping center and got on the road. Correct?"

"That's true."

"You stated that Skip really wanted to catch a bus to get away. Why didn't you just cut him loose at that point?"

"I've always been instructed by the FBI that if I got caught in the middle of somethin' to keep track of everybody."

"Oh, I see. Well, you didn't do a very good job of keeping track of Chuck or Mr. MacDonald, did you?"

Larry jumped from his seat, waving his arms, "Objection; harassing the witness!" As often as he could, Larry used this tactic to break the rhythm of the examination and, in this case, because he disliked the prosecutor's sarcasm.

"Proceed. Counselor," ordered the Court.

"Okay, at this point Skip has not told you exactly what he had done, and you still don't know if Mr. MacDonald is dead or alive?"

Larry noticed that both Rocky and the prosecutor were now referring to the victim as Mr. MacDonald. He was no longer "the MacDonald kid" or just plain "kid." They were now speaking about a dead man, and the tone had become a bit more reverent.

"So, now you have the suitcases packed and in the car and you are planning to run?"

"No!" Rocky said emphatically.

"Oh, I see…what were you going to do then?"

"I am gonna turn in Chuck and Skip and Dwight Fisher. That was the only reason I was involved in this case from the very beginnin'. Chuck was the FBI's target."

"Well, now, turning these fellows in would certainly blow your cover, wouldn't it? Weren't you worried about protecting your cover?"

"I knew it was too late for that and that I would have to testify. It would now be up to the FBI to protect me."

"Oh, I see…the FBI was going to protect you."

Larry had had enough of the prosecutor's sarcasm. Jumping to his feet, he said, "Your Honor, I am going to object to Mr. Lansing every time he doesn't like an answer, he says, 'Oh, I see…'" Larry drug out the seeeeee to make his point.

"Well, rephrase it, Mr. Lansing," admonished the judge.

"Yes, Your Honor. Now, Rocky, after making a couple of stops and then driving west on Interstate Highway 70, were you arrested and put into a car with Special Agent Davis and driven back to Columbus to the Federal Building?"

"That's true."

The prosecutor pushed on, "Isn't it true that you tried to make a deal with the FBI agents who arrested you, saying, 'If I can walk free, I will tell you who hurt Mr. MacDonald, and help you find him?"

Rocky stuck to his guns. "My words was to contact Special Agent Howard Bolton of the Detroit office and I could help in the investigation."

"Why didn't you tell them to check with Ed Marshall? After all, that was who you allegedly fed information to."

"Ed no longer worked for the FBI, so he couldn't tell the FBI agents in Columbus, 'Hey, he's free and clear'; only Howard Bolton would be the one to tell the Columbus agents that."

Larry realized that the wrinkle of Rocky passing information to Ed Marshall, but asking for Howard Bolton, revealed how painfully convoluted this case was. There was not even a scent of common sense to Rocky's communication with his handlers. He hoped the jury could figure it out.

The questions and answers flew back and forth like a tennis ball, with the prosecutor accusing Rocky of not cooperating with the FBI agents who had arrested him, and Rocky denying it. And all the while, Mr. MacDonald could be dying somewhere.

"Did you meet with the special agent in charge and tell him that if you gave them the body, you would have to have immunity?'"

"Yes. They was talkin' about chargin' me with murder, and puttin' me in the electric chair!"

Holding a handful of papers high into the air, Mr. Lansing said, "Okay, Rocky, I have here two reports written by Agent Howard Bolton, dated December 12th. Have you read them?"

"Yes."

"And is Ed Marshall's name ever mentioned in either report?"

"That report is not a true report."

Lansing kept up the pressure, pointing out item after item of Rocky's testimony that was not in the report, and then asking Rocky if he could give him any reason why this was so?

Larry knew he had to intercede. "Your Honor, I am going to object to asking the witness, Mr. Hamilton, to explain why someone other than himself is writing something in a report."

The judge told Mr. Lansing to give Rocky the report and ask him whether something was in the report or not.

Larry responded, "That is not his report; it is one that Agent Bolton made up."

"I realize that, but this is cross-examination, Mr. Strong," said Judge Abbot patiently.

"Okay, let's back up," said the prosecutor. "Did Agent Davis read you your rights in the car?"

"He may have. I don't recall. I just remember him sayin' I was charged with a homicide."

"A homicide! Now, how would he know it was a homicide at that point in time, when nobody knew whether Mr. MacDonald—"

"Objection!" Larry shouted, interrupting him mid-sentence. "That calls for conjecture."

The prosecutor went on, "Okay, Rocky, you were giving orders to the FBI agents in the car, telling them to hold radio calls, and telling them who you would or would not talk to. So why exactly would you not talk to the FBI agents in the car?"

"'Cause they wasn't my contact agent. My orders as an informant was to always get in touch with my contact agent;

those was strict orders. And, besides, these guys in the car acted like they didn't know who I was; like I didn't work for the FBI; and I never felt they was tryin' to help me."

"So, even though they were asking you where Mr. MacDonald was and if he was alive or dead, what was more important to you at this point in time, finding MacDonald, or talking to your agent?"

"Contactin' my agent."

"So, Mr. MacDonald's life was not important? The FBI certainly thought so since they had at least 150 agents working the case in Detroit."

"Yes, his life was important. I tried to protect him. But I was also concerned about my life, since the agent said he was chargin' me with kidnappin' and homicide."

"At that time, what evidence did they have of the murder of Mr. MacDonald?"

"None that I knew of. I didn't even know myself if Mr. MacDonald was dead or alive, but I believed he was dead, because Skip had said he used a blade on 'im."

The prosecutor asked Rocky if Howard Bolton ever came to visit him after he was arrested.

"Yes, on December 11th. As soon as he closed the door, I asked him what the hell was he doin' to me. I accused 'im of playin' them two tapes to Chuck to let 'im know I was a federal informant and had set 'im up and was workin' 'im from day one. Howard denied it. He said 'No, Rocky, I did not; the first I heard them tapes was when Agent Cahloun played 'em for me.' He was more agitated and excited than I was. Really frantic. I had never seen Howard acting like this. He told me it was out of his hands now since the Strike Force had took over the investigation and there was nothin' that Detroit could do for me at that time. He said that if I left the Bureau out of it and I didn't mention the FBI at all, he would be able to help me, but only as long as I left their names out of it." Rocky paused, taking a deep breath, as if he were reliving the moment when he knew the FBI had abandoned him.

"Go on," prodded Mr. Lansing.

"By then, I had lost my trust in the FBI and I didn't believe what he was sayin', so I told 'im I was gonna tell the truth. He told me that if in fact that happened, that I'd burn and that Shirley would burn and the most that would happen to him would be that he would lose his job. I stuck to my guns and told 'im that was what I was gonna do, and he said, 'Let me go back to Detroit before you do anything, and I'll contact you tomorrow and tell you what they say in Detroit.' That was the last time I saw Howard Bolton until last week here in this courtroom. I knew that the FBI was dumpin' me."

The prosecutor then began peppering Rocky with questions with machine-gun precision. Did you ever say, 'I can see the headlines now: FBI informant commits kidnap-murder?' Did you ever say that you were going to raise so much smoke that a jury will think everything I did was at the Fed's directions?"

"No! No! No! That's a lie! I never said that," Rocky vehemently denied saying any of these things, until...

"Did you ever make the statement, 'I'm going to make everybody think the Bureau supplied me with guns and ammunition?'"

"Did I ever say that? They have done that, but did I say I was gonna make people believe it? No, I never made that statement, but it is true they supplied both guns and ammunition to me."

"Did you say that they would have to let you plead guilty to guns or that you would ask for a Senate investigation?"

"No, I didn't say that. But I did write a letter to a senator askin' for help. I never said I would ask for a Senate investigation. My idea for a gun charge came to me just after I was arrested and took to the Federal Building, when they was chargin' me with kidnappin' and murder. They told me I would be goin' to the electric chair."

"When was the first time that you told anyone that the FBI had supplied you with guns and ammunition?"

"It was in the letters I wrote to the District Court, to the ACLU and the senator. When Mr. Strong was appointed as my attorney, I told 'im, too."

"So there is no way that Howard Bolton, on December 12th, just two days after your arrest, could be quoting you saying, 'I'm going to make everybody think that the Bureau supplies me with guns and ammunition?'"

Wow, thought Larry, *thank you Mr. Prosecutor for helping me prove that Howard Bolton fabricated his reports.*

"No way. I only said it in the letters I sent out, long after my meetin' with Howard Bolton. At the time I wrote 'em, a couple of days later the letters came back to me 'cause they had took away all my money and I had no stamps. They did finally get mailed, but they was out of my hands for several days."

"Where were the letters from Friday to Sunday?"

"I have no idea, but the police officials had access to 'em, and I raised the issue in federal court and the judge ordered 'em to take me out of solitary confinement and allow me to make phone calls and write letters."

"In your opinion, was Mr. Bolton not a very good agent?"

"In my opinion, no, I would say he wasn't."

The prosecutor changed tracks. "Mr. Hamilton, have you read the testimony given in this Court by Skip Nowalsky?"

"Not all of it."

"But it was provided to you. Right?"

"Yes."

"When?"

"When they gave it to me."

"When was that?"

"A few months ago."

"How many months ago?"

Obviously irritated, Rocky raised his voice. "I have no idea. You know when it was supplied to me; you give me the date."

"I'm asking you."

Rocky reached deep into his recollection and gave a satisfactory answer.

The prosecutor continued, asking Rocky, "Did you hear the tape of your conversation with Agent Calhoun?"

"I heard the second one; I never heard the first one."

"You are sure there were two tapes?"

"I'm positive. Howard Bolton admitted to me in the room where we talked that he had listened to two tapes."

"And you believed him?"

"Look, I'm the one that brought the tapes to the Court's attention. The FBI said there was no tapes 'til I insisted, and they finally came up with only one last July."

"Now, regarding the wiretaps. You stated in your direct examination that there were more than two. Right?"

"The FBI told me they had the authorization to tell me that there was five wiretaps—three in Detroit and two in Columbus. So that would be one at the house I stayed in when I was in Detroit—my Aunt Janet's house—one on Chuck's phone, one on Dwight Fisher's, and then in Columbus one at the house of my mother-in-law and one at my brother-in-law's house."

"Well, Agent Davis from the FBI said on this very witness stand that there was no mention of wire taps. Was he lying about that?"

"He sure was."

"And Agent Bolton was lying, and Agent Calhoun was lying?"

"Well, they certainly wasn't telling the truth."

The prosecutor finished by asking Rocky if he was crying during the interrogation after his arrest.

"I had tears in my eyes at times. I was highly emotional and confused because they kept saying they was gonna send me to the electric chair. What I couldn't understand was why they hadn't prevented Mr. MacDonald from bein' moved when they knew exactly where he was and was supposed to be watchin' the house. If they had, none of this would've happened."

"Just one more question, Rocky. Did you cry when you heard the MacDonald tape here in this courtroom?"

"No, sir, I did not."

"Thank you; that's all," said Mr. Lansing as he sat down.

CHAPTER 30

Redirect Examination of the Defendant – The Defense

Larry rose quickly before the judge called for a recess before starting his redirect examination, and told the judge he had only one question for his client.

"Mr. Hamilton, when the MacDonald tape was played, you mentioned that you did not cry in the courtroom. Did you notice whether Mr. Lansing was crying in the courtroom over that tape?"

"I didn't see him crying."

"Your Honor, I would like a recess before I continue."

After the recess, Larry told Rocky he had only a few questions to clear up some misconceptions that may have occurred. First, he wanted to clear up the prosecutor's accusation that Rocky had been sucking information from the FBI and feeding it to gang members so they could avoid prosecution. Rocky countered, saying that several gang members had been caught and were now in prison because of information he had furnished the FBI about their activities.

Larry wanted to leave an indelible mark on the memory of each juror about the fact that Rocky did not work for the FBI for money, but that his motive was to remain out of prison. He summarized how Rocky's lifestyle went way down after he signed on with the FBI, and that they still owed him as much as $12,500 in reward money. Because of the outstanding parole violation, Rocky knew that if he wanted to stop working for the FBI, he would be sent back to prison. Larry went on to remind the jury that Rocky was allowed to carry weapons and electronic equipment during the time he worked for the FBI.

"Rocky, you have testified that over the years you have worked with the FBI, you have furnished them a substantial quantity of information, and especially during the month leading up to the kidnapping, you met several times with Agent Bolton to keep him informed. Yet, in the file that the FBI gave to the defense, there were only two 209's that had been filled out by Agent Bolton. Did you have only two meetings with him?"

"I had many contacts with him, mostly by phone, and passed information through Ed Marshall, too. Most of the information I gave the FBI on Chuck Wilson, Jason Bintner, Jerome Madison, and Jimmy Wilson was missin' from the file."

"How about the information you furnished on Jimmy Hoffa?"

"That was missin' too. And all the information on union activities, and Mr. Fitzsimmons' car gittin' blew up; there ain't one paper in the file about that."

"Why did you assume that Agent Bolton knew about the kidnapping, since you did not get the opportunity to tell him until a couple of days after the fact?"

"Well, if you have up to twenty agents in the bank robbery squad at the FBI, and if a bank you've been tellin' 'em about goes down, and a kidnappin' takes place at that bank, he should've knew exactly who was behind it."

In closing, Larry asked Rocky how much Shirley knew about his involvement with the FBI and what was going on with the kidnapping. Rocky stated that Shirley knew he worked for the government and she knew something was wrong when he showed up in Columbus in the middle of the night and when they went out to the house where MacDonald had been held, but she did not know any of the details of the kidnapping.

"No further questions, Your Honor."

Larry hoped the re-cross by Lansing would be short and they could put this part of the trial to bed. He was anxious to begin working on his closing argument.

Re-Cross-Examination of the Defendant – The Prosecution

Prosecutor Lansing said he wanted to re-address the scarcity of the 209s in the FBI file. "You heard the testimony of Agent Bolton when he explained that most of the information you passed to him was simply street talk and not worth reporting. If you thought the information was so valuable, why didn't you demand payment for it?"

"That's not how it worked. I never demanded money from 'em. They'd just ask me from time to time if I needed some money. The bigger amounts came from the FBI when an arrest was made. I was also gittin' some living expenses from gang members."

"All right, now. You have said that Howard Bolton and Ed Marshall had all the information on the kidnapping that was about to happen. You heard the testimony of Howard Bolton, who said that he shared your file with the FBI Strike Force on December 9th, correct?"

"That's what he said."

"So, all they had to do was sit back and wait for you to call, since you were in control?"

"Howard could've called me from December 5th on. I gave 'im all the details of what was gonna happen at that bank, but I don't know what information he passed on to the Strike Force."

Mr. Lansing said, "Thank you; that's all."

Larry felt the need to clear up this last issue about control that Mr. Lansing had raised. "Rocky, do you control when the FBI arrests anybody or rescues anybody?"

"No, not at all. All I can do is give 'em the facts and tell 'em where I think the crime will be committed and what I think is gonna take place. I never know how they're gonna take action on a situation."

"You don't pull the strings?"

"No, I don't make no decisions of when they're gonna move. That's somethin' that somebody way above me would do. I give 'em the information, and what they do with it is up to them."

"Nothing further, Your Honor. The defense rests."

Rocky had been on the witness stand for four days straight. Larry marveled at his stamina and appreciated that Rocky had told the truth, no matter how tough the questioning from the prosecutor had become at times. For Larry, the most difficult part of the trial was over. He exhaled audibly.

CHAPTER 31

Rebuttal Witness–The Prosecution

"Your Honor," said Prosecutor Lansing, "I would like to call FBI Special Agent Michael Nielson to the stand as a rebuttal witness."

Larry was caught by surprise by this "hail Mary" witness. He had no idea what gem the prosecutor was about to present. Agent Nielson took the stand and was duly sworn in. The prosecutor got immediately to the point.

"Agent Nielson, I have called you to the stand because Defense Counsel has tried to persuade the jury that it was the defendant Rocky Hamilton who notified the FBI about the planning and execution of the kidnapping of Jamie MacDonald, but I believe you have testimony that will refute this claim. Are you or were you the handler of the informant Dwight Fisher?"

"Yes," confirmed Agent Nielson.

"And did Dwight Fisher tell you he had information about the kidnapping of Jamie MacDonald?"

"Yes."

"How and when did he give you this information?"

"It was by telephone at around 2:00 Monday morning, December 8th."

"What exactly did he tell you?"

"He said he had overheard Rocky Hamilton and Chuck Wilson talking on the telephone where ransom money was mentioned. Then he had noticed Chuck Wilson reading intently the newspaper article about the kidnapping. He also said he believed that they were holding the kidnap victim somewhere in Ohio. He gave me an Ohio phone number for Rocky."

"And with that information, the FBI was able to finally pinpoint the location of where Mr. MacDonald was being held?"

"Yes."

"Just to be perfectly clear; the information which led to the location of Mr. MacDonald came from your snitch Dwight Fisher, and not from Rocky Hamilton?"

Larry jumped to his feet objecting, "Your Honor, Mr. Lansing cannot draw such a conclusion as to where the FBI received its information. There were hundreds of FBI agents working this case and the information could have come to any one of them. Agent Nielson can speak only to what information he personally received."

Judge Abbot told Mr. Lansing to rephrase his question.

"Yes, Your Honor. Agent Nielson, you are absolutely certain that this is the exact information that you received from your informant Dwight Fisher?"

"Yes. Absolutely certain. He called me at 2:00 in the morning and since I was awakened from a deep sleep, rather than relying on my memory, I taped the conversation so I could refer to it later in the morning."

"Thank you. That will be all," said the Prosecutor.

Upon hearing there was a tape recording, Larry's antenna shot up. He turned and faced the judge. "Your Honor, may we approach the bench?"

"You may. At this time, though, we're going to go ahead and excuse the jury for an early lunch. We'll reconvene at 12:30."

The moment the jury was out of earshot, Larry started in angrily, "I would like to make it clear at this very moment for the record that the defense has never been provided any such tape or ever been told that any such tape ever existed. Weeks ago, upon my asking, Mr. Lansing stated that there were no records or recordings being held summarily by the prosecution that would in any way help the defense. And I said to him that I was in complete contradiction with him, and I felt there were things not made available to the defense that would be favorable for us. Your Honor even asked Mr. Lansing, 'Do you have any recorded statements made by any witnesses other than the two that have already been submitted.' And Mr. Lansing answered that he had no other written or recorded statements. He averred that nothing in his possession could aid us.

"Then we have FBI agents clearly lying on the stand, saying they have no records of taped conversations. And just last week, another agent testified that he has no original records of his contacts with Rocky, because, shock of all shocks, a week ago he got stricken with a catastrophic case of spring cleaning - in the autumn - and destroyed his original notes. A week ago! Your Honor, this is outrageous!

"The defense has been turned down time after time after time for funds to investigate and research, so we are at the mercy of whatever the prosecutor and the government deign to give us. Under these circumstances and this tomfoolery, there is no way that the defendant can get a fair trial."

Gary snapped back, "I don't think there is anything on that tape that in any way is helpful to Rocky Hamilton. Actually, everything on that tape points to him being the perpetrator of the crime."

"Mr. Lansing," said Judge Abbot, "we are not arguing the case here."

"The point is," charged Larry, "the Court specifically asked you if there were any written or recorded statements and you said unequivocally no. This is incredible, and I think the Court should direct a verdict and that this case should be dismissed."

"Your motion on a directed verdict, Mr. Strong, is overruled."

"Then, Your Honor, at this point I would make a motion for a mistrial."

"Counsel, your motion for a mistrial is overruled."

"Please note my exceptions to the record."

"You may have your exceptions," replied the judge.

"I would like to hear that tape right now," demanded Larry.

The prosecutor produced the tape and Larry retired to a conference room to listen to the tape over lunch. Agent Nielson's voice is heard first.

"Hello."

"Hey Mike, this is Dwight."

"How ya doing, Dwight?"

"I'm sticking my neck out a mile, but I might be able to get you some information on this MacDonald kidnapping thing. In a way, I think I've been used."

"Oh, yeah? What's the story?"

"Well, I'm pretty sure that Rocky Hamilton is in on this. I, uh, I just did somebody a favor, and now I'm afraid I'm gonna get caught in the middle, you know, and I don't need that."

"What kind of a favor did you do, Dwight?"

"I rented a car for Rocky. He'd been driving a blue one, a Monte Carlo, and then I got him a red Firebird."

"Sounds like you're onto something. I'll tell you this much, I did hear that Rocky Hamilton and Chuck Wilson were planning something like this."

What? Larry could not believe what he had just heard. He stopped the tape and rewound it a bit to be sure. He listened intently to Agent Nielson's voice, "I'll tell you this much, I did hear that Rocky Hamilton and Chuck Wilson were planning something like this."

There it is, Larry thought to himself. *There is the smoking gun! Agent Nielson had already heard about the kidnapping and was volunteering that information. He just confirmed that he had heard that both Rocky* ***and*** *Chuck were involved. The FBI knew all along who was involved in the kidnapping since Rocky had been keeping them informed. Why did they hold back when they had plenty of time to save Jamie MacDonald?*

He clicked the tape recorder on to hear the rest of the phone conversation. Dwight Fisher was speaking, "Yeah, it was Chuck Wilson who asked me to rent the car for Rocky."

"Do you know where either Rocky or Chuck is staying?"

"Chuck is somewhere in the city, and Rocky, I think he's down in Ohio, and what I mean is, well, I think they've got this MacDonald guy with them down in central Ohio, about a four-hour drive from here. I heard Chuck talking on the phone, saying they plan on getting two hundred and fifty grand and then wiping the kid out. I also noticed Chuck thoroughly reading every word of the newspaper article about the kidnapping."

"Do you have a phone number for Rocky?"

"Yeah, it's, uh, 491-8777. I believe that's an Ohio number."

"Okay. Let me know when you get any more information about this."

"All right," replied Dwight.

The tape clicked off and Larry was elated, but he would not let it show when he cross-examined Agent Nielson. He would keep it short and to the point as to not raise any red flags with the prosecution or Agent Nielson as to what had been revealed on the tape. The prosecutor had unwittingly used his "hail Mary" witness to prove Larry's case.

After lunch, the jury filed in dutifully; the witness was reminded he was still under oath. Both the prosecutor and the defense requested the Court to play the tape for the jury. Afterwards, Larry approached the witness stand. "Mr. Nielson, regarding the tape recording of the telephone conversation between you and your informant Dwight Fisher that we have just heard in this courtroom, has this tape been altered in any way?"

"No."

"Is this the exact tape you made of that conversation?"

"Yes."

"Thank you. Your Honor, I have no further questions." Larry sat down.

The prosecutor rose to inform the judge that he had no further questions. He added, "The prosecution rests on the rebuttal."

Judge Abbot then stated that closing arguments would begin at 9:00 the following morning. He dismissed the jury, tapped his gavel, and court was adjourned for the day.

Larry raced from the courtroom to a telephone. He phoned an intern law clerk in his office in Columbus and asked him to contact the visual arts company that did work for the firm and alert them he had a big project that had to be done right away. Then he told the clerk to race over to Newark, some thirty-five miles, to pick up a transcript of the tape. When the intern arrived, the court reporter had just finished the transcription.

The intern sped back to Columbus to have a 5 ft. by 6 ft. poster board made of the transcript, word-for-word, since Larry would need it the following morning for his closing argument. Larry's staff and the visual arts guy worked at breakneck speed late into the night, and Larry picked up the large poster board the next morning on his way to the Newark courthouse.

CHAPTER 32

Closing Argument – The Prosecution

Larry was grateful that the prosecutor always goes first. Although he had the wrap-up of this case firmly in his head, he would need to work in points raised by the prosecutor. Thankfully, there would not be many.

Mr. Lansing very politely approached the jury and gave them the customary gratitude for their patience and attentiveness. He extended his gratitude to the defense counselors, Messrs. Strong and Steinwell, his co-counsel, Mr. Stancil, and the judge. Then he got down to the business of convincing the jury to find Rocky Hamilton guilty of aggravated murder and kidnapping. After cautioning them to base their decision solely on evidence, he referred back to his opening comments of eight weeks earlier, which he remarked were only his opinion.

"In my outline that I gave you at the beginning of this trial, I laid out that I would show you prior planning of the kidnapping of Mr. MacDonald. You have heard how they staked out his house the night before the kidnapping, on December 4th, and when that did not pan out, they actually carried out the kidnapping on the morning of December the 5th."

Mr. Lansing went on to summarize all the salient points that followed the kidnapping, reminding the jury how Rocky Hamilton tried to hide his tracks by taking Mr. MacDonald to Jason Bintner's house, how he rushed to get rid of the blue Monte Carlo, how a tape was made to show that Mr. MacDonald was still alive, how he was involved in the ransom calls, and how he snuck Mr. MacDonald from Michigan to Ohio. Although Rocky Hamilton did not plunge the knife into Jamie MacDonald that killed him, he had masterminded the entire kidnapping. Yes, Chuck Wilson was brought in to help with the ransom, but Chuck had abandoned the bank. He did not show up that morning, and it was Rocky and Skip Nowalsky who actually did the kidnapping. And it was Rocky who did all the planning subsequent to the kidnapping. It was Rocky who decided where Mr. MacDonald would be hidden until he and Chuck could get the ransom money from the bank. They had already planned how the money would be split. It was Rocky who told Skip to clean up the house, which meant to get rid of the fingerprints and evidence.

"Rocky Hamilton would like for you to believe that he was hiding Mr. MacDonald in Ohio for safekeeping until the FBI could intervene and save him. If that was the case, why did Rocky wait for three days—**three days**—before calling the FBI? A lot can happen in three days, especially when you are dealing with desperate criminals looking to get their payoff.

"Actually, the FBI got their first break in the case when another informant, Dwight Fisher, told his agent, Michael Nielson, exactly who he thought was involved in the kidnapping, who told the FBI main office, and it was they who called Howard Bolton. It wasn't Rocky who called Howard Bolton. Now, Rocky had many opportunities to call his FBI agent. He made a lot of phone calls during those four days.

"Let's talk about the phone calls he made on December the eighth, the day before Mr. MacDonald was killed. Rocky called his Aunt Janet Peterson, who told him that the FBI had been to her house in Detroit to check on the blue Monte Carlo. So Rocky feels the heat and decides it is time that he finds out what the FBI knows. Does he call his agent Howard Bolton? No! He calls his old buddy Ed Marshall, who no longer works for the FBI. They have a casual conversation, with Rocky trying to pick up any information that Ed may have heard from his buddies at the FBI.

"If he had called Howard Bolton on Friday soon after the kidnapping, do you think for one minute that Mr. Bolton would sit on this information and go hunting on the weekend? That is not how the FBI works, ladies and gentlemen. You have heard testimony that there were 150 FBI agents in the Detroit Office working this case." At this point, Mr. Lansing held up his hands and touched the fingers on one hand one by one with the other hand, as he rattled off the remainder of his sentence to emphasize how many agents were working the case. "As well as another 100 agents in the FBI offices in Columbus, Cincinnati, and Zanesville, ***and*** the Detroit Police Department." He continued, opening his arms grandiosely, "They were looking all over God's green earth to find Mr. MacDonald. Once the FBI put the pieces of the puzzle together, they knew that Rocky Hamilton was their man who masterminded the kidnapping, and they zeroed in on him like a laser beam. Rocky knew it, and that was why he was preparing to make a run for it just before his arrest."

In closing, Mr. Lansing told the jury that they would have the tape recordings and a summary brief in the jury room that they could refer to. He told them the brief included the testimony of Chuck Wilson. He pointed out that sure, Chuck aided and abetted Rocky Hamilton in this crime and was just as guilty as Rocky, but he had been granted immunity for his testimony. "Chuck Wilson is not on trial here; Rocky Hamilton is.

"The brief will explain that any person who knowingly helps and assists and associates himself with another in the commission of a crime is regarded, by law, as if he were the principal offender and is just as guilty as if he personally performed every act constituting the offense. This is true even if such person was not physically present at the time at the exact place where the crime was committed. I never said that Rocky Hamilton actually stabbed Mr. MacDonald thirty times, but he put it in motion with the kidnapping and by bringing him to the house in Ohio and by giving that fateful message to his wife to have the house cleaned up, which resulted in Jamie MacDonald's death, just as surely as if Rocky had been there himself.

"Rocky was definitely calling the shots. He testified on this stand that he was considered the planner for the Ashton-Keely Gang. You don't become a planner without a brain. He's an expert at playing both ends against the middle. And that is why Rocky Hamilton is guilty of aggravated murder while kidnapping. In deciding this case, ladies and gentlemen, I admonish you not to leave your common sense outside the jury room. Thank you."

The Court went into recess. As the jury headed off to lunch as a group in the company of the bailiff, Larry had lunch with Co-Counsel Gus Steinwell to discuss several points that the prosecutor had brought up in his closing argument, but they felt comfortable that Larry's closing argument yet to come could stand as planned.

CHAPTER 33

Closing Argument – The Defense

As he entered the courtroom after lunch, Larry wore a knowing half-smile over what he would be presenting to the jury. He felt the prosecutor's closing argument had been predictable and actually a bit boring. It was time to wake everyone up. It's showtime!

Wearing his best, and most expensive, navy-blue suit, Larry loomed in his full six-foot-four-inches frame before the jury. In a friendly tone, he addressed the jury. "Ladies and gentlemen, it has been a long eight weeks. Especially for you," he said as he waved his arm to include all of them. "I was not aware until today that this has been the longest case in the history of this county, and I want to start by sincerely thanking you. My co-counsel, Mr. Steinwell, thanks you—and especially Rocky Hamilton thanks you.

"The way the law works in court trials like this is that the prosecutor gets to tell you first what he thinks he has shown. Mr. Lansing has done that. Now it is my chance to show you what I think the evidence has shown, and then the prosecutor gets a second chance to rebut anything I may have told you. But, I don't get a second chance to rebut him, although I would certainly like to. Neither does Rocky get a second chance. This is our only shot at showing you what we think the State proved or did not prove.

"You will recall that when we started out, we talked about the elements of crime and of this offense especially, and how each element stands alone. It is the responsibility of the prosecution to prove each and every element, separately, beyond a reasonable doubt. The most substantial element in this case is whether Rocky Hamilton purposely caused the death of Jamie MacDonald, as he is charged. In the State of Ohio, no one can be convicted of murder unless he has intent, culpability, or wrongdoing. I would like to make specific reference to whether Rocky was working for the FBI during this kidnapping as an informant—or was he moonlighting, as the prosecutor would have you believe?

"Although the judge will instruct you about the law, I would like to read to you one short paragraph that is extremely critical to this case, and I quote:

A person who by prior arrangement with a law enforcement agency, honestly and in good faith, acts solely for the purpose of enforcing the law and assisting the law enforcement agencies in the apprehension of others involved has no criminal interest, i.e., no intention of violating the law and is not guilty of any crime in connection with such acts, but where such person acts on his own volition, he is guilty of violation of the law.

"So the point is, if Rocky was acting solely for the purpose of enforcing the law and assisting the FBI to apprehend others, there is no crime, there is no intent on his part, there is no *scienter*. You may recall that we talked about *scienter* in my opening statements. *Scienter* refers to intent or knowledge of wrongdoing prior to committing the crime. The best way I can describe it to you now would be, let's say, you were selling a car that had bad brakes, but you did not know that the brakes were bad, then you would not have *scienter*. However, if you sold the car and knew there was a problem with the brakes before you sold it, you would have *scienter*. If there is no intent, or *scienter*, on Rocky's part in this crime, you must return a verdict of *not guilty*.

"May I remind you that Rocky is innocent until proven guilty, and the State has the burden of proving him guilty beyond a reasonable doubt. Rocky does not have to prove innocence or guilt. The burden is on the State of Ohio."

Thinking he had adequately made his point and not wanting to bore the jury, Larry moved on. "At the outset, I told you we had proof that Rocky Hamilton had been working for the FBI. You have heard testimony that everyone has agreed and confirmed this as fact. Rocky considered himself an FBI agent without a badge. Considering the amount of work he did for the FBI over the past couple of years, that would appear to be true.

"I encourage you to listen with common sense and watch for credibility and believability when considering your decision. Who to believe and who not to believe? This is the toughest part for a jury. You have heard testimony where one witness told a story one way and another witness told the same story a different way. Which one do you believe? You heard Rocky Hamilton specifically testifying about telephone communications with Howard Bolton and Ed Marshall. And each one of them said, 'We don't know what you are talking about. We weren't getting any information from this man about a kidnapping.'

"Who do you believe—Rocky or the two FBI agents? Actually, I have proven to you that Rocky is telling the truth that he did in fact contact Ed Marshall on Monday, December the 8th, the day before Mr. MacDonald was killed. Mr. Hartwell from the Newark Telephone Company showed us a record that Ed Marshall's unlisted home phone number in Detroit received a collect, long-distance telephone call from the pay phone that Rocky always used at the Kroger grocery store at exactly the time Rocky testified that he had placed the call. Then I showed you the phone records where Ed Marshall called his old buddy Bob Wallace in Nebraska shortly after the phone call from Rocky. We are all pretty certain what they talked about.

"Ladies and gentlemen, this is the smoking gun that has blown this case wide open. Rocky was definitely keeping the FBI informed about the kidnapping, through Ed Marshall, because he couldn't get through to Howard Bolton. He kept getting a busy signal at the phone number he always had used to contact Howard Bolton. Mr. Bolton testified that the FBI changed that contact phone number around the same time that Rocky was trying to get through. Rocky testified that during the times he was in Detroit, he made several local calls from pay phones to Ed Marshall, but those records were destroyed by Ma Bell Telephone Company, so we have no record of them. I'll bet the FBI was able to get those records before they were erased, but they were never furnished to the defense.

"As you know, I called Mr. Marshall and Mr. Wallace to the witness stand a second time, showed them the telephone records, and asked why they had denied earlier that they had received any communication from Rocky for several months. They both lied when they said they could not explain the recorded phone calls. Mr. Marshall said he had no recollection of a call from Rocky on December 8th and neither of them could remember even talking with each other. Well, the telephone records do not lie. These two men did talk to each other—for *ten minutes*. Their testimony was most likely rehearsed from the same playbook, with both saying they knew nothing of the kidnapping and that Rocky must have been working on his own. This proof of timely contact between Rocky and his handlers proves our case without a reasonable doubt. I ask you, ladies and gentlemen, were the responses of these two agents believable to you? Clearly, they were lying!" The body language of the jurors made it obvious to Larry and everyone else in the courtroom that the jury did not believe the two agents' claim of lack of knowledge. One juror was shaking her head slightly.

"Now, let's talk about the question of telephone numbers and addresses. You heard statements like, 'We never knew where Rocky lived.' Why is this important? Well, because the FBI and the prosecutor both say they only knew about two telephone numbers, which they tapped. Now, the most significant telephone number with regards to Rocky Hamilton ends in 8777. That is the number of the Edwards' house, Rocky Hamilton's mother-in-law, from where he made the most telephone calls to the FBI while he was in the Columbus area."

Larry paused and picked up a stack of papers. It was Exhibit A, which was a telephone log listing calls that Rocky made to the FBI. Running his finger down the page, he said, "You will see on this telephone log the number 8777, 8777, 8777. But the FBI agents testified that they did not tap the 8777 number. They tapped only two phones, according to their testimony—Dwight Fisher's house in Detroit and the 2256 number at the Columbus house of Hugh Paddock, brother-in-law to Hamilton's wife, Shirley Stevens. Yet, Rocky testified that when the FBI arrested him, they told him they had tapped five phones. Which sounds more logical to you? You don't see the

2256 number, which they said they tapped, on the telephone log. Why not? Because nothing was happening at that number! Rocky never went over to the Paddock house to make phone calls. So why would they bother to tap that one? The question to be considered here is whether there was a phone tap on the 8777 number and the State and the FBI withheld this information. If that were the case, it would have a huge impact on this trial. It would prove there is a conspiracy by the FBI against the defendant. What is believable here? You must keep this in mind as you deliberate."

Larry noticed that some of the jurors were taking notes, especially juror number three, the brunette with big hair. He remembered in *voir dire* how articulate she had been, as well as attentive throughout the trial. He hoped they would choose her to be the forelady.

Larry continued, "The FBI claims they did not know Rocky's whereabouts, and they had agents running here and running there looking for him. I think we have shown you that the FBI knew all along exactly where Rocky was. I think that Rocky's story of the FBI holding back on making an arrest because they wanted to snare Chuck Wilson in the act of picking up the ransom money is more believable than the FBI's denial. Chuck had slipped through their fingers twice already, and this time they were not going to let him get away. So the question we are dealing with here is, did the FBI know where Rocky lived and the phone number where he could most likely be reached? That would be at his mother-in-law's house in Columbus, Ohio. His aunt in Detroit, Janet Peterson, testified that she personally gave the 8777 phone number to the FBI when they visited her on Sunday, the 7th of December. She even tore it out of the phone book and gave it to them.

"FBI Agent Nielson testified that on the following day,

December the 8th, he got that same phone number—491-8777—from his informant, Dwight Fisher. You can hear it for yourself on the taped telephone conversation in Exhibit RR. Now the FBI had the telephone number from two sources, and moreover it was undoubtedly in Rocky's file at the FBI office. You heard the testimony of the Assistant Deputy Director of the Special Investigative Division of the FBI who came from FBI headquarters in Washington, DC to testify at this trial, that it is absolute procedure," which Larry emphasized with air quotes, "and that the agent always knows how to contact his informant, and that contact information is always kept in the file. *Always, always, always*!" Larry slammed his hand onto the lectern, startling not only the jury, but the gallery as well. He paused until the murmurs receded.

"We reviewed some internal reports, called 209's, that the FBI kept on Rocky. They reported that Rocky was excellent and effective in his work for the FBI. He had never shown any indication of emotional instability, unreliability or furnishing false information. *Never!*" Larry practically was shouting now as he slammed his hand onto the lectern a second time. "And not one of them reported that contact information was missing. I would submit to you that his address has always been known, and that the FBI knew from the outset who was involved with the kidnapping, and for some reason they were holding back in making any arrests.

"I do not wish to cast aspersions on the FBI as a whole. A few bad apples don't spoil the whole barrel. Most of the agents are good people and do a good job, and if I were in trouble, the first people I would call for help would be law enforcement. But we have a problem here with a few specific people. Somebody is lying here. You have to decide who you believe is telling the truth.

"To be able to prove something, you have to know the players who are involved. In this case, there are ex-agent Marshall, current agent Bolton who is the man in the middle, and Rocky Hamilton." Larry couldn't help but slip out a little chuckle, while admitting it was a twisted communication system that Rocky used. "He passed information to Ed Marshall, who had been fired from the FBI, to pass on to Howard Bolton. Why would Rocky do that? Well, for one thing, it was easier to find Ed Marshall, who was always available. Rocky had even been to Ed's house on several occasions. Isn't this proof that Rocky felt that Ed was a good friend, that they had a close working relationship, and he felt comfortable talking to him? He trusted that Ed would pass the information along to Howard in a timely manner. He knew that Ed missed working with the FBI, so Ed had no objection to still being a part of the organization he loved.

"Rocky Hamilton was involved with the FBI because he wanted to stay out of jail. Up until June 1973, Rocky lived in the underworld and was a very effective criminal. But when he was arrested in Albuquerque, he had just finished a nine-year sentence and was now facing life in prison. Agent Jones convinced Rocky that one way to stay out of jail was to cooperate and work for the FBI. From that time until now, Rocky's relationship in working for the FBI was as strong as it had been to the underworld. The information he was passing to the FBI helped to fight crime in many areas, including labor union activities, arson, attempted hits, murder, kidnapping, the Ashton-Keely Gang…you name it. Rocky had to walk a tightrope. He was now playing both sides of the fence, and if the Gang found out about his relationship with the FBI, he would have been blown away by his criminal compatriots. He did a very effective job for the FBI. You heard testimony that he got special bonuses that had to be approved by the Director of the FBI. I can't think of any better proof that Rocky was well-liked, well-known, and a very effective informant for the FBI.

"Yet the prosecutor wants you to believe that Rocky was a double agent, getting information from the FBI agents and feeding it back to the underworld. If that is true, then why are members of the Gang sitting in prison, having been arrested based on information from Rocky? Rocky's involvement in the underworld was very valuable to the FBI. It's like they had a front-row seat."

Larry walked over close to the jury box, and leaning in like he was having a fireside chat with them, he said, "Let's talk about the masks. The prosecutor said that Rocky was very attached to those masks. Well, that's true. And with good reason. Mr. Marshall testified that the FBI had taken pictures of the masks when Rocky bought them. They kept them in the file, so that they could identify and trace them when they were used in a bank robbery. And they were, indeed, used in two subsequent bank robberies—the one in Garrettsville and another in Indiana. Rocky did not go out and buy new ones each time at a costume store. Instead, he managed to get them back into his possession each time so that the FBI would recognize them.

"I ask you, what would be the logic of Rocky putting on his mask to kidnap Mr. MacDonald? Rocky is no dummy, and he would know that the FBI would recognize him. This proves he was surprised when Skip Nowalsky suddenly decided to grab Mr. MacDonald on the morning of December 5th. Skip put on his mask, so Rocky had no choice but to put on his mask also. If Rocky had been planning this kidnapping on his own, he would have gone out and bought new masks so he could not be recognized by the FBI. I want you to consider ***logic*** in your decision.

"Rocky also testified that during the three weeks leading up to the kidnapping, he was working several jobs. Let's name them—the kidnapping of lawyer Nathan Schuler, robbing the Commonwealth Bank on Joy Road, and kidnapping Mr. MacDonald from the National Bank of Detroit. He was constantly feeding information to the FBI through Ed Marshall. He even stopped by Ed's house in the blue Monte Carlo, which he parked right by the side door where Ed greeted him. Ed couldn't help but see the car; he could practically touch it! Is that how you hide a getaway car? By taking it to a FBI agent's home? How logical is that?

"And there is another point of logic, or *illogic,* that I want you to consider. Remember the scanner—or the lack of a scanner? If Rocky were planning this kidnapping, don't you think he would have had a scanner in the car that worked so that he could know where the police were and what they were saying? May I reiterate—and emphasize—that it was Chuck Wilson who was doing the planning and calling the shots. Rocky found himself in the middle of several things that Chuck was planning. Nothing was definite enough to give the FBI exact dates. Maybe this week; maybe next week; only when the time was right for Chuck. Personally, Rocky thought they were about a week away from the kidnapping.

"It is my honest belief that if Ed Marshall were still with the Bureau and monitoring all the information that Rocky was feeding the FBI, he would have had a better sense of things about to happen. You recall that Howard Bolton was not a street person, but Ed Marshall certainly was. That is why he and Rocky got along so well.

"Yes, Rocky was caught in the middle, and he felt the responsibility to protect Mr. MacDonald until the FBI could intervene. Did Chuck Wilson feel that way about Mr. MacDonald?" Larry raised his voice and emphatically said, "*Not exactly*! He wanted to put him in the trunk and forget about him. Or get rid of him. Rocky, on the other hand, took him to his house in Ohio. Why? Well, for one thing, he really had no other place to take him, and he wanted to keep him safe from Chuck Wilson. And, secondly, Rocky knew that his agents would know where he would be. No, he didn't pick up the phone and say, 'Hey, I'm driving down the road right now, going to Ohio.'

"The FBI knew that Rocky had been working that bank for nearly a week already, so now that the kidnapping had happened, Rocky felt confident that the FBI knew exactly where to find him. They knew where he lived and how to contact him. Remember, Rocky told Shirley, 'If Howard calls, tell him I have got what he wants at the Madison house.' He expected Howard to call, since he had the 8777 number at Shirley's mother's house. And that was where Shirley was staying while Mr. MacDonald was being held out at their house on Pointer Run Road, which they rented from Jerome Madison. There was no grandiose plan about where he was going or what was going to be done. In Rocky's mind, everything was cool, and the FBI was going to rescue Mr. MacDonald. He felt MacDonald was safer being away from Chuck Wilson.

"The FBI had been telling Rocky they wanted to arrest Chuck Wilson. They wanted him *bad*. On Monday, December 8th, Rocky called Ed in Detroit from Ohio and told him that Chuck was in Detroit trying to get the ransom drop arranged, but he couldn't give them an exact location. He told him where he was holding Mr. MacDonald. Rocky's intentions were to stay with Mr. MacDonald to be sure he was safe until the move was made and the FBI could grab him at that point, but Chuck called him back to Detroit on Tuesday, December 9th, to help with the ransom arrangements. Because Chuck Wilson was calling the shots in this kidnapping. Rocky reluctantly went, thinking that the sooner he could get this ended, the better.

"Now, let's look at what is happening at the Kempfer residence across the road from the Madison house on Pointer Run Road. You heard testimony that the FBI arrived there at three o'clock on Tuesday the ninth. Some of the agents set up surveillance inside the house next door, and a couple of agents were actually placed in the back yard of the house where Mr. MacDonald was being held. They gently hammered spike mikes into the side of the house so that they could hear everything that was being said inside the house. They also had sophisticated parabolic sensors that could detect sounds and movement inside the house. It was a long, cold December night, and they all fell asleep, *all of them*, inside the house, as did the two men outside in their car.

"For some reason, Skip Nowalsky took Mr. MacDonald out to the woods at around 11:30 that night and killed him. Had the FBI agents been awake, they could have saved Mr. MacDonald when Skip was putting him into the car. Ladies and gentlemen, this shows how unprofessional the FBI acted in this case. Falling asleep on the job cost a man his life. This was sheer buffoonery and incompetence at its worst! And that is the reason the FBI agents have lied to you to cover up their embarrassing performance.

"This was all happening while Rocky was driving back to Ohio to release Mr. MacDonald the next day. You will recall the car ran out of gas. What should have been a four-hour trip turned into a six-hour trip because he had to walk two miles in the cold freezing rain in the dark to find gas. Rocky was frustrated, angry and confused. He couldn't understand why the FBI was not doing anything in this case. He was feeding information to the FBI and it was not being acted upon. He had done nothing wrong. All along he had been protecting Mr. MacDonald to the best of his ability.

"He arrived very late to his mother-in-law's house, around 4:30 in the morning and found Skip there and found out the shocking news that Mr. MacDonald had been hurt or killed. He bundled up the kids, and he, Skip, and Shirley went out to the house on Pointer Run Road to look for Jamie MacDonald. They arrived around 5:30 in the morning. Although Rocky was not aware of it, the FBI was camping out in a house across the street, but they were still sleeping and missed seeing Rocky at the house. You will recall it was Mrs. Kempfer who went over to the house where the FBI agents were camped out and woke them up and told them that someone had been at the house across the street that morning and the night before. How embarrassing is that for the FBI?" Larry couldn't help but see the reaction of the jury. Although they were familiar with the "asleep story", upon hearing it again, their reaction hovered between being flabbergasted and disgusted.

"After the house was cleaned and everything was put in a large plastic garbage bag, Rocky demanded that Skip take him to where he took Mr. MacDonald. Up until this time, Rocky was still not clear on what Skip had done to hurt Mr. MacDonald. Skip directed him to some nearby woods, but after wandering around in the area, they could not find Mr. MacDonald, so Rocky did not know if Mr. MacDonald was dead or alive.

"Rocky now had all the evidence from the house in the plastic bag in his car. Now I ask you, if Rocky was the master planner of this crime, what was the logic of having the evidence in his car? He had plenty opportunities to dump it. He could have dumped it in the woods when they were looking for Mr. MacDonald.

"When Rocky was arrested, what was the first thing he said? 'I want radio silence. I need to talk with my agent immediately.' It is FBI protocol that a snitch talks only to his agent. But the arresting officers were unable to reach Howard Bolton and instead connected Rocky by phone to Agent Calhoun. Actually, there were two such phone calls, but Agent Calhoun testified that he taped only the second phone call and not the first one. So—he—says." Larry stretched out those last three words and paused just long enough to let that sink in.

"Rocky believes that Agent Calhoun did tape both calls. The FBI is very professional, and something this important would certainly get taped. At the end of that phone call, Rocky felt like he is being set up to take the fall for this crime and being dumped by the FBI. They told him that they had picked up Chuck Wilson, who was singing a different tune. Rocky now feels certain that the first phone call was taped and played to Chuck Wilson. Unfortunately, you cannot hear that phone conversation because the FBI never provided it to the defense. In that tape, Rocky unloaded on Agent Calhoun, saying things like, 'What the hell is happening here? What have you guys been doing?'" Larry used the same tone of voice and frustrated motions with his hands that he thought Rocky would have used.

"So why is the FBI dumping Rocky Hamilton? I'll tell you why! In his testimony, Mr. Falsom from the FBI Headquarters in Washington, DC said it pretty clearly. He stated that the FBI doesn't get involved when somebody's life is in danger. Mr. MacDonald's life was in danger, and now he was dead, and so suddenly what had seemed like a great idea of how to catch Chuck Wilson during a case they were monitoring—they no longer wanted to be involved with it. Can you imagine the headlines? 'Bank Manager Found Dead with FBI Knowledge' or 'FBI Blows Kidnapping Case.' The article would spell out how the FBI knew all the details of the kidnapping from an undercover agent, and the man got killed anyhow. Surely the articles would mention that the FBI agents fell asleep on the job. The FBI would become a laughingstock. They couldn't stand the heat. They couldn't handle one more scandal, piled on top of their illegal activities that were exposed last December. So, good old Rocky is getting dumped.

"Then we have one more item to cover. When I spoke to you in my opening statement, I told you this would be a tough case. I told you there would not be anyone standing up in the back of the room, such as often happened in the popular Perry Mason television show, and say they knew something pertinent to the case that would make your decision easier. Ah, but surprisingly, in a way that has happened. Someone did say they knew something important about the case."

Larry caught the surprise on the prosecutor's face and the quizzical expression of every juror. They had not yet connected the dots. So Larry would do it for them. The Court had approved in advance that Larry could bring in a visual aid to help make a point of what Larry felt was the most crucial element of the trial. A very large 5 ft. by 6 ft. poster was brought into the courtroom and placed on an easel where it could easily be seen by the jurors. Printed in large type was the text of the audio tape of the telephone conversation between FBI Special Agent Michael Nielson and his informant, Dwight Fisher, which the jury had heard the previous day in the prosecutor's rebuttal.

With everything in place, Larry continued, "That person would be FBI Agent Michael Nielson, the handler for informant Dwight Fisher. He testified that he was a close friend of both Ed Marshall and Howard Bolton. He also testified that he had heard that Rocky Hamilton *and* Chuck Wilson were planning something like this kidnapping. Each one of you has already heard it on the tape for yourselves. And we are going to play it again for you right now."

Larry followed along, pointing to each word printed on the large poster with a pointer as it was spoken from the tape. He then asked the jury if he had typed out the spoken words properly. They all nodded yes. Larry then read the text out loud and circled with a bright red marker the first mention of Rocky Hamilton's name by Dwight Fisher, and then in the response of Agent Nielson, Larry circled "Hamilton *and* Wilson." The gasp from the jury was audible.

"That, ladies and gentlemen, is a Perry Mason moment. An FBI agent willingly offers information that he has heard about the kidnapping of Mr. MacDonald. And note the date of that tape—December the 8th. That was **before** Mr. MacDonald was killed. You no longer have to rely on Rocky's testimony that the FBI knew exactly what was going on in this case. Here you have an FBI agent admitting he had already heard that Rocky Hamilton **and** Chuck Wilson were involved. We know that he could have heard about the kidnapping from many sources. Ed Marshall could have told him, or Howard Bolton, or his girlfriend who was a friend of Chuck Wilson's girlfriend. Or they could already have been having meetings about the kidnapping at the FBI.

"Ladies and gentlemen, when you get in the jury room, I want you to listen to the tape all the way through, and you will see that Agent Nielson already knew about the kidnapping ahead of time. Dwight Fisher did not bring up Chuck Wilson's name. It was Agent Nielson who brought it up. This is not a small thing; I want you to understand it is a major part of this case.

"But now, Rocky Hamilton finds himself in the middle. Someone is dead, and the FBI claims they knew nothing about it in advance. And they just chose to forget about old Rocky here." Larry had walked over to where Rocky was sitting and placed his hands on Rocky's shoulders. He stayed there near Rocky, as if defending him physically. "I suppose their thinking was that Rocky is a convicted bank robber, a bad guy with a criminal history, so no jury is ever going to believe what Rocky Hamilton has to say. To them, Rocky is disposable. They liked Rocky okay when he was doing a good job for them for two and a half years. But now something has gone wrong, and they think that Rocky Hamilton would never testify against the FBI because it would blow his cover and all the people he has caused to go to prison would surely have him killed. Well, they miscalculated. Rocky is on trial for his life, so he decided to tell the truth, exactly as it happened.

"Ladies and gentlemen, this has been a long trial and I don't want to keep you much longer. The burden is on the State to prove Rocky Hamilton is guilty beyond a reasonable doubt. They have had the might of the FBI, investigative power and money, and people testifying that they were not associated with Rocky, saying that he was on his own. We, on the other hand, tried to show you the holes, where the logic is or isn't, and pointed out to you that certain FBI agents have testified under oath and have committed perjury. Ed Marshall lied about his relationship with Rocky; so did Bob Wallace. We couldn't get Howard Bolton to admit 'Yes, Rocky, I received your phone calls.' Howard had seen what had happened to both Ed Marshall and Bob Wallace for minor infractions. They had both been fired over something so trivial. Howard Bolton was not going to take the rap for this, so he lied to protect himself.

"We don't know who in the FBI was calling the shots in this case, saying 'Get as close as you can, but stay back at arm's length.' We are not making accusations that the FBI was planning all the way through to let Mr. MacDonald get kidnapped and then go along with it. But, Rocky did stay with it to the end, as he had been instructed. From the very beginning, he told them everything that was happening on this case. He would stop along Highway I-75 and make phone calls from pay phones to keep the FBI informed when he was on the road. Unfortunately, we do not have records of those telephone calls, because records are kept for only twenty-four to forty-eight hours.

"Rocky trusted that the FBI would come in at some point and pull Mr. MacDonald out of the fire. But the FBI couldn't protect Mr. MacDonald, because at the very moment that Mr. MacDonald was murdered, they were all fast asleep!" Larry felt he had to get in that one last dig.

"And that, ladies and gentlemen, is what I call a royal double cross. Dumping Rocky so coldly while all along he was doing their bidding and keeping them informed, and then the FBI trying to cover up their incompetency by lying.

"Rocky was feeding information to the FBI through Ed Marshall and, at times, directly to Howard Bolton solely for the purpose of the FBI's effectiveness in aborting the crime from even taking place. But in this case, the FBI could not stop it from happening, and Mr. Jamie MacDonald is dead. I don't feel good about this, and I am sure that you do not either. What Skip Nowalsky did was terrible, and he has been tried and sentenced, and justice has been done. And that is where it should stop. Rocky did not do anything wrong and did everything in his power to control specific acts to protect Mr. MacDonald from being harmed.

"The State has to prove criminal intent, and that Rocky purposely caused the death of Mr. MacDonald, beyond a reasonable doubt." By this time, Larry had walked back over to the jury box. "Ladies and gentlemen, I would submit to you that we have shown you reasonable doubt. We established that Rocky clearly was working with the FBI. I have shown you all the inconsistencies of this case. I know that you will do what you feel is right. You are aware that justice means that you bring in the right verdict—whether Rocky is guilty or not. I am sure that you will do the right thing and bring in the verdict of *not guilty*. Thank you very much."

Larry sat down and glanced at Rocky as if to say, *"Well, it is done."* He had done the best he could in handing the jury a beautifully wrapped package with a large satin bow. It contained all the facts and the common sense they needed to make their decision. He wished he could have told members of the jury how deep corruption ran in the ranks of the FBI. If the law had permitted him to do so, he would have told them about the assassination attempts on both his life and Rocky's. Orders to kill your own citizens come from the very top. In Larry's estimation, the FBI should serve as the conscience of a country, not as its executioner. They were no better than the organized crime establishments they investigated.

CHAPTER 34

Rebuttal Argument – The Prosecution

Shortly after the Court had reconvened after lunch, Mr. Lansing stated to the jury that he wanted to shed a little more light on certain salient points of Mr. Strong's closing argument, and that he would move quickly so the jury could begin deliberations. He talked about there being only two wiretaps, not five or fifteen or twenty or thirty as the defense would have them believe. If there had been more than the two wiretaps that the FBI said there were, then everybody in the offices of the FBI in Columbus and Detroit would be lying. They were all just a bunch of liars. They would have committed a legal offense by lying to a judge, and that carries an extreme penalty and a fine. Larry was nodding his head in the affirmative with every word that Mr. Lansing uttered, and he made sure the jury saw it.

The prosecutor went on to remark how the defense absolutely crucified both former FBI Agent Ed Marshall and Rocky's handler, FBI Agent Howard Bolton, on the witness stand, and had inferred that they both had lied, lied, lied. "Yes, you should use your common sense, as Mr. Strong has requested you to do. In that regard, why would it make any sense that Mr. Ed Marshall would be passing information to the FBI, after they had already fired him? Why would he want to help them in any way? Why would he lie on the witness stand when he had nothing to lose? That just makes no sense at all!

"Mr. Strong would want you to believe that the FBI let this case ride out too long because of their desire to catch Chuck Wilson in the act of collecting the ransom money. That's the guy the FBI was really after, according to Rocky Hamilton. If the FBI wanted Chuck so badly, they had many other things on him already, such as breaking and entering, parole violation, and interstate transportation of narcotics. They didn't need this kidnapping case to get him.

"But I will tell you, Rocky Hamilton masterminded the whole thing. He participated in the kidnapping and then brought Chuck Wilson in to collect the ransom. He even left Ohio to go back up to Detroit to try to get the ransom payoff delivered. It was Rocky Hamilton who gave the order to the junky Skip Nowalsky to clean up the mess, which meant to get rid of Mr. MacDonald.

"It is not difficult to understand why Rocky wanted that ransom money. He wanted it bad. He testified that in the last six months he was constantly working for the FBI and was paid only $55 for his service. He told us that for living expenses, he had borrowed thousands of dollars from Fred Bunker. We all know that borrowed money has to be paid back at some point, or someone is going to get hurt. I think Rocky's note had come due and he needed money, and this kidnapping was going to pay off handsomely.

"Rocky had already assisted the FBI earlier in putting away most of the Ashton-Keely Gang. So he had formed his own new gang, picked his own people to carry out this crime—Skip Nowalsky and Chuck Wilson—who would take orders from him, and he borrowed money to finance it until he could collect the ransom money.

"It was Rocky Hamilton who lied on the stand. He said he suspected he was under constant surveillance, but if that was so, why did he go back to Ohio to check on Mr. MacDonald? Why would he go clean up the house on Pointer Run Road where Mr. MacDonald had been held? Why would he have gone out to the woods to see if he could find Mr. MacDonald? Why would he do any of that if he thought he was under surveillance? Actually, Rocky was not under surveillance. The reason was the FBI did not know Rocky's whereabouts, and Rocky was not working with the FBI on this case.

"When he could not determine whether Mr. MacDonald was dead or alive, he panicked and knew he was in big trouble, and that is why he was making a run for it when he was arrested, and that was why he tried to make a deal with the arresting officers. He already knew that the FBI would not be there to help him, because he simply had not informed them of this case. If he had, he would have been busting a gut to find and help Mr. MacDonald. But he did neither.

"Ladies and gentlemen, it is now time for you to consider all of the evidence. Judge Abbot will give you all the instructions and explanations of the law. I am asking you to think about it just the way it happened—step-by-step, right down the line. Thank you very much."

CHAPTER 35

Judge's Instructions of Law

"Members of the jury," intoned Judge Franklin Abbot in a friendly voice, "you have heard the evidence and the arguments of counsel. It is now my duty to instruct you on the law which applies to this case. The Court and the jury have separate functions. You decide the disputed facts, and the Court provides the instructions of law. It is your sworn duty to accept these instructions and to apply the law as it is given to you. You are not permitted to change the law or to apply your own concept of what you think the law is or should be.

"The criminal case begins with the filing of an indictment. A defendant is presumed innocent unless and until his guilt is established beyond a reasonable doubt. A plea of not guilty is a denial of the charges. The defendant must be acquitted unless the State produces evidence which convinces you beyond a reasonable doubt of every essential element of the crimes charged in the indictment.

"Allow me to define a number of legal words, which have specific meanings in law. What is reasonable doubt? Reasonable doubt is present when after you have carefully considered and compared all the evidence, you cannot say you are firmly convinced of the truth of the charges. It is a doubt based on reason and common sense. It is not mere possible doubt, because everything relating to human affairs is open to some possible or imaginary doubt.

"If, after a full and impartial consideration of all the evidence, you are firmly convinced of the truth of the charge, then the State has proved its case on the charges beyond a reasonable doubt, and you must vote to convict. If, on the other hand, you are not firmly convinced of the truth of the charges, even one of them, then the State has failed to prove the case beyond a reasonable doubt, and you must vote to acquit.

"What is evidence? Evidence is all of the testimony received from the witness stand, together with the exhibits admitted into evidence during the trial and the stipulations entered into by counsel. Evidence may be direct or circumstantial, or both.

"Direct evidence is the testimony given by a witness who has seen or heard the facts about which he testifies. Direct evidence includes exhibits admitted into evidence and the stipulations of counsel. On the other hand, circumstantial evidence is the proof of facts by direct evidence from which you may infer other reasonable facts or circumstances.

"Evidence does not include the indictment, nor the opening statements and closing arguments by counsel. Those are designed to assist you in following the case. The view of the scene of the crime is not evidence, but it may help you understand the evidence.

"Now, you must not speculate why or what the answer might have been to a question to which the Court objected. Just remove that from your mind. You are the sole judges of the facts, the credibility of the witnesses, and the weight to be given to the evidence. In considering the credibility of a witness, you will rely upon the tests of truthfulness which you apply to your daily lives. Consider each witness in his or her appearance, manner of testifying, reasonableness of the testimony, the opportunity he or she had to see, hear, or know things they were testifying about, accuracy of memory, frankness or lack of it, intelligence, interest, and bias, if any.

"You are not required to believe the testimony of any witness simply because he or she was under oath. This applies to the defendant, as well as all witnesses.

"Generally, a witness may not express an opinion, unless they are identified as an expert witness based on their profession or special line of work, as well as their education, knowledge, and experience. We had expert witnesses in this trial in the persons of the fingerprint examiners and the pathologist who performed the autopsy. In reviewing their testimony, consider their skill, experience, knowledge, veracity, and familiarity with the facts of the case. Such testimony was admitted to assist you to arrive at a just verdict.

"In this trial there was testimony by persons who had previously been convicted of criminal acts, including the defendant. You should use the same tests of credibility and weight of their testimony as you would of any other witness.

"I would like to specifically point out that one witness by the name of Chuck Wilson was an accomplice and testified about his involvement in this crime. An accomplice is one who purposely, knowingly assists, or joins another person in the commission of a crime. His testimony should be considered together with all the other facts and circumstances in evidence. You must determine if his testimony is worthy of belief. No person shall be found guilty of aggravated murder or any lesser offense based upon the testimony of an accomplice unless the testimony is supported by other credible or believable evidence of the essential element of the crime.

"You should consider with caution evidence of any statement by the defendant to law enforcement officers. In weighing such evidence, you should consider whether it was made by the defendant, whether it was truthful, whether it was accurately repeated or recorded, whether the defendant understood what was said, the circumstances under which it was made, or the emotions of hope or fear that might have existed. It is your duty to apply the same general rules for testing the credibility of witnesses and decide what weight should be given to all or any part of such evidence.

"What is immunity? In this case immunity was granted by this Court to Chuck Wilson at the request of the State, and to Jerome Madison at the request of the attorneys for the defendant with the approval of the State. I granted those two requests for immunity."

Judge Abbot read to the jury the Ohio statute titled *Immunity of Witnesses Turning State's Evidence.* In its simple form, the statue simply states that a judge has the authority to grant immunity to a witness if it appears in the interests of justice to do so, in that the person is in possession of evidence or knowledge necessary to a full and complete investigation of criminal conduct, or that such testimony of the person will secure or conclude a prosecution. However, that witness can still be prosecuted for perjury or tampering with evidence. The judge had been quick to remind the witness of this fact when he took the stand.

Judge Abbot then read the Ohio statute which explained aiding and abetting. It pertains to a person who knowingly and purposely aids, helps, assists and associates himself with another in the commission of a crime. In law, that person is just as guilty as the principal offender, as if he personally performed every act constituting the offense. This is true even if such person was not physically present at the time and exact place that the crime was committed. When two or more persons have a common purpose to commit a crime, and one does one part and a second performs another part, those acting together are equally guilty of the crime. Defense Attorney Larry Strong had driven this point home to the jury during his closing arguments, but in the sense that Rocky was working with the FBI to solve the crime, not to be a party to it.

Judge Abbot specifically linked Rocky Hamilton to each part of the statute. "Now, the defendant in this case is charged with the crime of aggravated murder. Aggravated murder is the purposeful killing of another while committing, or fleeing immediately after committing kidnapping. Before you can find the defendant guilty, you must find beyond a reasonable doubt that Mr. Jamie MacDonald was a living person and that his death was caused by the defendant in Licking County, Ohio, on or about December 10th, 1975; that the killing was done purposely; that the killing was done while the defendant was committing or fleeing immediately after committing kidnapping. If you find that the State has failed to prove the killing was done by the defendant under the circumstances just mentioned, then you cannot find him guilty of aggravated murder, and may consider a lesser crime of murder. The crime of murder is distinguished from aggravated murder by the State's failure to prove that the killing was done while the defendant was committing the crime of kidnapping.

"This provision of a lesser offense is not designed to relieve you from the performance of an unpleasant duty. It is included to prevent failure of justice if the evidence fails to prove the original charge, but does justify a verdict for the lesser crime."

Inwardly, Larry was marveling over the clarity of Judge Abbot's explanation of the law. He hoped the jury was listening carefully and that the legal terminology was not too tedious for them. He had been impressed with the jury throughout the trial. This was not surprising to him, since he felt he had hand-picked each one himself in *voir dire* at the beginning of the trial and had used just enough aplomb and charm to veer them to his side of the argument. A smart, savvy jury can make a big difference in how a defense attorney presents the case. He never felt he had to talk down to them. He trusted them to find Rocky *not guilty.*

Showing total fairness to the defendant, Judge Abbot then pointed out to the jury, **"A person, who by prior arrangement with a law enforcement agency, honestly and in good faith, acts solely for the purpose of enforcing the law and assisting the law enforcement agency in the apprehension of others involved, has no criminal interest, which means no intention of violating the law, and is not guilty of any crime in connection with such acts, but where such person acts on his own volition, he is guilty of a violation of the law."**

The judge then explained the various verdict forms, informing the jury that when all twelve jurors have arrived at a verdict, the foreman, or forelady, should fill in the blanks in ink of the verdict—guilty or not guilty—and the charge—aggravated murder or murder. Then all twelve jurors should sign and date the verdict in ink.

"Now, you may not discuss," said Judge Abbot with a short pause, and then raising his voice, he continued, "and I repeat, you may not discuss, nor may you consider the subject of punishment. Your duty is confined to the determination of the guilt or innocence of the defendant. In the event that you should find the defendant guilty, the duty to determine the punishment is placed by law on the Court alone. It is your duty to carefully weigh the evidence, to decide all the disputed questions of fact, to apply the instructions of the Court to your findings, and to render your verdict accordingly. Consider all the evidence, and make your findings with intelligence and impartiality and without bias, sympathy, or prejudice, so that you can arrive at a fair and just verdict and so that the State of Ohio and the defendant will feel that their case was fairly and impartially tried. A verdict in a criminal case must be unanimous. When you reach a verdict, you will complete the forms which correspond to your verdicts, as I have instructed you.

"Your initial conduct on entering the jury room is a matter of much importance. It is not wise immediately to express a determination to insist upon a certain verdict, because if your sense of pride is aroused, you may hesitate to change your position even if you later decide that you were wrong. Consult with one another, consider each other's views and deliberate with the objective of reaching an agreement, if you can do so without disturbing your individual judgment. Each of you must decide this case for himself, or herself, but you should only do so after a discussion and consideration of the case with your fellow jurors. Do not hesitate to change an opinion if you become convinced that you are wrong. However, you should not surrender your honest convictions just to be congenial, or to reach a verdict solely because of the opinions of your fellow jurors."

Judge Abbot then turned to the three alternate jurors and addressed them. "Your duties have now come to an end. The Court takes this opportunity to thank you for your service. We are most appreciative of your time and effort in attending these proceedings. I indicated to you at the beginning of this trial that you would be seated in the jury box in the event of an emergency, and that indeed did happen when one alternate juror, Mr. Willard Buckner, replaced juror number five when he, Mr. Albert Kassling, became ill. You remaining three are at this time excused.

"However, before you depart, I have one instruction that applies to you as an alternate juror. You are not permitted to express to any person how you would have voted, had you gone into the jury room. You are not permitted to express your opinion as to the guilt or innocence of this defendant while this jury is deliberating. The moment the verdict is returned, you are free to say anything you please. You are free to agree or to disagree with their verdict.

"I am sure that counsel most sincerely thanks you as well. You are perfectly free, if you wish, to remain as a spectator. Since you have put so much time and effort in this case, you may wish to know the outcome."

Returning his attention to the jury, he said, "In a moment you will be given the records and exhibits. After you retire to the jury room, your first act will be to select a foreman or a forelady from among yourselves. Do this first. That person will be in charge of the records and will see that your discussions are orderly and that each juror has the opportunity to discuss the case and to cast his or her vote. When you have reached a verdict and filled in and signed the proper forms, you will contact the bailiff by using the buzzer in the jury room.

"From this moment on until we have a verdict, you are sequestered, which means you may have no contact whatever, other than through the bailiff, with any person outside your own fellow jurors. You are not permitted to leave that jury room under any circumstances until you have buzzed for the bailiff, who will take the appropriate action for whatever problem may occur. I want to emphasize to you, if there are any problems, you will be accommodated. You are not permitted to use the telephone. If you must make an emergency phone call, so long as it has nothing to do with this case, the bailiff will make the call for you.

"If, during your deliberations, the jury has a question to propound to the Court, you should do it in the following manner. First, you should reflect upon it and discuss it in the jury room. Then it should be reduced to writing so that there will be no misunderstanding as to what has been requested. You should keep in mind that any request may not reflect the status of your deliberations. The request should be signed by the foreman, or forelady, and delivered to the bailiff, so that he in turn can hand it up to the Court."

Judge Abbot told the jurors that he would send into the jury room a copy of the charge he had just read to them, and asked counsel if they were in agreement with that. Mr. Lansing and Mr. Strong answered yes, they were in agreement. The judge then asked counsel to examine the jury forms to see if they were in proper order. Yes, they both agreed that all was in order. With that, Judge Abbot addressed the jury one last time, "Members of the jury, the case is now yours for a decision."

Led by the bailiff, the jury filed out of the courtroom to the jury room. They seemed a bit weary to Larry. They had just been handed the weight of the trial. It had been a long day already, but there were still a couple of hours left in the day. The terrible wait for a verdict now began for Rocky Hamilton and his attorneys.

CHAPTER 36

Jury Deliberations and the Verdict
November 17, 1976

The jury had been deliberating an hour and a half when Judge Abbot decided to bring them back into the courtroom to see if they had made progress toward a verdict. "Let the record show that the defendant is present with counsel, and also the prosecuting attorney is in attendance. Now, Mr. Hamilton, at this time we will call the jury in here to see if they are near a verdict, and if they are not, we will recess for the evening and sequester them in the Sheraton Hotel with the bailiff, Mr. Peter Statler, and Mrs. Statler to look after them. Is that satisfactory, Mr. Hamilton?"

"Yes, Your Honor."

"Are you satisfied, Counsel?"

Defense co-counsel Steinwell answered, "We are, Your Honor."

Prosecutor Lansing nodded. "Yes, sir."

"Bring in the jury," the judge ordered. The jurors filed into the courtroom one by one and took their seats.

"Now, at this time ladies and gentlemen of the jury, the Court realizes that this is a rather touchy time to interrupt your deliberations; however, have you selected a foreman or a forelady, and who is it?"

Mr. Jeffrey Gifford, juror number seven, stood and said, "I am, Your Honor."

Judge Abbot asked him if there was any chance of reaching a verdict this afternoon or this evening. Mr. Gifford answered, "No, sir."

"Well then, we will recess for the evening and you will be sequestered at the Sheraton Hotel, where arrangements have been made for you, under the supervision of Bailiff Statler and Mrs. Statler, his wife." Judge Abbot then asked the clerk of the court to administer the oath to Mrs. Statler to be sworn in as bailiff also.

"Mr. and Mrs. Statler will keep the jurors together at all meals. You may leave your cars in the parking lot here at the courthouse, or if you wish to drive your own car to the Sheraton Hotel, you will be accompanied by a bailiff. Is that all right with you, Mr. Hamilton?"

"Yes."

The judge continued, talking to the jurors. "I want to caution you again, do not communicate to any other person, to another juror, any thoughts, opinions or comments relative to your deliberations of this case except in the jury room of this courthouse. Do not listen to any news media, or watch any news on television, or read anything involving this case. We will recess now until you are ready to resume your deliberations tomorrow morning at 7:00 or 8:00, or whatever time you are ready. Is that satisfactory, Mr. Hamilton?"

"Yes, it is."

The twelve jurors returned to the jury room of the courthouse the following morning after an early breakfast. At 11:30 a.m., they recessed for lunch in a private dining room at the Sheraton Hotel. The judge had sent them off to lunch with the same cautions they would hear every time they left the courtroom. Later that afternoon, the jury foreman sent a note to the judge through the bailiff. The judge called both counselors and the defendant to the courtroom to read and discuss the request.

When everyone was in their place, Judge Abbot stated, "No one has read this question posed by the jury except me, and I will now read it to you. It says, 'If someone feels he, Mr. Hamilton, participated in the kidnapping, but had no intent to harm Mr. MacDonald and the act of murder was purely the act of Mr. Nowalsky—Skip's doing, in other words—legally what is Rocky Hamilton guilty of?' That is the question. Does the prosecution have an opinion?"

Following a short conference with his co-counsel, Mr. Lansing told Judge Abbot that the answer to the question was fully addressed in the written charge the judge had sent into the jury room, and that the jurors should read the charge in its entirety. This message was passed to the jurors. The question brought great relief and hope to both Larry and Rocky.

At 4:30 p.m., after a total of six hours and fifty minutes of deliberation, the jury sent a message to the judge that they had reached a verdict. But the reading of the verdict had conditions attached to it. The jury said it would render the verdict only if the judge and the attorneys for both the prosecution and the defense would meet with them in chambers after the reading. All agreed, and the jury was brought into the courtroom. Word had spread quickly that a verdict was imminent, and the courtroom had become crowded and abuzz with reporters and spectators. Members of the MacDonald family sat in the front row. Not one person in support of Rocky Hamilton was present except his legal team.

Larry was wondering what this request from the jury might be about. He stared at the jurors, but with downcast eyes, they would not make eye contact with anyone. This was not a good sign. He felt sure this jury was savvy enough to see through all the lies spouted by the FBI agents. Larry had proven to them that Rocky was working with the FBI all along and was keeping them informed through phone calls, yet the FBI had deserted Rocky after MacDonald was killed, because it couldn't stand the heat. He had clearly pointed out to the jury that the FBI could not admit that it knew what was going on because they had messed up so badly. They could have saved Mr. MacDonald by intervening. Larry knew that not one of the jurors would forget that all the FBI agents had fallen asleep. His thoughts were interrupted when the bailiff intoned, "All rise!"

When Judge Abbot had taken his seat and brought the Court into session, a deafening silence fell over the room. "Let the record show the defendant is present with counsel. Has the jury reached a verdict?"

"We have Your Honor," answered Mr. Gifford.

"Would the defendant please stand for the reading of the verdict?"

Larry and Rocky stood in unison, along with Co-Counsel Steinwell. Rocky appeared nervous, constantly pumping his hands into a fist. Larry wondered what was going through Rocky's mind at this moment. In mere seconds he would learn his fate that would determine the rest of his life.

Judge Abbot's voice interrupted Larry's thoughts, "Mr. Gifford, would you please hand the verdict to the bailiff and would the clerk of the court please read the verdict?"

In a loud and clear voice, the clerk read, "We, the jury being duly impaneled and sworn, do find the defendant *guilty* to the charge of aggravated murder as charged in the indictment and also *guilty* of the specifications of kidnapping. Both verdicts have been duly signed by each of the twelve members of the jury."

Rocky had slumped forward holding onto the table, his eyes closed, his face disbelieving. Larry placed his hand on Rocky's arm and felt it stiffen. Rocky did not hear another word of the proceedings. Neither did Larry, but he felt he should stay alert in case the judge addressed him in some way.

The gallery had come alive with voices, gasps, and restlessness. Judge Abbot slammed his gavel, restoring order. He then polled each of the jurors separately asking if this was their verdict. Each said it was.

"The Court will accept your verdict of *guilty* on the charge and on the specifications. I am required to have a pre-sentence investigation, and Mr. Hamilton will be required to have a psychiatric examination, after which a report on this examination will be submitted to the Court. So at this time the Court will defer sentencing in this matter until statutory requirements are complied with. The Court wishes to thank you for taking time out of your busy lives to perform this important function."

After the courtroom was cleared and Rocky had been taken away in handcuffs, the judge and counsel for the prosecution and the defense met with the twelve jurors in chambers as promised. The foreman of the jury spoke for the entire group. "The defense proved to us beyond a reasonable doubt that Rocky Hamilton did this kidnapping with the full knowledge and assent of the government. If we found Mr. Hamilton *not guilty,* this criminal would be released onto the street and the FBI would get the green light to let innocent people get kidnapped for their conviction rate. So we found Mr. Hamilton *guilty*. We hope you will execute him.

"Also, we felt that the FBI agents—especially former FBI Agent Ed Marshall and current FBI Agent Howard Bolton—were not telling the truth, and in actuality were co-conspirators in the murder of Jamie MacDonald because they did nothing to stop his death although they had full knowledge of the circumstances leading up to it. We ask the prosecutor to indict these two men and we hope you execute them, too. Only then will the FBI change its conduct." The jury had spoken.

Outside the courthouse, Jamie MacDonald's sister, who had testified at the trial about how she had been contacted as to where to find the tape recording in the bushes proving that her brother was still alive, stated to the press that the family felt that justice had been achieved.

Larry rehashed several points of the trial as he sped down the rural back road of Ohio on his way home. He always came to the same conclusion: He had done his best in defending Rocky. He felt he had proved his case to the jury beyond a reasonable doubt—proved through phone records that Rocky was working for the FBI. In his estimation, the jury had not exactly followed the law in the strictest sense. They admitted they knew Rocky worked for the FBI, but they had erroneously attached *scienter* to him. They were using Rocky to teach the FBI a lesson—just as Rocky did by taking the witness stand against Larry's advice. Nevertheless, Larry nodded his head in admiration for this rural group of twelve jurors. In the end they had the capacity to step back and figure out the whole thing and actually try to do the right thing by getting bad guys off the streets.

He hoped that the public was now more aware of the misdeeds and arrogance of the FBI, and that their lily-white reputation was tainted in the minds of the people who had followed the trial. Larry felt his greatest triumph was when he made the fourth most ranking official of the FBI admit to the embarrassing, bumbling mistakes of its agents in the field, but, unfortunately, he could never get any of them to admit to the cover-up. They were a ruthless, righteous, dirty power unto themselves.

Now that the trial was over, Larry hoped the long arm of justice would protect him from this unexpected outcome of a guilty verdict. He knew that Rocky had thugs on the outside who might come after him and squash him like an ant. But if he could survive an attack by that orange FBI helicopter on this very road, he might be smart enough to outwit common thugs. Nonetheless, he would be looking over his shoulder and in his rearview mirror for months to come. Right now, he could only think how great a cold beer would taste, and of his lovely wife waiting at home for him.

EPILOGUE

Jamie MacDonald, Jr., Twenty-Five Years Old

Jamie MacDonald's family immigrated to the United States from Scotland when Jamie was seven years old. He was a bachelor who lived at home with his parents. After graduating from Wayne State University in Detroit, he was employed at the National Bank of Detroit, where he had risen to the position of assistant branch manager. This young, dedicated man had a bright career future in banking. He wasn't feeling well the day he was kidnapped, but went to work anyway because he knew that Fridays at the bank were always busy.

Although he was heavily drugged by his kidnappers, he fought valiantly during the stabbing attack that killed him. His body was found six days after his kidnapping along a backwoods road fifteen miles from Newark, Ohio. He was laid to rest on December 15th, 1975, in Grosse Pointe, Michigan.

Rocky Hamilton, Forty Years Old

As required by law, prior to sentencing Rocky Hamilton was sent for a psychiatric examination. He refused to talk to the Columbus psychiatrist assigned to examine him. Subsequently, he was sent for sixty days to Lima State Hospital for a psychiatric examination. He also refused to speak with the psychiatrist there and was characterized as a deliberating, calculating, heartless person with an anti-social personality, but without mental disorders.

Sixteen days after the verdict, Rocky asked for a new trial based on two issues: Ohio had reinstated the death penalty in 1974, but Judge Abbot had prevented his attorneys from asking prospective jurors about their feelings on the death penalty. The second issue was that the misconduct of the FBI agents as State witnesses during his trial prevented him from receiving a fair and impartial trial. Supporting the latter issue was an affidavit by jurors stating that while they entered and exited the courtroom during the trial, they overheard agents of the FBI making derogatory, sarcastic, and demeaning remarks about the credibility of defense witnesses.

On March 17th, 1977, Rocky Hamilton was sentenced for aggravated murder with the specification of kidnapping to be executed in the electric chair. Three months later, Rocky was implicated in yet another murder that had taken place in 1973 in Michigan.

Subsequently, his death sentence was appealed and reversed, and he was sentenced to thirty years in prison. He would have been eligible for parole in 2007. However, Rocky never saw freedom outside the gates of prison. He died in 2005 at the age of sixty-nine.

Skip Nowalsky, Thirty-Eight Years Old

On June 8th, 1976, Skip Nowalsky was found guilty of aggravated murder with the specification of kidnapping of Jamie MacDonald. Prior to sentencing on November 29th, 1976, Nowalsky said he felt his trial was not a fair one because of statements his attorney made following his conviction. He was sentenced to death by electric chair. His psychiatric examination characterized him as having a passive personality with a need to go along with the ideas and behaviors of others, which could lead to aggressive actions. He sought an appeal based on several errors in his trial and insufficient representation. The appeal was denied, and he was executed in the electric chair in Ohio.

Shirley Stevens, Twenty-Four Years Old

Shirley Stevens, Rocky Hamilton's common-law wife, was initially arrested and then released. She was re-arrested when her mother called the police to report that her daughter was withholding information about the kidnap-murder of Jamie MacDonald. Stevens pleaded guilty to the charge of aiding and abetting the kidnapping, although she stated she never was aware that a kidnapping had taken place. At Rocky's request, she delivered a message to Skip Nowalsky to clean up the house. Skip Nowalsky mistakenly thought that meant to kill Mr. MacDonald, who was put into the trunk of Stevens's car. She drove to the woods, where Skip took Mr. MacDonald from the trunk and told her to drive down the road and come back in five minutes. When she returned to pick up Skip, Jamie MacDonald was not with him. She stated that she felt that something wasn't right.

On April 7th, 1977, she was sentenced to twenty years in federal prison for aiding and abetting in the kidnap-murder of Jamie MacDonald. The presiding judge said, "All your troubles have come about because you have been mixed up with the wrong people, but you were also a willing participant in a horrible, horrible crime."

Chuck Wilson, Thirty-Seven Years Old

Chuck Wilson was a career criminal who preferred kidnappings to bank robberies. In this case, he was granted immunity from murder charges in exchange for his testimony, which helped convict both Skip Nowalsky and Rocky Hamilton. He was sentenced on March 30th, 1977, to fifteen years in prison for aiding and abetting the kidnapping.

FBI Agent Howard Bolton
and Former FBI Agents Ed Marshall and Bob Wallace

Subsequent to the Rocky Hamilton trial, all three agents were indicted for perjury in Licking County by a grand jury. The FBI spirited the three out of Michigan and Nebraska, located them elsewhere in the United States, and gave them new identities. None of them has been found nor tried. They are still free today.

Defense Attorney Larry Strong, Thirty-Five Years Old

The trial of Rocky Hamilton was the first and only case of capital murder that Mr. Strong defended. By his second year of practice, Mr. Strong had already proven his ability to his colleagues and was awarded partnership status in the nineteen-member firm. From the notoriety generated from this case and his reputation of rarely losing a case, his practice flourished and he became recognized and respected for his expertise in complex, high-profile civil litigation for private and publicly traded companies. During his career, he successfully represented individuals and companies of great prominence in numerous criminal and constitutional cases.

He served as lead trial attorney in over 400 jury cases, winning over 98% at the trial level. He honed his focus to represent business entities in corporate formation, governance issues, transitioning private companies to public companies, and mergers and acquisitions. During his career, he handled five cases before the United States Supreme Court.

Subsequently, Mr. Strong left private law practice and became general counsel to a growing public company, and eventually became its president and board chairman. Afterwards, he returned to practice law, specializing in complex business litigation until his retirement.

Co-Counsel for the Defense Gus Steinwell, Thirty-Five Years Old

Gus Steinwell was a well-known local criminal defense lawyer in Newark, Ohio. He had a wealth of criminal law experience and was a bit more scholarly and less theatrical than lead Attorney Larry Strong. He proved to be an excellent trial partner and often questioned witnesses during the Rocky Hamilton trial. Later in his career, Gus Steinwell became probate judge in Licking County, Ohio.

The Jury

The jury was composed of seven women and five men and four alternates of two men and two women. All of them resided in rural Licking County, Ohio. After the trial, one of the jurors reported in Newark's newspaper, *The Advocate,* that three votes had been taken. At the first vote they were split six to six. At the second vote, four had swung to the *guilty* side, and finally all twelve agreed on the third vote on the second day of deliberations.

One juror reported that at one point the jury was ready to find Hamilton innocent until they re-read the laws involved and better understood them. According to Ohio law, if a person is involved in a kidnapping and the kidnap victim dies as a result of the kidnapping, the person is also responsible for the victim's death. The juror said this law convinced him of Hamilton's guilt because he was involved in the planning and the kidnapping.

The Trial

The trial of Rocky Hamilton took place in the historic Licking County courthouse in Ohio. Lasting eight weeks, the trial began on September 17th, 1976, with jury selection and ended on November 18th. The defense called 150 witnesses, while the prosecution called 50.

LEGAL TERMS

Confession and Avoidance Defense — A confession and avoidance defense is when the defense admits the truth of the evidence as put forward by the prosecution, but the defense avoids legal responsibility for the reason established and recognized by law.

Ex parte — a Latin legal term meaning "from (by or for) [the/a] party". An **ex parte** decision is one decided by a judge without requiring all of the parties to the controversy to be present.

Fi-sur — A FBI stakeout.

Indictment — A formal charge or accusation of a serious crime.

Scienter — The law governing *scienter* is called "confession and avoidance defense." The law dictates that for one to be guilty of a crime, he/she must have "*scienter* — guilty knowledge and intent." This is why insanity is a defense. If one is legally insane, they lack intent and knowledge of right and wrong. In this case, if one is doing a robbery or a kidnapping for the purpose of catching bad guys and assisting the government, the act of robbery lacks *scienter*, and there is no crime.

Voir Dire — Originates from the French language meaning "to see/to speak." In actuality, it is the questioning of prospective jurors by a judge and attorneys in court. *Voir dire* is used to determine if any juror is biased and/or cannot deal with the issues fairly, or if there is cause not to allow a juror to serve (knowledge of the facts; acquaintanceship with parties, witnesses, or attorneys; occupation which might lead to bias; prejudice against the death penalty; or previous experiences such as having been sued in a similar case). Actually, one of the unspoken purposes of *voir dire* is for the attorneys to get a feel for the personalities and likely views of the people on the jury panel. In some courts, the judge asks most of the questions, while in others the lawyers are given substantial latitude and time to ask questions. Some jurors may be dismissed for cause by the judge, and the attorneys may excuse others in "peremptory" challenges without stating any reason.

CPSIA information can be obtained
at www.ICGtesting.com
Printed in the USA
FFHW02n1315120918
48351239-52191FF